Andrea Michael writes books
relationships and might be aim
just a little.

You may know her from her previous romantic comedies, written under the name 'A.L. Michael'.

She works in marketing, runs writing for wellbeing workshops, and lives in Watford with her fiancé and their crazy cat.

www.andreamichaelwrites.com

facebook.com/Andreamichaelwrites
twitter.com/ALMichael_
instagram.com/andreamichaelwrites

Also by Andrea Michael

The Book of Us

THE THINGS THAT MATTER

ANDREA MICHAEL

One More Chapter
a division of HarperCollins*Publishers* Ltd
1 London Bridge Street
London SE1 9GF
www.harpercollins.co.uk
HarperCollins*Publishers*
1st Floor, Watermarque Building, Ringsend Road
Dublin 4, Ireland

This paperback edition 2021
First published in Great Britain in ebook format
by HarperCollins*Publishers* 2021

A catalogue record of this book is available from the British Library
ISBN: 978-0-00-837023-7

Printed and bound in the UK using 100% Renewable
Electricity at CPI Group (UK) Ltd

Content notice: miscarriage

For my husband:
Above all else, adventures.

Damaged people love you like you are a crime
scene before a crime has even been committed.
They keep their running shoes beside their souls
every night, one eye open in case things change
whilst they sleep.

— Nikita Gill

Prologue

2006

Aylesbury Prison and Young Offenders Institute

He looks different.

That's all I can think as I see him walk out of the prison and into the fresh air. His dark brown hair is cut short, and he's muscled, like he's a troubled American teen from the movies, returning from military school.

He holds himself differently, taking up space. Squared shoulders, like he's daring anyone to bump into him or look at him the wrong way.

The Dan I knew before was lithe, his sixteen-year-old body showing only the faintest muscle beneath pale skin.

Now, even though it's only been a few months, he looks… he looks like a man.

It's happened so gradually, I shouldn't be shocked. But it's different seeing him out here in the world.

I've been visiting every week since he was sent here, bunking off lessons whenever I needed to. School have been pretty understanding about 'everything that went on' and if I've learnt anything from my mother, it's that you've got to take advantage of that kindness when it comes along. People don't give it often. It's reserved for when something really bad happens.

The journey from Luton took me about an hour and a half each way; three buses and a walk either end. But I didn't mind. All I wanted to do was see him. To smile so he'd know I was okay, to tell him funny stories and keep his mind off everything. To give him a countdown of the days until he was out and back to me again.

I put every last bit of energy I had into making him happy, or as happy as he could be in there. I counted his smiles on each visit, collecting them like it was a video game, a little 'ding' in my head when I made one appear.

Dan was trying hard for me too, I knew. He didn't ask me about the foster home they'd tried to put me in after everything happened, because there was nothing he could do. When I told him Sharon next door had agreed to take me in, at least until I could finish my GCSEs, he breathed a sigh of relief and his smile was like sunshine.

Three months. It didn't seem that much, not really.

But for a nice boy from a nice family, who'd done nothing wrong, three months seemed like a lifetime. Especially when the nice family didn't want to know Dan after everything happened – they couldn't handle the embarrassment.

People like us don't do things like that, Daniel. Your father's business, his contacts, you know how people are. How they talk. We can't risk it, you must understand. Be reasonable, Daniel.

I'd been there when his mother said it, when she explained why she wasn't coming to court the day he was sentenced. How he didn't hear anything from them, not his parents or his brother or sister. I didn't ask about his family any more. We were each other's family now, that was the promise we made.

He looks across the yard at me in the bright daylight and holds up a hand to shield his eyes from the sun. He looks… strong. Strong and capable and yet, somehow like a stranger. Fear clutches at me, just for a moment. Has he changed? Have our plans, a teenage romance and big dreams of escape and new starts, have they been foolish? Are we just stupid kids like everybody said?

'How will you make money Natasha? Love doesn't feed an empty belly, or pay the gas bill,' Sharon said this morning when I packed my backpack with the few things I owned and hoisted it onto my shoulders. I knew I wouldn't be taking the three buses back to Luton again.

'I know how to survive, don't worry about that.'

She hadn't looked convinced. I wanted to tell her I'd been looking after myself for most of my life. That it had been years of rifling through coat pockets at school for change to buy dinner, or making a Mars bar last two days. I knew all about food banks and clothes exchanges and every single way there was of surviving. And I would teach Daniel. If he wanted to learn.

Daniel, who was used to living in a four bedroom detached home, and had never once considered that he wouldn't have a hot meal and a pressed school uniform. Who had never gone to bed hungry and angry. At least, not before prison.

He never blamed me. Even as we stood in that court room and the judge declared he was guilty of manslaughter, even as his face lost all colour and his knees buckled. It took less than a second for Dan to compose himself, smile at me and hold me close as he told me it was worth it.

In that moment I had promised myself that I would do everything I could to make it up to him, to make it true. To be worth it.

Dan approaches me, suddenly within arm's reach, and he smiles that same soft smile. That hasn't disappeared. Neither have the butterflies in my stomach or that voice in my gut that says, *'This one, this one is for you.'*

We stand looking at each other awkwardly.

'I can't believe you're finally here.'

'Me neither. The outside world. First thing I want to do is eat a huge steak and chips. Or a burger. Oh, or Thai food!' He grins at me, those beautiful blue eyes still warm and loving, unchanged. He's still here, he's still mine. 'Actually, no, this is the first thing I want to do.'

He kisses me, and I know. I know I've been right all along. That every time I fell asleep on the bus home from the prison and missed my stop, or every time one of the other inmates had leered at me during visiting hours, or the number of times Dan's mother had called me a 'grubby little bitch who ruined everything' whenever I pleaded with her to visit her son. It was worth it, it had all been worth it.

Dan takes the backpack from me, putting it over his shoulder, and taking my hand in his as we start walking in no particular direction. Just, away. Our fingers interlink the way they always did, his thumb tracing my palm. Even that simple gesture feels like home.

'So, what now? Where do we go?' He kisses my hand.

'Anywhere we want,' I say, desperate to be that little ray of sunshine, to make this moment everything he's been dreaming about for the last three months. 'Anywhere we want. We go and we build a life. Where do you want to go?'

'Anywhere! Somewhere brilliant. Shall we flip a coin? Find a globe to spin?'

I want to tell him it won't be easy. That we'll have to work and struggle. That he's never really had to think about it before. But that sounds negative. In many ways I'm so much older than him.

I need to give him the option. I stop walking.

'There's still time to back out, Dan. Go home, apologise? See if they've changed their minds?'

He tilts his head as if it's a trick question. Those blue eyes meet mine and he shrugs.

'I've had as much time as they have to think about this. If they don't want me, then I don't want them. Let's… let's go live *good* lives, Taz. Great lives! And one day they'll come crawling back and I'll tell them to do one. Because we're each other's family now, that's the deal, right?'

'Right.'

He's still in there, the dreamer, the one who sees the good, who sees the light. The one who reaches for happiness above all else. They didn't take that away.

We're going to be okay.

Better than okay.

We're going to be perfect.

Chapter One

2020

London

'Are you almost ready to go?'

Angela raised a perfect eyebrow and tapped the Champagne flute with her nail. She was annoyed with me, that much was clear.

'What's your hurry?' I said. 'Pre-drinks were your idea, so we could catch up. I haven't seen you in forever.'

'And whose fault is that?' Angie flicked her dark hair over her shoulder and fixed me with a stare.

'Well, you run a tech empire and I don't work, so I'm going to say *yours*.' I smiled at my friend, bumping her with my hip. I felt like I was doing well, keeping the smile on my face, staying light and happy. It was exhausting, but I was managing it.

I was determined that today I was going to do better, be better. I was going to be the friend Angie deserved.

I leaned across the kitchen island and topped up her glass, willing her to let it go. But that wasn't Angie's style. We'd been friends for about four years, ever since she waltzed into a 6 a.m. yoga class still in her clothes from the night before, fell asleep on the mat for the whole hour, snoring loudly, and without a whiff of shame thanked the teacher for such a '*rejuvenating savasanna.*'

I thought she was absolutely mad, and really we made no sense as friends except for the fact that we both loved shopping in charity shops, mocking the rich and famous, and proving people wrong. Although Angela, as some sort of heiress, was kind of at a disadvantage with the rich and famous thing – they were her people.

But these days we moved in the same circles and sometimes you really needed someone who was willing to join in mocking the woman who spent fifteen grand on a dog house for her toy poodles. You just needed back-up. A spark of reality in with the excess.

'You took a call from the Wah Wah centre when I arrived and were gone for forty minutes!'

'Don't call it that.'

One of the few things Angie and Dan agreed on was

that I spent too much time helping on the grief helpline. They thought it wasn't good for me.

But I was helping people. That's what they couldn't understand, that I desperately needed to do something useful, something *good*. Something that wasn't sitting around miserably feeling guilty.

We could have Champagne any time. We could spend any day we wanted sitting in my huge Hampstead flat and drinking expensive wine out of expensive glasses and talking about things that didn't matter. The people who called me had *real* problems.

'They needed help, I was there. I'm sorry I ignored you, okay? I've put the phone away and we're focusing on you.' I tried to soothe her and Angela snorted into her glass.

'It's *your* birthday, moron! We're meant to be focusing on *you*!'

'Well, I'd quite happily skip it, thanks.' I smiled tightly, trying to make it sound like a joke. 'Who's excited for thirty, anyway?'

I sounded ungrateful, I knew. I was trying so hard to seem *okay* again after everything. To have enough time pass that people didn't tilt their heads and wince when they asked how I was. To not have them exclaim in those pitying tones that *it was really awful, what happened*. And then you have to say *sorry*, or *thank you*, or some other weird thing to make the conversation end.

And then if you're me, you take your drink and you hide in the toilet until your husband comes and gets you, makes excuses and takes you home.

Unsurprisingly, Dan hadn't taken me out much in the last few months. I can't *quite* be trusted on the corporate dinner party circuit anymore. The offers that used to pour in, ski trips to Chamonix and weekends in Monaco, they've dried up. I can't say I'm disappointed. But I think Dan might be.

The only person I liked out of that group was Angela anyway, and she still dropped by every week with huge takeaway cups of coffee to chat and moan about how awful they all were. At the beginning I didn't even say anything, just gripped the coffee cup with both hands and stared at her face, but it was honestly the best thing anyone did for me. Just came into my day, asked nothing of me, and told me stories.

'You wouldn't believe who was there, Taz, this woman was wearing so much gold she may as well have been carried in on a lounger.'

'Taz, honestly, I think everyone got food poisoning. Must have been the sushi. I heard later in the evening there was projectile vomiting!'

'Oh god, babe, you know Nicola's best friend Yvonne? Her wanker banker husband had an affair with the cleaner and now they've run off to Mauritius!'

She didn't require anything from me. She didn't talk

about life before. She didn't talk about Dan, who still had to go and build his career and play nice for his daddy. Show him that nepotism really did pay, that it was worth it to let him back in, to promote him to that nice corner office, even with his council estate wife.

I'm not quite over it yet, in case that wasn't obvious.

The huge bouquet of birthday flowers Dan sent me was on the side in the kitchen, and every time I looked at them I noticed some other extravagant detail. They were huge, colourful, audacious things. Exactly the kind of thing Dan would have bought me when we were younger, if we'd had a spare seventy quid to spend on things that weren't food or rent.

It made me feel better, that he picked something fun. He'd been tip-toeing around me for so long that seeing something bold felt hopeful. The card said, *'To my darling Taz, happy birthday. You deserve all the good things this year. All my love, Dan.'*

Something in there hinted at pity and survival, just a little, but I wasn't going to dwell. I was incredibly lucky, I had a lot to be grateful for. Thoughtful husband, beautiful home, good friend looking at me like she was about to drop a bombshell…

'What?' *Please don't be pregnant.*

'I feel like I should tell you something, but Dan told me not to…' Angela untangled one of the huge gold hoop earrings stuck in her hair, and I snorted, relieved.

Poor Ange. Never could keep a secret. And my lovely Dan, always plotting and planning, as if he'd let my birthday pass quietly, even this year.

'He's throwing me a surprise party.'

She raised an eyebrow, 'You knew?'

'No, but it's a Dan way to approach things.' *To try and fix things.* 'He's a go big or go home type. My husband has never found an over the top gesture he didn't like.'

Angela looked at me like I'd grown two heads. 'Taz, you *hate* big events and fancy parties. You hate having to dress up and pretend to be interested in the stock market whilst frat boys in suits look at your boobs and your husband pretends he likes these people. It's why we get along so well.'

I laughed and shrugged, sipping my wine. 'I know.'

'So why wouldn't you be annoyed?'

'Because he wants to do something nice for me. Even if I would rather stay home in my pyjamas and eat pizza—'

'—which he *knows* because you've been married since you were *children*—'

'Babe, this is how Dan shows love. He likes to make a big show, he feels like it means more if he has an audience.'

I tried to not make it sound like a judgement. That had been the difference between us – Dan's parents had taught him to care what things looked like. It was so hard to get used to the idea that people gave enough of a damn about what you were doing to form a negative opinion. My parents had more of a 'fuck anyone who criticises you' approach. But as far as I was concerned, neither of us lucked out in the family department. Except in finding each other.

'Sweetie, aren't you a bit tired of this Stepford Wife shit? I mean, I know you wanna stand by your man and all that but… don't you think it's time to stop trying to be perfect?'

I recoiled a little. 'What?'

Angela put a hand on mine, 'Look, you know I don't do all the warm and fuzzies, and I would rather go bond by getting simultaneous bikini waxes, *but* you went through some stuff, and you're pretending everything's fine.'

'That's what people *do*, Ange. They get on with their lives. They pretend they're fine until they are fine. Otherwise you mope and get bitter about how unfair the world is, and you wake up five months later and your husband's left and your friends are bored of you and you're bored of yourself…' I could feel myself getting choked up, and Angie squeezed my hand.

'I'm not trying to upset you, I'm just saying you don't have to be perfect. Not for me, not for Dan.'

'I'm not trying to be perfect. I'm just trying to be okay.'

The thing is, all these people, these well-wishing bystanders to your life, they say things like that just because it's what you do. They say 'take all the time you need' but what they *really* mean is 'hurry up and get over this, we want you to be normal again.' Grief makes people uncomfortable in a way I've never experienced before. Like you're handing them something and they don't know where to put it.

When we went through everything as teenagers, we didn't have to talk about it with anyone but ourselves. Even now, these people Dan surrounds himself with don't know about his stint in prison, they don't know our story. They just know enough: that he was the good boy from the nice family, and I was the girl with nothing who still doesn't like seeing how much of that catered food is thrown away at the end of the night. I always end up sweet-talking the caterer into packing half of it up so I can drop it off at a shelter. The other half is for the staff, obviously. I worked enough catering gigs as a teenager to know a lot of them are surviving on leftover canapés for dinner.

The thing is, before I didn't mind being the kooky leftie wife. I was doing good things, even if it made them uncomfortable. I wasn't on display. *Now* the problem is that every time someone asks me how I am, I get closer and closer to telling them the truth.

That wouldn't be good for anyone. It's better to put on a smile and gloss over the cracks. What's that saying, about pouring yourself a drink and putting on extra lipstick? These last few months I've been buying a lot of lipstick.

I've been buying a lot of everything, actually. Dan sees the credit card bills, all these charges to late night shopping channels, stupid stuff we'd never need. Stuff the old me would be horrified by. Pointless expense, just because. But he hasn't said anything about it. Either he doesn't want to embarrass me, or he doesn't want another conversation about why I'm still not sleeping. Doesn't want to bring up medication again.

There were a lot of things we weren't talking about at the moment.

'Well, now that the surprise is good and ruined, I'm meant to have you out of the flat and on the way to the pub in the next ten minutes, so chin chin.' Angela topped up my mostly full glass, and filled her empty one again.

'Is it subterfuge? We go for a drink and they come here?' I was hopeful, but it was unlikely. Dan would have had a cleaner come in if it was at home. And then I would have pointed out we don't need a cleaner, and he would have said I was being difficult for no reason, and it would have been a *thing*.

Angela shook her head, 'But it's at the Star and Anchor, so that's not bad, right?'

The Star and Anchor was our local pub, and although it was a little fancy for my tastes, I liked it. The food was good, the drinks weren't insanely expensive and there was never anyone from Chelsea auditioning for a TV show on a Saturday night. Dan and I sat drinking in the garden one summer's evening before we moved to the area, when we used to walk around Hampstead and dream of living somewhere lovely. We bought the cheapest pints possible with a pack of salt and vinegar crisps and just sat quietly in the garden, people watching. When I closed my eyes I could still conjure him sitting there, ivy behind him, impossibly young as he told me all about the big fancy home we'd live in on *this very street*. I'd called him a dreamer, but he was someone who turned dreams into reality. He mapped out our future over a packet of crisps, and when we'd left the pub he'd pulled me along to skip with him.

'Why are we skipping, we're not kids!' I'd laughed, happy to be dragged along.

'Maybe we should be, they have more fun!' he'd replied, and kissed me. All we'd been through and he was still my dreamer. My dream maker.

And so if he wanted to make me happy with a big party, I'd be happy with a big party.

'The Star and Anchor is great. It was really nice of him to try and do something for my birthday.'

'Ugh, Robo-wife, stop with all the *gratitude is the new attitude* bullshit or I'm going to boycott your party on principle.'

'You are a very angry lady,' I stuck my tongue out at her.

'I don't know if you've looked at the world, turned on

the TV lately, but there's a lot to be angry about.'

I raised my glass to hers, 'Fair enough. I've just got to find my keys, then we can go.'

Fair play to my friend, she didn't even blink. I'd been losing things all over the place the last few months, and half the time I was holding them in my hand whilst I searched. She always just went with it, joined in the search without judgement.

'Shall I check your coat pockets?'

I gave her a thumbs up and emptied my handbag onto the counter. The way I'd been recently, my keys could easily have been in the fridge, the soap dish or the fruit bowl. All equally as likely.

'Taz, what's this?'

Angela appeared in the doorway, holding an array of snacks. A couple of cereal bars, a mini pack of biscuits, clementines. 'You've got food in all your coat pockets!'

I tried to think of a reason to wave her concern away.

'Oh,' I shrugged, 'it's when I go to the shop and don't want to buy another plastic bag, so I stick stuff in my pockets and forget about it. Drives Dan mad.'

I'd always done it, squirreled away food in unexpected places. If you've never been unsure of what you're going to do for a next meal, if you've never been saving up to leave, you wouldn't understand. Even years later, with more material comforts than I ever could have imagined for myself, when I get nervous, I start to hide food. Dan never noticed. And I wanted to keep it that way. He already worried enough about me.

Angela seemed to accept my excuse, as 'scatty confused woman' was an acceptable reason for anything for me these days, and we walked down the street, arm in arm to the pub.

'Are you going to practise your surprised face?' she asked. 'Or your pleased face?'

'I don't need to practise! I'm a master!' I put my hand up to my mouth and widened my eyes. 'Oh my god! All this, for me? That's so lovely!' I faked a few tears and Angela snorted, nudging me as I dabbed at my eyeliner.

'Alright, calm down Olivier, I get it. You're good at pretending to be happy.'

I frowned, 'Low blow, Ange.'

Angie just shook her head and smiled, the light catching in her hair as she linked arms with me again. I couldn't help but smile back. My beautiful, unlikely friend.

'You need me. I am the antidote to your life. The only friend you have who tells you the truth.'

'You're the only friend I have, except Dan.'

'Husbands don't count.'

'Mine does,' I said and she looked pleased with me, like I'd said something she'd been waiting to hear.

I followed Angie into the pub, and of course, suddenly everyone turned around and yelled 'Happy birthday' and it was noisy and Dan was in my face, that puppy-dog look of excitement and slight trepidation as he bounced around.

'Happy birthday! Were you surprised, did you guess?' He kissed me on the cheek, and I closed my eyes briefly at the comfort, the feel of him grasping my hand. 'I never manage to surprise you!'

Looking at my husband still takes my breath away sometimes. Those bright blue eyes with the dark lashes. The thick wavy hair run through with the beginnings of grey. He complains, but it only makes him seem more attractive to me. I like seeing him age, seeing signs of the time we've spent together, growing up together.

More than that, I love how he always looks happy to see me. I'm never invisible when I'm with Dan.

'I *am* surprised! How did you arrange all this?' I plastered a smile on my face and I could see him searching my features for a giveaway, signs that I was unhappy. He wouldn't have had to look far. My ideal night would be staying in with a super cheesy pizza, a movie and a five quid bottle of wine. He knew that. But it was clear this was important to him.

Dan handed me a drink and I looked around at the faces in the room. I didn't know half of these people, and the ones I *did* know, I didn't like. Most of them were from Dan's work; his colleagues and their girlfriends, people we'd hung out with because I'd been told it was good for Dan's career. Most of them were insensitive knobheads who only cared about money and one-upmanship. If I had to hear about one more person's holiday chalet or how many of the latest sports cars were made I was going to pull my hair out. Dan said I was a snob about snobs. I just found the excess tiring. All that money and they were still just concerned with what everyone else had.

'Oi oi birthday girl! You look like you've lost the weight then! A bit too much even, maybe? It's a shame you've lost your tits though.'

Case in point: Paul. Possibly the biggest shitstain on humanity I had ever met.

'Erm, security, I think someone's let a wanker into my party by mistake!' I trilled as Paul kissed me roughly on both cheeks. I'd never properly called him out, and he must have been important enough at work that Dan never had, so now I just thinly hid my hatred under a veil of 'banter'. That seemed to be the way these people did business.

'What do you think of Danny boy's party Taz? Let me guess, all a bit too *opulent* for you? Shall we trade in the sushi bar for a Maccie D's and a few Bacardi Breezers?'

I opened my mouth to say something, anything, but he got there first, that big greasy grin in place.

'Oh don't mind me Taz, you know it's all just banter. You know what it is?' He clicked his fingers, 'You remind me of this bird from school, Jemma, and if you gave her a few cigarettes she'd give you a blowie round the back of the bins. Some of the best times of my life.'

I looked over to my husband, disappointed, almost waiting for him to storm in and beat the shit out of Paul. He would have, years ago. Before this job and these people became normal to him. He looked pained, shrugging at me apologetically as he tried to steer me away. But I wouldn't be led.

'Sorry, *why exactly* do I remind you of this bird who sucked you off behind the bins, Paul?' I could feel myself gear up for a fight, and actually, I was gagging for it. I'd been *so good* for so long. I'd been kind and understanding and cheerful. The good little wife, like Angie said. I *deserved* this.

But I supposed punching your husband's colleague at your birthday party probably wasn't the best way to show people you were better.

'Is it that she lived on a council estate? Was she poor, Paul, is that what it was?' I asked, smile firmly in place, not even blinking. 'Was she not impressed by your stories of your daddy's fancy car? Or did she have a constant look on her face like she'd enjoy punching you in the dick?'

Paul hooted, clapping his hands. God, I hated him. 'Hilarious, Taz, you're *hilarious*! Such a riot! Always good for the bants, eh White? You've got yourself a handful there. Or you did before she lost her boobs. Bet you're glad you dodged a bullet with those sleepless nights though, eh mate?'

I heard myself gasp.

Dan just looked at him, stony-faced and I felt my hands shake, wondering which one of us was going to say something. Surely *now*, surely that was enough to make Dan *say something*? But no. He glowered, but stayed perfectly still until Paul put up his hands and walked off, muttering.

Even though I was disappointed, I put my arms around Dan and rested my head on his chest. 'Why is that *awful man* here?'

'Because I invited the others and it would have looked bad. Plus you like Jasmine.'

'I feel sorry for Jasmine as I assume a part of her brain is missing in order to date that moron. Pity is not the same as liking her.'

I could hear myself moaning, and how ungrateful I sounded. I pasted my smile back on. 'But thank you for this, it's nice to be out, dressed up and celebrating.'

Dan's smile was sunshine and for a moment, I felt that same obsessive love I did at sixteen. The smile that had caught me then, that hopeful, proud one. He loved to spoil me, to show me things. But most of the time when we were teenagers, we just sat in the library writing notes to each other, both escaping from our parents and going home and never feeling like we fit. Dan was better at pretending in a crowd, and I guess that's what he taught me. Even though this party felt like the stupidest idea he'd ever had, I was happy to be held by my husband. It felt like we hadn't touched each other in months.

I knew it was my fault, but it was like there was this canyon down the middle of the bed that we never crossed. Before, I'd fall asleep folded into him and we'd always wake up forehead-to-forehead, hands clasped. A side effect of spending so many years in shitty studio flats with single beds. But we never cared, we could never get close enough.

What I wouldn't give to just lie in bed, with my husband stroking lazy circles on my arms and talking about the places we'd go, the things we'd do. It felt like a lifetime ago, away from all this.

The next few people to talk to me weren't much better than Paul:

'God, you look good! How do you look so good?'

'You've lost the weight, haven't you? How are you feeling?'

'It's so good to see you up and around. You deserve a good party.'

That head-tilt, the wide-eyed questions, rushed through in the hopes that I wouldn't reveal anything too awkward. *Don't bring down the mood, Taz, we don't want to hear about all that awful stuff.*

That's why I'd been volunteering on the grief helpline. Sometimes you *do* want to talk about it. You want someone who will listen without judgement, won't shy away or offer empty platitudes to try and make it better. Most people don't know how to listen, and that's okay. But they shouldn't ask if they don't want a real answer.

Of course, I didn't actually *use* the helpline, I think that's what irritated Dan more than anything else. I wanted to help. I wanted to be the fixer. I had enough bad memories of school counsellors and the power they had with their solutions and suggestions. How they could change your life. I didn't want to be beholden to anyone. So I stayed the soothing stranger in the dark for other people's pain, listening and 'mmn-hmm'ing and doing all those human things that say, 'I'm here.'

I survived the party by nodding and smiling, taking the glasses of Champagne that were thrust into my hands and saying very little. Dan's parents were there, of course, basking in their son's achievements and I tried to smile, to show I was the good, appreciative wife. His dad, Timothy, was a stern man, with none of his son's warmth. He had very little interest in people, it was *things* that made him tick. Numbers and items. But he was still a tropical island retreat compared to Dan's mother. Miranda hated me. And I couldn't blame her – I had ruined her son's life. And then I called her every day for three months, begging her to see him. I was a reminder that she'd abandoned her child, and she had to see that every time she saw my face.

Miranda gripped my arm in her spindly hand as she air-kissed me, 'Happy birthday.'

I got the same comments: I looked thin, I looked well,

it was good that I was getting out and about. I was starting to wonder if I'd spent the last few months in a facility and just didn't recall it. Everyone was acting like I'd been sectioned.

'It's good to have Daniel around again, back to normal and all that.' Tim seemed to boom everything he said, never making eye contact. It was always like he was lecturing to a room rather than having a conversation. He had his hands in his pockets as he surveyed the room; most of the people there were his employees. It had always been the plan that Dan would go into the family business, and in the end they got what they wanted.

Dan's parents showed up under the guise of making amends two years ago, and our lives changed. From the outside it looked like they waved a magic wand: got Dan a well-paid job, got us our fancy flat. We went from living like students to living like socialites.

But he was meant to be an artist, my Daniel. The boy who took my hand outside that prison and walked until we got on a bus into London, he was going to be a painter. He was going to tell the truth with a paintbrush, paint things that mattered, that's what he said.

Instead now he worked on investment portfolios, played golf with his father every Saturday and visited his mother afterwards for a 'cheeky gin and tonic'. It was made very clear that the flat, our new life, came with strings. These people had abandoned their son when he needed them, and everything still turned out the way they wanted. Except me, obviously. I marred an otherwise perfect picture.

'I've been around, Dad. Everything's running smoothly.' Daniel's smile was strained.

'Well if you want to take over from me, you're going to have to show you're hungry for it. You can't lose your drive just because you haven't got a family to support anymore.'

I blinked, trying to figure out if my father-in-law had really just said that, or if I'd imagined it.

'Yes, darling, now you can focus on what matters.' Miranda did that thing where she picked an invisible piece of fluff from Daniel's top, a power move that I'd hated since the first time she'd done it. 'And really, maybe it's all for the best, you know? Babies can complicate things.'

I coughed, a dry, sharp sound that sounded like choking. It felt like choking. Choking down every terrible thing I'd ever wanted to scream at this woman who seemed so capable of dismissing my pain. My husband's pain.

'Complicate things,' I tried to keep my lips pressed together but I couldn't. I took a shaky breath. '*Complicate* things?'

Miranda turned towards me, and I could tell she wanted to roll her eyes, but that wouldn't be polite. She always spoke more slowly to me, letting me know she thought I was stupid. 'Now don't be *overly sensitive*

Natasha, I just meant…'

'You meant that a baby would have tied Dan to his trashy wife forever,' I said, smiling through clenched teeth. *And maybe now he'll see sense and leave me for one of those trust fund Barbie dolls you've been parading around him ever since he came back into your life.*

We had laughed about it, at first, Dan and I, when she started turning up with these women. Young, successful women with tailored clothing and job roles *just* high up enough to be impressive, but not so high as to intimidate the menfolk. They would quit their jobs to raise their kids, and think nothing of throwing away a decade of work. They were a particular type, and I often wondered if Miranda was growing them in her greenhouse.

But I wasn't laughing today. Babies can *complicate things*. Good God.

Miranda curled a lip. 'You're being incredibly vulgar, though I don't know why I'm surprised.'

'Yes, I never did manage that way you people have of hiding a snide comment behind a smile.' I looked to Daniel, who seemed to be on the verge of tears. 'I assume you have nothing to say about this?'

Dan looked between us. I waited for him to back down, to take their side, the way he always did. He'd been so desperate to please them, to make up for disappointing them. The number of times in the last two years that he'd asked me to be patient, to be understanding, to let his family do what they wanted. To do it for him. I'd lost count.

There was the fake second wedding that his mother organised just so she could be in the photos; the new flat that was so big, it made me uncomfortable when I was there alone. The big fancy job that meant he was never around. These last couple of years had been about what they wanted for us, and I had bitten my lip and stayed silent, because I owed Dan everything, and this was what he wanted.

I was waiting for him to take their side again.

Instead, he smiled at me and reached out a hand for mine, before turning to face his mother. We were united, and I could have cried in relief.

And then he spoke.

'Mum, we're incredibly sad about what happened, and I'd like you to be a bit more sensitive please.'

Oh wow, you told her.

I felt my stomach dip in disappointment.

His mother was right, of course, I'd never managed their lingo, their way of pretending to be interested when they were laughing at you. It was a particular skill and I figured you probably had to grow up hearing it to recognise it. Like Morse code or a certain frequency. *'Oh, how riveting.' 'Oh you really are the most interesting person.' 'I'm so pleased you actually managed to make it. I thought you'd be too busy.'*

I'd never caught on. I said what I thought or, more

likely, I said nothing at all. And that marked me out, more than the way I spoke, or my distaste for caviar and macarons or bottles of wine that reached triple figures.

'Oh darling, you know I only want what's best for you. Daddy and I are just so pleased you're back to focusing on work and building up your career.'

Instead of focusing on the family we're so disappointed by. The woman who begged you to save your child instead of her.

It was no one's fault, obviously, and nothing we'd done would have made any difference, the doctors were eager to make that clear. But there was a brokenness in me that hadn't been there before, like I was a walking bruise being bumped by every single thing or person I passed. Dan had been there, a vague outline in the greyness. It was like those visiting hours. He came and he talked, he held me and he gave me hope.

And one day I woke up and I could see things properly again. I could shower and dress and make breakfast. I could eat lunch and watch television and think about something other than this huge festering wound of loss.

But now we were meant to be back to normal, and I was letting the side down.

I had carried my baby inside me, all those months, and then he was gone and I was so very unused to being alone in my body. It was a loneliness that I couldn't explain. Almost like still expecting a flash of tail or a twitched ear from a pet you'd always had, and finding the house empty.

Angela raised her eyebrows at me from across the room, and when I made a face she bounced over, drinks in hand. 'Sorry ladies and gents, I'm going to have to steal the birthday girl here, you're hogging her. Toodles!'

As we escaped into the garden, I kissed her on the cheek, 'You are a *goddess*. A jail breaker, my knight in shining armour, whatever, I love you.'

'Wicked Witch of East Hertfordshire causing problems again?'

'Oh, she's still waiting for Daniel to wake up and realise he never loved me, that I was a gold-digging bitch who tricked him into staying with her, and I only got knocked up to spite her.'

My voice broke a little as I reached the end of my sentence, so I sucked down half the glass of Champagne. Angela handed me a cigarette and I paused.

'I quit.'

Angela's warm brown eyes were frank, 'Yes. You quit because you needed to, and now you don't need to, so you may as well.'

'Or I've quit, so I may as well carry on with it. You've always been the devil on my shoulder.'

'I've been the antidote to the bullshit in your life, sweetcheeks,' she flicked her dark hair back, those gold hoops getting caught again. 'But do as you like, it's nothing to do with me.'

I looked through the window as yet another swishy brunette was introduced to my husband by his parents, exactly the kind of woman they'd wanted for their son. Someone with airs and graces, or at the very least from good stock. Someone who knew when family came first and when to step back. Someone who would shut up and do what they were told.

'Ha,' I pointed her out to Angela, 'called it.'

We got married when we were twenty years old. It's been ten years. And still, *still*, they just can't comprehend why their son would saddle himself with someone like me. Someone who didn't go to university, who came from nothing. Who worked for a charity, 'begging people for money all day' (Dan's dad referred to charities as 'useful for reducing taxes but not much else'). What could I possibly have had to offer him that would make him give everything up for me? That would keep him here all these years later?

The answer was simple – devotion. And gratitude. Daniel had saved me at the worst moment in my life, and I'd saved him during his. Those months and years after, when we'd lived off dented tins of beans and tuna pasta bake for weeks on end, they weren't a hardship. Not for me. I just got to be with him, wake up to him, spend my life loving someone who loved me. Poverty didn't even touch the sides, I was happy.

But I'm starting to wonder if Daniel wasn't. He never complained, never said anything. But when his parents offered him this job two years ago, he took it and ever since then it's been a steady stream of corporate bullshit. They're grooming him to take over, and when he does, I half expect them to offer an ultimatum: *You've had your fun now Daniel, but it's time to grow up. Leave Taz, she'll be just fine without you, her kind always is.*

I didn't know what bothered me more – that they still thought I wasn't good enough for their son after all these years, or that one day soon Dan might think it too.

I held my hand out for a lighter and lit the cigarette, 'Fuck it.'

'Atta girl.' Angela nudged me, 'Vices are important.'

'Hmph,' I replied, non-committal. I watched Dan smile at people, shake hands and slap backs and raise his glass in greeting. He was so good at all this, as much as he professed to hate it. He was a natural. He belonged in this world.

'So, are you going to try again?' Angela said lightly, and I suddenly felt like I was going to throw up. I stubbed the cigarette out on the wall, and buried the butt in the soil of the planter behind me.

'None of your fucking business,' I felt myself harden.

'Good,' Angela nodded, unruffled, 'no one else has asked that yet then. I wanted to prepare you. These people have absolutely no tact.'

'And you do?'

'When it comes to the people I care about, sure.'

'Are any of them here tonight?' I nudged her, half-smiling and Angela leaned against me.

'I'm just looking out for you kid, I don't know why you put up with these people. This is my livelihood, I need them, you don't.'

But I needed Daniel. And no one told me at the beginning that this life was part of the deal. This privileged, perfect life.

I paused. 'They're not gonna ask me when we're trying again.'

Angela raised an eyebrow.

'It would be tacky, these people aren't tacky.'

She snorted, 'You *were* at that Christmas party at the Ivy last year, right?'

'I love that you're such a snob.'

She rolled her eyes and stubbed out her cigarette, 'Well I wouldn't mind if they weren't all so *dreadfully dull*, darling. You're the only one here who ever does something I don't see coming.'

'I don't do anything! I sit quietly and nod and let people look at my boobs, like you said. Although apparently they're less impressive these days.'

Angela's grin was wicked, 'I think you're rewriting history a bit. What about when you cornered that MP who voted against the homeless bill? And the summer party when you tore that private school headmaster a new one when it came to charitable status? And that time you got every woman in the room to calculate how much they'd spent on their periods in the last twenty years and made the bosses donate the equivalent to charity?'

'Ah, the *Looney Tunes Leftie Wife*, I guess I did give them a run for their money at the beginning.' I had a lot more energy back then. I'd still been working at the charity and I was strong-willed and confident. If I riled up the right old man at the right party with the right journalists present, I could raise more for charity in that night than I did in a month. It was like a game, and I'd loved to play it. I was good at it, too.

'You have never been boring, and it's why we're friends. Also I'm hoping if I hang around you long enough, your morals will rub off on me.'

'Oh no, don't bother, they're terribly inconvenient. Especially in this crowd.' I clinked my glass against hers, and then rested my head on her shoulder. 'Thank you for being here. I know I haven't been… I haven't been right for a while.'

'You never have to apologise for that sweetcheeks,' I felt her rest her head on top of mine. 'I just miss Taz the fighter. She made me hopeful.'

I had been so tired, so very tired. Too tired to fight about anything. All I'd wanted to do was lie in bed every day staring at the ceiling. Ignoring the voicemails Miranda left for Dan (never for me) and avoiding that grey and yellow bedroom at the end of the hall with the mural we'd painted so beautifully.

'I miss her too,' I said, tapping my fingers until Angie handed me the remains of her cigarette.

'So… what's the plan to get her back?' she asked, and I sensed the hesitancy. *Tread carefully Ange, don't spook her. She spooks easy these days.*

'What do you mean?'

Angie exhaled and leaned back so she could meet my eyes. She looked scarily sincere. 'Babe, your birthday present from me is some tough love. I adore you, you went through shit, it's okay to wallow and take time to heal…'

'But?' I could feel it coming.

'But I'm worried you're getting bitter. You're like… clenched. A waiting fist. But you never punch. You just stay there, frozen. Time doesn't heal all wounds, right, sometimes you've got to take responsibility for some healing.'

'Wow,' I croaked, looking up to try and avoid my eyes filling with tears. *But I thought I was doing so well. I was trying so hard to seem happy. To seem okay.*

'But… but you told me I didn't have to pretend with you.'

'Oh darling, no, you don't. That's not what I'm saying. You can be sad. You can be quiet and hurting or raging or whatever you like. But you're not being any of those things.'

'I am!' I sniffed, embarrassed at how weak I sounded, like a child scolded and trying to reason with the adult.

Angela smiled kindly, and tucked a piece of hair behind my ear. Even that caring gesture made me want to burst into tears. 'You're not expressing anything, Taz. I asked you to come to that yoga retreat, I invited you axe-throwing, and to that therapeutic writing class. Gong baths and weekends away, you didn't want any of it. You won't even talk to that helpline you're so attached to. You've got all this pain and you're not *putting* it anywhere.'

I wanted to deny it, but I couldn't. I desperately searched for something that I'd done in the last few months. Something to show I was trying to get better, trying to find myself again.

Instead, I just met her eyes and nodded, and we sat silently, clasped hands as I tried to compose myself.

'I knew you were pissed off about bloody axe-throwing,' I grumbled, smiling at her. 'Who drinks a bunch of cocktails and then throws sharp objects?'

'Well-adjusted people, apparently,' Angie grinned and stuck out her tongue, before pausing. 'So, we're okay, right? It's okay that your birthday present was a kick up the bum?'

'From anyone else, no. From you… maybe,' I nudged her. 'I know I've been stuck. I'm just… I'm working up the energy, you know?'

'It's why you need the axe-throwing,' she grinned. 'I'll even print out a photo of your mother-in-law's face for the bullseye, I bet that'll motivate you.'

I snorted, 'Why didn't you say? I'd have been there in a flash.'

Angela pulled me into a hug, brief and rough. 'I love you, little one. And if you ever tell anyone that I said that…'

'I know, I know, you've spent years cultivating an image of a bitchy entrepreneur and you've got to protect it.' I kissed her cheek. 'But I love you too, you softy.'

I watched as Angela's body language changed, how she peered behind me into the pub and looked suddenly alert.

'Come on, we better get inside. Here, drink the rest of mine,' she switched our glasses as she hustled me up.

'I'm sure I can wait the five minutes until we get to the bar,' I snorted. But Angela's eyes were trained on something inside, and she shook her head.

'I have a feeling Dan is making a speech, and he's missing the guest of honour.'

'Oh shut up, he wouldn't make a speech. It's my thirtieth, not my hundredth.'

Angela tapped the glass in my hand, 'Think of it as one of those things American girls get, cotillions? Coming out parties? You're being reintroduced to society as Natasha "I'm completely fine, really" White.'

Angela was right. Daniel was standing at the raised edge by the bar, microphone in hand and tense smile on his face as we walked in. 'Ah there she is, finally, the birthday girl! Call off the search party!'

Oh no, he was annoyed. I knew that fake smile and clenched look around his jaw. He wanted his moment and I'd embarrassed him.

'Taz, come on up babe,' Daniel beckoned me, holding out a hand as if knowing I wanted to scarper, and the crowd seemed to part for me, all those smiling faces with flitting eyes, scanning to see what I'd do.

He positioned me awkwardly next to him, slotted into his side, and I just watched him, wondering how much that expensive suit cost, and how much this party had cost, and whether the ornamental bird cage that I bought online at midnight last night had been dispatched yet. And where the hell I'd hide it when it arrived.

'Now, as most of you know, it hasn't been the easiest year for us…' Daniel started, and I had to stop myself from physically wincing. *Oh please don't. Please don't put all my pain and shame out in front of these people. These awful, awful people.*

I pasted a vacant smile on my face and let Dan squeeze my hand, even as I searched in the crowd for Angela's eyes with a kind of panic. She looked outraged, mouthing 'What the fuck?' as my husband continued.

'But we're really happy we're able to celebrate Taz's birthday with you all, and we appreciate all your support and patience over the last few months as we get on with everything. And well, I basically just want to say that my wife is amazing.' He turned to me, beaming. 'A lot of people said we wouldn't make it, getting together so young, getting married so young, but I always knew we were meant for each other.'

One of Dan's banker bros imitated vomiting loudly and everyone laughed. I suddenly really wanted to cry. I wasn't Fighter Taz anymore, I was just a very tired woman who wanted to be at home, eating ice cream in her pyjamas.

'Yeah, I suppose that was a bit sappy,' Dan smiled at me as though he didn't care, and I desperately pushed down on my irritation. He was trying to do a good thing, he was trying to make me feel better, be better. 'But I don't care. Here's to my wife, the one and only Taz White, fearless, brave and a survivor, always, no matter what. Happy birthday, sweetheart.'

'To Taz!' someone in the crowd yelled, and they raised their glasses to me, my husband kissing my cheek as I realised this portion of my life had been closed without my permission.

That's what this whole night was for, to tell me I'd had my time. Now I was just being selfish. I was stopping my husband from focusing on his career. I was costing all of these people money because they had to cover his work when he couldn't leave me, just lying on the floor staring at the ceiling, because I hadn't slept in forty-eight hours.

I had been given my grace period and now I was taking the piss.

No more grieving, Taz, no more just surviving. It was

time to get on and feel better. Not just pretend but actually be better.

I'm not sure I'd ever hated my husband before.

I took the microphone, and Dan looked a little surprised. They were expecting me to nod and smile and accept my accolades, my congratulations on making it through another year, for *surviving*. I was meant, like the other wives and girlfriends would have, to take this graciously, sip my expensive Champagne, nibble at the sushi platter and blush prettily when people said nice things to me.

But I was Taz White and like fuck was I from this world.

'I'd like to thank you all for coming. Well those of you I know, not so much, but those of you I don't know, you might be alright, so cheers to you!' I held up a glass and there was a brief tittering, but the flash of panic in Dan's eyes told me I was onto the right track.

'Daniel's right, we've had a bit of a shitty year, and definitely your main priority when you've been unhappy and unwell and generally drowning in your own grief is to have a big knees-up with a hundred and fifty of your "nearest and dearest"… or "nearby and alrightest".

'I've got the message, loud and clear. You love Daniel, just like I do. And you need him, just like I did. So, yes, he will 100 per cent be back at work making you all lots of money in that way you like!' I laughed drily and there was actually a hoot and some applause at the back. I was sure it had to be Paul. 'His top priority will be the business, and you don't have to worry about me getting in the way anymore, I promise. Scout's honour.' I held my hand up to my temple. 'So, let's get this party started, shall we? That thousand pounds of sushi isn't going to eat itself!'

I stepped down through the crowd, hearing Miranda tut as I walked past. I made a beeline for the toilets and when I got there, Angela was already waiting with a bottle of wine, and led me out into the garden, right at the back, hidden by the shrubbery. I didn't really say anything, Angela just held my hand and filled my glass and told me funny stories about going on tour with a band when she was nineteen, and living in Greece, and the artist she was in an on-again-off-again relationship with. She didn't say anything else about taking control or channelling my anger. Because at least I'd done that, finally. Angie was kind, and funny and full of stories. I didn't smile, but I felt better.

At least until Daniel came to get me and said it was time to go.

We sat in silence in the car, the back filled with balloons and flowers and presents, colourful ribbons contrasting with the dark mood in between us. God, I was the *worst*.

'I really screwed up, didn't I?' I said.

Dan didn't say anything, just stared straight in front of him, tapping his fingers on the steering wheel. He hadn't even turned the engine on, so I knew he wanted to do this now.

'Come on, let it out. I know you're angry with me.'

'I'm not…' Dan took a breath, clenching and unclenching his fists. 'Do you now how hard I work not to be angry around you, ever? Not to shout too loudly or get too close? I need to prove that I'm still the good guy. I'm not some thug who ended up in prison, I'm calm and kind and in control. All the time.'

'I… I hadn't thought of that.'

He turned to me, and I was almost ashamed to look at him.

'You really embarrassed me tonight, and I don't understand why.' Daniel ran a hand through his hair, 'This was a chance to show we were okay, we were back on the right path…'

'What path, Dan?' *What path is it that you and your parents are constantly talking about, like there's only one way to live?*

'I was just trying to do something nice and you just… ruined it. Threw it back in my face.'

'Oh, you can't honestly believe any of those people were there for me tonight,' I scoffed, and watched as he clipped in his seatbelt. Apparently he was calm enough to have this conversation whilst driving. I hated being a passenger at times like this, it felt like a hostage situation.

'They were there for *us*.'

'Oh yes, every woman's dream, a "we're sorry you

lost your baby" party,' I snorted. 'And your mother! Your *mother* said to my face that it was a good thing our son was dead, and what was your response?'

'I asked her to be more respectful!'

'Oh, please be nicer to my wife, Mummy. It's not her fault she lived on the estate and doesn't know how to act,' I mimicked like a child.

'Well you proved her right, didn't you?' he spat back and I felt a frustrated growl escape my throat.

'You shouldn't be driving.'

'I'm fine.'

'You were drinking.'

'You want me to leave forty portions of fucking birthday cake in the car? All your presents bought by people that you just belittled? We can park the car here if you want, leave it on the side of the road?'

I took a breath, 'Fine, let me out. I'll walk the rest of the way.'

Dan laughed, that hollow, sarcastic chuckle that I hated. 'God, how can you be so incredibly selfish? I put a lot of time and money into arranging this party for you—'

'This party was for *you*,' I snorted, 'for you and your family and your family's friends to tell everyone that Daniel White and his wife are *just fine* and that *everything's okay* and you won't be distracted any more! What is it with you people and what other people think?!'

'You people?' Dan laughed again. 'And if we're going to talk about people *pretending to be okay*...'

'I'm trying to be okay! I'm trying my best! I didn't need to be paraded in front of strangers like a fucking show pony tonight. What did you have to prove? Got tired of defending your working-class wife who didn't go to uni?'

'Oh, right, you're *so* much better than these people, just because they've got money and like skiing and fly first class? That's what this is?'

I took a breath, trying to bring down the argument. I hated yelling, I hated loud noises and big emotions and the way Dan's driving became more erratic when he answered me.

'I don't know what this is,' I said quietly, 'but clearly it's not working.'

We sat in silence for a few moments, the traffic trundling along. We wouldn't have long before we were back home, and somehow I didn't want this argument to escape from the car. Once it was out there, it was in the real world and we'd have to deal with it.

'I'm sorry I was embarrassing. I'm sorry I seemed ungrateful and I was rude. But this party wasn't really about me, Daniel, be honest.' I made my voice soft and sweet, I reached for his hand on the gear stick. 'I know you were trying to do a nice thing for me, I get that, but this was about painting a pretty picture for everyone.'

Dan didn't talk for a moment, just breathed deeply,

slowly, and I knew he was gathering his thoughts, finding a way to say what he really meant. It was only in these times, just us, that I managed to find him again. But they were becoming fewer and farther between.

'You're acting like you're the only one who lost a baby.' His voice shook and I loved him and wanted to hold him, but I also wanted to scream.

Because yes, he'd lost a child. He lost the hopes and dreams he had of a family. Something to stop it just being *us* anymore, tangled up in a complicated past. He'd lost the chance to see a version of himself in a new life, a new chance with none of our bullshit.

But he doesn't know the pain of your body turning on you, betraying you. The life you've carried all those months suddenly gone, the friend that doesn't talk to you any more.

'You never want to talk about it…' I said gently.

'And you *always* want to talk about it, Taz. It's too much. You want to talk about whether he looked like me or you, or if he would have grown up to like the same stories you loved as a kid, or if he would have been a painter or gone to private school, and it's just too much! It's like you want to jump head first and just swim around in it all. I don't want to do that. It hurts. It fucking hurts.'

'You want me to shut up and pretend to be okay?'

'I want you to be okay. That's it, that's literally it.' He

huffed as he pulled up in front of the flat. 'And I don't know why that makes me a monster.'

'Because I'm not ready yet. And this, tonight, it was you telling me, telling all of them, that I had to be! That's not fair!'

Dan looked at me, frustrated, like I was a child who didn't understand the adult world. Those blue eyes that I had so fallen in love with when we were sixteen, the eyes I searched for whenever I needed someone to ground me, they were disappointed.

'Life's not fair, Taz. It's important to get on with things, and I've got to show them that I'm on top, that I'm capable of being the boss. They're looking to me to step up, and I haven't been able to…'

'I'm sorry your wife and her miscarriage were such an inconvenience to you,' I spat out, crossing my arms.

'Now *you're* not being fair.'

I didn't know how to argue with my husband anymore. I didn't know how to talk to him beyond this big wall of hurt.

Dan took a breath, 'You've changed. I don't know if it was the baby, or before then, but it's like you're full of poison now. Always thinking the worst of people, always ready for drama and trauma. You don't forgive. Everyone's always out to get you… I know you went through stuff as a kid, but it's like you *enjoy* it. You enjoy the drama. Your fucked-up family are gone and it's like they've still got power over you.'

I blinked. Dan looked straight ahead, as if he wasn't sure what I was going to do. Was he afraid of me?

I *enjoyed* the drama? The drama that stuck him in prison and left me homeless. That left me with a runaway mother and a dead father. I thought I might explode with rage, my veins thrummed with it. Full of poison, indeed!

The problem was, I'd been raised to survive, no matter what. And when you're backed into a corner, the only way out is to scratch and bite. No matter who you hurt.

I made my voice calm and collected.

'You do realise, babe, no matter how good you are, however many promotions or title changes you get, it's never going to make them forgive you? You do understand that, Daniel? They wrote you off the minute you were in trouble, and giving you a fancy corner office, or throwing us a stupid second wedding doesn't undo that. They didn't love you enough to stay. All this is shit rolled in glitter, a decade too late. The minute you step off the path they want, they'll leave you again.'

Daniel looked like I'd slapped him, but his voice was calm, soft, muddled with hurt and loss.

'You knew what you were getting with me, Taz. I don't know why it suddenly makes you unhappy. I've given you everything I had.'

He simply shook his head, gave me the keys and got out of the car, walking into the flat. When I followed him ten minutes later, I found a glass of water out on the side waiting for me, and the door to the spare bedroom closed.

No matter what argument we'd had, if we were both home we hadn't slept apart in thirteen years. Most of the time because we hadn't had the luxury. When we lived in the studio there was nowhere to go. If you had an argument you had to get in the damn bed and try to radiate irritation whilst sleeping.

And somehow, in the night, our bodies would take over, pulling each other close, enveloping the other with love, and by the morning it would be hard to stay mad, because touch reminded us how much we needed each other.

Another reason this big stupid flat was bad for us.

I padded along to the bedroom and paused at the door to the spare room.

'Thank you for the water.'

There was no answer, not that I expected one.

'I'm sorry. I love you,' I tried again, whispering. 'Goodnight.'

I tucked myself up in that beautifully heavy duvet and snuggled down into the pillows, trying to figure out how the hell to fix my marriage and myself.

It hadn't always been like this. We had lived an entirely different life. One that wasn't opulent or filled with fancy dinner parties and expensive mini-breaks. When Daniel got out, we started with nothing. We crashed on sofas for a few weeks, and then I managed to wangle jobs, and got us a small studio not far from Tufnell Park. It was damp and little more than a room with a microwave, but it was ours.

I worked at a café during the day, and at a bar in the evening. I was in my element, I knew how to survive, I knew how to work hard. Daniel struggled a little more, mainly because his record now made work more difficult, even if he had been a minor when he was convicted.

However, he had savings and he was learning to be thrifty. He got work with a painter and decorator at the weekends, a friend of my boss at the bar, and whilst it wasn't the kind of painting he'd dreamed of doing, he liked it. He was achieving something.

Those were honestly the best times of my life, curled around Daniel in the evenings as we ate tuna pasta bake or three-bean chili for the third night in a row, watching VHS tapes that we used to find at a little shop on the corner for 50p. He drew in his sketchbooks, and I learnt to sew, fixing our clothes to keep them in good condition. I brought home leftover cake from the café, read every book I could from the library, and life was good. We'd book days off and go walking through London, visiting art galleries and eating our pre-made jam sandwiches in front of monuments.

We were surviving, all on our own. We didn't need anyone. And it was wonderful.

We got married on a Wednesday, skipping down to the registry office and paying our thirty quid. I wore a white Oxfam summer dress that I sewed daisies onto, and Daniel wore a blue blazer over his nice shirt and jeans with a ridiculous top hat, perched slightly askew. He picked flowers from the grass verge near our flat and we asked two strangers on the street to be our witnesses. We took photos on disposable cameras, and when we were done, we walked around Camden Market, bought a bottle of Cava and some Chinese food, and sat by the river, toasting our own brilliance. We were twenty years old, and it was the best day of my life. I'd never been so sure of things being *right* before. But I had this person and this life, and we were happy and strong, working towards our dreams.

It was another eight years before Daniel's parents reached out, and by then we were actually doing really well. We'd moved into a slightly bigger (but still damp) flat, and had actual furniture. I had a job at a charity, starting out as a fundraiser on the street but quickly moving into their in-office department, working in comms. I loved it, feeling like I was doing something good every day, helping people. I'd never dreamed of doing anything like that, and I was good at it. Telling a story, grabbing attention, tugging at heart strings. I still worked in the bar a couple of nights a week, because being scared of being without never quite leaves you, no matter how well things are going.

Daniel had been able to work on his art alongside the decorating – he'd been creating murals and feature walls. He'd decorated a café on our street, painted the entire wall in a scene of local people and worldly adventures, and I was so proud of him. He was starting to get commissions, and the decorator he worked for suggested setting up his own company. He even had a small exhibition of his line drawings in a space in Camden. He was at the beginning of his career.

And that's where his parents found him.

They didn't even look at his artwork. There was no apology, no 'we missed you' or 'we were wrong'. The Whites didn't do that, they were too cold for all that messy emotion. The least they could have done was nurse some tepid wine from plastic cups and tell their son they liked his drawings. Instead, it was a simple command:

Enough of this silliness now, it's time to come home.

Oh, when they realised we were married they hit the roof. Even Miranda broke the ice queen persona long enough to start a screaming match. Daniel was tied to me now, and they realised what a mistake it was to have let him go. Their baby boy, not only with a criminal record, but a wife like me?

But Daniel couldn't see that, he saw only the family he'd lost suddenly back again. He heard stories of his brother and sister, and what everyone was up to. The school friends who went to uni and were now in graduate schemes or high-flying jobs. They talked of the holidays they went on, and the people they spoke to. The things he'd missed and people he'd never even mentioned to me.

But more than that, I realised, he missed the comfort of not having to worry. Living like poor artists was fine for someone like me. This was the best I'd ever had – savings in my bank account, food in my belly, no fear of the flat being taken away at a moment's notice. A safe, loving home. But that wasn't enough for Daniel.

His dad offered him a job. He said he'd still be able to do his murals, work on his art in his spare time. Dan said it was an olive branch, and he should take it, show he accepted their apology. He wanted us to get along, it was the right thing to do.

He's always been quicker to forgive than I have.

So Daniel got the little office, started wearing suits to work and I didn't need to keep sewing up jeans or darning socks. We started to go to fancy networking events, and at the beginning it was fun, so fun.

We'd see how many spring rolls and cheese puffs we could fit into my handbag, and drink their free drinks and mock everyone. We'd pretend to be different people, joining in conversations about holiday homes and tax brackets. We'd jump into talking about ridiculous things we knew nothing about, and then disappear before anyone could question us.

Then we'd sit on the tube home and eat our stolen snacks, and laugh until our stomachs hurt:

'Did you see the guy who looked like Winston Churchill?'

'The one who breeds Arabian horses?'

'No, the one who went to the Playboy Mansion back in the seventies and couldn't stop staring at the lady in the black sparkly thing.'

'Did you speak to the woman who's made her entire house gold leaf? She says she's inspired by the works of Gustav Klimt and might get a column in Home and Country*.'*

'Her dog was wearing a gold headpiece!'

'Yes!'

It was play-acting. We'd go into their world briefly, us against them, and then retreat back to our little flat, entirely sure of our place in the world. We were living right, with soul, with *purpose*. Their lives were trifles, basic and ridiculous.

They must be such unhappy people, we used to say.

But the lines became blurred over the next two years. The play-acting became harder to stop, because Dan so very much wanted to please his father. After all, he had more than enough to make up for. Dan stopped making up stories. He'd frown if I said something outlandish, and when I tried to mock them, he'd say, 'Oh well, he was actually very nice, if you gave him a chance.'

Sometimes he'd say, 'This is important to my family, Taz, please just go with it,' and I'd struggle not to remind him that *I* was his family, that was the deal we'd made. They'd abandoned him and I'd been there. But no, he felt that he'd deeply disappointed them and wanted to fix it.

And everything that happened was because of me, so I had to go along with it. Had to play the happy little wife to the big-shot banker. He rose through the ranks (largely through nepotism) and we had to go to more parties, more galas, more charity events. I still insisted on buying my dresses from charity shops in fancy areas of London, but Dan bought expensive suits. He got comfortable with money again. Once at a charity auction he spent two thousand pounds on an ugly vase and I didn't talk to him for a week.

We were losing ourselves. We'd become the lie.

And somehow, time had passed, and we were here. In a fancy Hampstead flat financed by Mummy and Daddy, and a second wedding that was befitting for their baby boy.

It meant more to Daniel than he'd admit. But I've known women like Miranda White my whole life, doesn't matter if they're on the estate or in an ivory tower – they never do anything unless something's in it for them. It was more than just being in the photos or inviting great-aunties. It was about controlling the narrative.

I remembered hearing someone say, 'And who are the

bride's *people*?' during the reception, and snorting to myself, almost hysterical with giggles before I walked myself down the aisle. My *people*. The notion of it!

I had a person. I had Daniel. And he was all I'd ever wanted.

Lying alone in bed whilst my husband slept next door, it was hard to remember a time when he might have felt the same.

Chapter Two

When I woke up the next morning, Dan was already at work.

Most mornings he woke at five, and went down to the shed in the thin patch of garden we owned to use the punch-bag he'd set up. In the summer I'd look out of the window to see him doing push ups and burpees on the grass, and watch with this sort of wonder before rolling over and going back to sleep. Then there'd be shower, breakfast, prepping paperwork and off he'd go to the tube, returning anywhere from eight p.m. until midnight.

These days, it was more often the latter.

I padded downstairs and found he'd left me a mug and the remains of a cafetière of coffee. It was still warm. No note this morning, but still more kindness than I deserved. I'd been awful last night. I'd embarrassed him. I'd been so incredibly ungrateful.

He was right. He was right about so many things.

My fucked-up family.

That he'd given me everything.

I knew exactly who he was when I'd married him.

Except… well, I *hadn't* signed up for this life. I know it's the one everyone aspires to, but the money was never what it was about for me. I need a little hunger to get out of bed in the morning, a reason, a use. Dan's family and friends will say differently, of course. I'd never stop being the girl off the estate with the greasy hair and the thumb-holes in her jumper who won the lottery the day Daniel White saved her life.

At school, we seemed an unlikely pair. He was the perfect son with the good grades and the easy laugh, who everyone wanted to be friends with. Yet he used to hide out in the library after school to avoid going home, just like me. He'd sit and draw these cartoons, things that had happened, funny stuff teachers said, or arguments his parents had.

Then after about an hour he'd run his hand through his beautiful dark hair, scrunch up the papers and throw them in the bin on the way out. And I, like the little creep I was, would go and rescue them, because they were wonderful and deserved to be seen.

This carried on for weeks, watching him draw as I pretended to do my homework, or read the same page five times over from across that huge table in the library. It was like I had an insight to him that no one else had, I knew him, the *real* him. Not the boy who laughed so easily, or played the clown or kicked a football around at lunch. We were from different worlds in that school, but in the library, we were the same.

The arguments his parents had, in those cartoon strips, they'd been so similar to the ones my parents had before my mum left. Sure, my dad held a beer and his mum had a martini. Mine swore in ways I was used to, and his speech bubbles used words that sounded posh and sharp, like *bah-stard* and *ahrsehole*.

He discovered my snooping, in the worst possible way. He bumped into me in the hallway and his sketches fell right out of my bag. I stood there, waiting to be shamed, accused of being a freak, a stalker. Instead Dan just smiled, asked if I was okay, and how I'd found his drawings. Speaking in that spooked animal voice he still uses on me. No fear, no worry. Always assuming the best.

I opened my mouth and I spoke, more than I ever had before. About how beautiful his drawings were, how they deserved to be seen, how I related. An embarrassing spew of word vomit and I got redder and redder until eventually I turned on my heel and ran.

After that, Dan always sat next to me in the library. He started asking for my opinion, sliding the cartoons across so I could fill in the speech bubbles, writing me notes, drawing me unicorns and sassy dragons smoking cigars, wizards DJing supernatural parties. He made me laugh so loud that the librarian glared. He said he was collecting my laughs and counting them.

And that was it, that was the beginning of us. The girl who was always hungry, growing out of her uniform, itchy from being soaked in washing-up liquid in the sink. And the boy from the nice bit of town who only went to the comprehensive because his dad thought it would 'build character'.

I caught sight of a photo of us in our early twenties on the fridge, sticking our tongues out. We grew up together. There are no photos of us in our teens, but it's probably better that way. Dan likes to pretend that time didn't exist. This version of Daniel White is not the sort of man who went to prison for manslaughter.

At the time he said he didn't regret it, but I think he's changed his mind. Last night he looked at me like I was the worst thing that ever happened to him.

That's more true than even he knows. There are secrets about back then that I can't ever tell him.

Some things become unforgivable the moment they're said out loud.

My phone buzzed, making me jump, and I leapt for it, hoping it would be him. But no, it was Angie.

'Alright princess? Did he lock you up in the tower for being bad?'

'Oh don't. Why didn't you stop me from being an absolute dickhead last night?'

'Um, because you didn't say anything that wasn't

true?' Angela's voice softened, 'Come on now babe, you were fine. You were being funny. It maybe missed the mark a little, but most of those arseholes were so plastered, I bet they didn't notice.'

'Dan noticed.'

'Well, yeah. I imagine he would. But maybe he should have focused on what you needed rather than what he wanted?'

I considered it. The problem was, Angie was always on my side. And she had no problem being ruthless when the occasion called for it. So who was right? Was I the ungrateful wife addicted to drama, or was he the workaholic husband bored of his wife's grief?

Or were we just two people who got married too young and grew up suddenly?

'So he'll be hiding himself at work the next couple of weeks then? Do you want to go away? I've got to go supervise an influencer shoot in Milan, you could tag along?'

I frowned, 'I thought you made an app?'

'Yes,' Angie said, 'and now we're marketing it.'

'Why do you need a photoshoot for a non-physical thing? In fact, why do you need a shoot in Milan for a British app?' I felt suddenly incredibly old.

'Babe, why do you ask me questions like you think I'm lying about my life? Believe me, I'd rather not fly for a couple of hours to watch some twenty-year-old pout at a screen with two hundred euros' worth of balloons, but it's my business and I take it seriously.'

'I know you do, sorry, that wasn't…'

'I thought you were going to start saying yes again?' Angie prompted, and I remembered her words from last night. Start feeling, start doing.

'Yeah but…' I started, and Angie laughed. 'No, let me explain. If I go now, I'm running away from a fight. And that's not fair on him.'

'Because you have to be here to show you're miserable? You have to be waiting for him whilst he gets to stay at work and punish you?'

'It's my marriage.' I wanted to explain that it was the longest thing in my life, the thing I'd cultivated and cherished from the moment it started. I was going to be a brilliant wife, I'd decided from the moment he asked me. I wore the title like a crown.

We did that thing everyone does when they first get married, calling each other 'husband' and 'wife' all the time like you're getting the pronunciation right, getting used to the taste of the words you'll use for the rest of your life.

But we still did that now, still cherished those names because they meant something.

'Actually, I've been thinking about what you said last night and I'm going to take action.'

Angie's voice rose in surprise, 'You'll see a therapist? I can recommend a couple.'

Fear clutched at my chest, 'No, but I'm going to sort my CV out and start job hunting. Maybe start something different. Or go back to school? I can now, can't I? Might as well take the opportunity to get my degree, do what I couldn't do before.'

Dan had attained his degree eventually, but I'd been focusing on making money, and by the time I fell into charity work, I didn't need to go to uni.

I loved feeling like I was doing something useful, helping people find housing. And I was *good* at it. My education didn't matter. All that mattered was that I could explain exactly why a human being should help another, and I could get that through to someone in under thirty seconds. Sometimes, they'd even thank me for it.

They'd said my job was there for me whenever I wanted, but the idea of going back, of people asking how the baby was, before they realised… or worse, not asking because they'd all been briefed about my 'situation'. I spent nights imagining interactions with my colleagues. The pity, the awkwardness. I had to start fresh, stop looking back.

'Well that sounds good, what do you want to study?' Angela's voice cut through my pointless imagined scenarios. She thought I was just telling her what she wanted to hear. Another half-hearted attempt to seem better.

'I… honestly? I have absolutely no fucking idea.' I'd never really thought about it before.

'Well lucky you, about to find a new passion!' Angie teased. 'Though I bet you could moon over syllabuses on a flight to Milan?'

'Next time,' I said, and the silence at the end of the line told me she didn't believe me.

I paused.

'Hey Ange?' I asked. 'Don't stop asking me, okay? I know… I know what I'm like right now, but please keep inviting me places?'

She was quiet for a moment, but when she finally spoke I could hear the smile.

'You know me, your friendly neighbourhood pitbull. I won't let go. Love ya, kid.'

'You too. Safe flight.'

When she hung up, I wondered where to start. I was going to make her proud though. I was going to *do something*. I had to do more than just put on a good show. I wanted to be able to look at this day and say I did something.

Today, I decided, was going to be a good day.

In the world of business, as Dan had so recently learnt, there was the idea of 'eating the frog'. Whatever the hardest, worst task you need to do is, you get that done first. Which was why I was standing in my hallway, grasping my cup of coffee like a lifeline, staring at a closed door.

The room needed to be emptied. I hadn't been in there in months, not beyond dumping the useless pieces of tat I'd bought online and throwing the door closed behind them, like the room was haunted. But today was the day. My husband thought I was poison, and my best friend thought I was lost, and as much as I regretted the argument I'd had with Dan, it had felt *so good* to finally say something. To finally take the mic and tell those people what I thought.

So, I was going in.

I watched as my hand trembled on the door. I shook out the tremors, clenching and unclenching my fist, annoyed at myself.

'Oh come on, you *stupid* woman,' I muttered, and threw the door open.

Silence.

It was just a room. A beautiful room with light streaming through the window, the grey striped walls like something out of a magazine. And then that perfect back wall that we'd painted the mural on. Well, Dan had painted it obviously, but he'd let me help, didn't mind when my messy brush strokes went outside the lines. It was a lush jungle, so beautiful you could almost walk right into it.

'I want him to crave adventure, right from the beginning,' Dan had said when he finished sketching it out, and I'd kissed him, so thrilled, so excited to see him be a dad. I was quite far along by then, and I had these dungarees and a pink bandana to cover my hair, and it felt like we were in a movie, having this perfect moment. We blasted the radio and sang along, and Dan hovered when I got on the stepladder, even though he pretended he wasn't worried. That night we ordered pizza, and he rubbed my swollen feet, and we kept going back to the hallway and opening the door to look at our work.

'We are really doing this, it's really happening,' Dan had whispered, hugging me from behind, his hands on my stomach.

'It's happening. And no matter what, even if we absolutely suck as parents, we know that our kid is gonna have the best-looking nursery ever. I mean, look at it. We're already doing an awesome job.' I patted his hand.

'Thank you,' he said, kissing my neck. 'None of this would have happened without you.'

'Well, you had a rather important role to play too,' I laughed, twisting to kiss his cheek.

'No, I mean… I mean our life. I'm just really grateful.'

I'd probably made a snarky comment, or said something stupid, but after that he tucked me in bed and he went back downstairs to do some more stuff for work. I remembered falling asleep noticing how much my face hurt from smiling, and thinking how lucky I was.

I was still lucky.

That's why I had to clear this room out. Paint it over and start fresh. It was meant to be his room, it didn't seem fair to save it for another baby. Even the thought of that felt sharp and painful.

I started with all the stuff I'd bought, dragging it out into the hall and assessing what I could do with it. Some of it wasn't even opened, forgotten about as soon as it was ordered. Efficiency and action was the key here, so I got to work sorting them by date. If they were unopened I checked the order details and made arrangements to return them. The ones that were opened, I checked the same, and if it was too late, I put them up for sale online.

Within minutes I had people on local groups buying things and by midday I'd had more people at my door than I'd seen in six months. Friendly faces, perhaps a little worried that the price was too good to be true. But I just wanted the stuff gone. I wanted Dan to come home and see how much I'd done, how hard I was trying.

By early afternoon the nursery was empty of all the boxes and rubbish and everything else I'd stuffed in there. It felt like I'd pulled a dead body out from under the bed. Something in my chest was lighter.

But now I was left with the perfect nursery we'd worked so hard on. I didn't have the heart to dismantle the beautiful crib, or take down the mobile with the felt sheep I'd spent hours sewing and stuffing. I'd stabbed my fingers so many times with the needles that I kept smearing blood on their little white bodies, and I had to keep starting over. At one point I even wore gloves, and Dan had laughed at my dedication. I'd put all the love I had into that mobile, even if it had none of the skill. I couldn't throw it away.

What I *could* do, was bag up all the beautiful baby clothes in the chest of drawers and take them down to the charity shop. And then cover the furniture in dust cloths and get the white paint out. I picked up a new paint roller and a pot of paint on the way back from the charity shop on the high street, feeling buoyed by purpose.

Painting was therapeutic, making everything blank again. A new start. I worked hard and didn't stop until late afternoon. The only thing I left was that jungle wall. I couldn't cover it over, it was just too beautiful. I tried to tell myself I could use it as an office when I decided what I wanted to study, that I wanted to turn it into something new.

By the time I collapsed onto the sofa with a cup of tea and a sandwich, it was 4 p.m. My first truly useful day in a long time. No calls on the helpline, no feeling sorry for myself. Just action. I liked it.

I was going to continue. I'd cook steak for dinner, open a nice bottle of wine and we'd sit down and talk everything out. I could fix this. It was my life, my marriage. I could control this. Yes, I was tired and a bit broken. I wasn't the spirited, driven woman I was before, but as long as I tried hard enough, I could do it.

On the kitchen counter I noticed the pile of post I'd collected when I came back from the shops. I rifled through, wondering if there were any more birthday cards, perhaps from my old colleagues. There was only one that wasn't a bill, my name and address written in bright blue ink. On the back of the envelope, the return address was in Scotland. The Highlands. I couldn't think of anyone we knew there.

The card was an artsy black and white photo of some sunflowers in a vase, the type you'd find in a museum.

Inside it read:

Happy birthday Natasha,

I hope this year brings you all the things you deserve.

I know there's never a good time to reach out with things like this, but I'm not very well and I'd really like to make amends.

I know that's probably not fair of me to ask, and I'm sorry about that.

I'd really like to see you, if you were willing.

Love,
Mum
xxx

I actually forgot to breathe.

I dropped into one of the bar stools, reading the sparse words over and over, as if each line might reveal a secret coded message, something that made more sense than the one she'd actually written.

If you had let me guess who sent a mystery birthday card, my mother wouldn't have even made the top twenty.

She left when I was eleven.

Nina's focus was always on survival, and that's what she taught me. Start with what you've got and take what you can. She thought she deserved more than we could give her. She blamed Dad for 'tricking' her. He'd promised her a good life, but their ideas of good were very different.

When she left, we were hounded by debtors. There were the typical ones, the banks and store cards who hired professionals to knock on the door politely and discuss a payment plan. But Dad wasn't home and it was just me, and I didn't understand. They were sympathetic, but they kept coming back.

The guys on the estate were worse, the ones who sent their sons with threats, holding cricket bats. I just kept thinking, *Why are they telling me? What am I supposed to do about this?* Even if I'd wanted to help, I couldn't have. I'd had my little secret saving places, boxes and pots under my bed or behind my books on the shelf. Money I'd saved, found, pilfered on occasion. It was much like my little collection of pre-packed biscuits, the odd cereal bar or treat we got at school – I saved them up in case I needed them.

But Mum found all my hiding places. By the time she left I had nothing. At that point, I wasn't even crying for her, because she'd gone. I was crying because I'd have to start all over again from scratch, that I'd never escape now.

I didn't really want to think about any of this today.

I had the kind of life she'd always dreamed of, the true-love, big-home, fancy-holiday sort of life. I'd won the lottery, reached the end of the fairytale. I'd been rescued.

Why would I want to revisit all that now? I had bigger problems than an old lonely woman who had finally realised that she'd been a bad mother.

I folded the card neatly in half, chucked it in the bin and went to get the steaks out of the freezer.

Dan didn't come home for dinner.

I was in bed when I finally heard the front door. I didn't leave the dinner out in a passive-aggressive message that he'd messed up my attempts at a loving reconciliation. I thought about it, and God was it tempting, but I resisted, wrapping the plates in cling film and placing them in the fridge.

At least he came to sleep in our bed. I kept gravitating

towards him in my sleep, waking slightly when I realised I'd reached out to touch his skin, and he'd shifted away.

I dreamed of my first birthday in London, when Daniel had woken me up at some ungodly hour, and cajoled me awake with the promise of coffee. I'd called him a bunch of unfair names as we walked up Primrose Hill in the darkness, panting and sweating. He hadn't cared, my cheerful love, just grinned and squeezed my hand and told me it would be worth it.

When he'd eventually stopped at the top, I had thrown myself down on the grass dramatically, whispering that it would be a terrible shame for me to die on my eighteenth birthday.

'Oh hush. Here, stick this in your gob,' he'd chucked me a croissant from his bag, and poured a cup of coffee from a thermos.

'Charming!' I remembered laughing, 'Happy birthday Taz, stick this in your gob!'

Daniel had just grinned at me, that eager-to-please look I knew so well. 'This is my favourite place at my favourite time, and I wanted to share it with you. Watch.'

He had pointed out in front of us, and put an arm around me. His leg against mine, the smell of him on the hoodie I'd stolen. And as if by magic, the sun rose over London, bathing it in glorious pinks and yellows, awakening the town from slumber. Of course, there were cranes and angled buildings in the imperfect skyline, but even they looked majestic as shadows of the sun.

I'd never seen anything like it.

'You are the strangest, most wonderful person,' I'd nuzzled into his chest. 'Thank you, this is the perfect birthday.'

'Better than a lie in?'

'… yes, *okay*, better than a lie in. Are there more croissants?'

'Don't you want your birthday present?'

'Oh Dan, you didn't go overboard, did you? We don't have the money, and it's really not important.'

'Taz, don't ruin a perfectly lovely day worrying about things you don't need to worry about. It's not like I'm gonna spend the rent money. I've got a little set aside for birthdays and Christmas. I'm responsible. You've taught me well. Don't make it a thing, yeah?'

He'd produced a small envelope made of wrapping paper, with a little ribbon around it.

I opened the little envelope and tipped it open into my palm, feeling the weight before I recognised what it was.

'The one from the market?'

The ring was perfect, silver with an oval opal in the middle, reflecting the light. I slipped it onto my right hand and wiggled it to catch the light. 'Oh, Dan, I love it, but it's too much.'

Dan crouched, shifting in front of me, and placed a hand over mine. 'I don't think it's too much. In fact, I don't think it's enough. But…' he slipped the ring off my finger, 'I was thinking it would look better on the other hand?'

He paused, looking at me with those hopeful eyes, a little smile on his face as he waited for my answer.

I laughed, almost giddy with the realisation. 'Baby, you want a real answer, you've gotta ask a real question.'

Daniel laughed too then, shaking his head at me. 'You're right, one chance to do it properly. What d'ya say Taz? You wanna spend your life with me, be my family, us against the world?'

God, those eyes. Daniel was the only person who had ever looked at me like I was the best thing in the world. It was intoxicating. It made me feel powerful, beautiful. Like I was looking at every good decision I'd ever made and ever would make.

I paused, feeling my heart beat in my throat. 'You know… I really, really do.'

I seemed to dream about that sunrise at least once a week. Just the two of us, that perfect silver ring sitting heavy on my hand as we curled into each other on the hilltop and watched the day begin. It was the place I went to in my mind when the world got a little too cruel. My oasis in the past.

When I woke up at 5 a.m., and rolled over to see Dan was still in bed, I breathed a sigh of relief. I looked at the ring on my finger, a sparkling solitaire and the gold band that went with it. A new piece of jewellery to match our second wedding; Miranda had insisted that Daniel had to go pick something more appropriate. God, I missed my old ring.

But there was no time to wallow – I had a plan. I made a thermos of coffee, and grabbed a packet of biscuits from the cupboard before pulling on my leggings.

'Daniel, come on an adventure with me?' I whispered, placing a hand on his arm.

'What? What time is it?' he muttered, blurry with sleep.

'Time enough to walk up a big hill and watch the sunrise with your wife?' I said hopefully, praying that my enthusiasm was catching. That he'd see what I was doing. That I was trying.

'What?' Dan rolled over and frowned at me in confusion.

'I've got a thermos of coffee with your name on it! Let's walk up to Primrose Hill? I think we can make it in time?'

He paused for a moment, looking at me, and I wasn't sure if it was that he wanted to say yes, or he was just taking time to fully wake up and understand my words.

'What time is it?' He rolled over to look at the clock. 'Shit, I'm gonna be late!'

'What, how?!'

'I need to do my workout, and then I need to get to the office early. I've got back to back meetings.' He was already up, pulling on his workout clothes, and I wanted to stand in front of the door to stop him getting away.

'Well, switch your workout for a morning hike with me instead? I promise you'll still burn calories!' I smiled, waiting. 'More fresh air than working out in that little shed too!'

'I can't, I've got my routine. I can't just change it because you suddenly feel like it.'

'Oh.'

Dan pulled on his trainers and went to brush past me, but paused, touching my arm. 'It's a nice idea. Maybe we could do it at a weekend sometime?'

I nodded as he kissed my cheek and darted from the room.

I went back to bed and didn't get up until midday.

A cafetière of cold coffee sat on the side for me when I finally made it down to the kitchen. After this morning, it felt like more of a polite gesture than one of affection.

I chewed toast without tasting it, sitting at the kitchen counter as I scrolled through social media posts. New home, new baby, wedding, engagement, new career. Lives moving on as I sat still. I didn't even like half these people I followed online, so why was I comparing my life to theirs? Was I only bothered because I didn't have anything good to share?

I looked through Angie's photos of Milan and regretted not going, just as she'd known I would. I'd been part of 'Taz and Dan' for so long, it didn't feel natural to do something for myself. But Dan had prioritised his workout, his job, his day.

I should have done the same. After all, he now had his job and his colleagues and his family. I only had him and Angie. That was stupid of me, to leave myself vulnerable. Put all my eggs in one basket. That was always my mother's lesson to me – *First you've got to take care of yourself Tashy, make sure you survive. Then you can worry about everyone else.*

She had clearly lived by her philosophy.

I went over to the bin and peered inside, saw the birthday card still sat on the top. I fished it out and looked at it again.

Her writing was neat and to the point, no swirls or exclamations. Capital letters felt aggressive but clear. There was no falsity. She was being honest in a way I couldn't remember as a child. That said, who really knows their parents when they're a kid? Who knew what she was going through back then?

When I thought I was going to be a mother, I harvested those memories desperately, wondering what she'd done, and what I wouldn't do.

There had only been one memory I'd loved with my

mum. She'd let me have the day off school, and we made a fort in the living room, pulled all the blankets and duvets off the bed and curled up in there, watching Disney movies. She'd made melty cheese on toast and big sugary cups of tea, and I laughed as she did impressions of the mice in *Cinderella*. She'd stroked my hair and called me her special girl, holding me close until her perfume almost choked me. I'd felt cherished.

And that was my only good memory. Eleven years, and one memory. So I had looked elsewhere for inspiration. I had known I didn't want to be like Dan's mother, pinning all of my hopes and expectations onto her child, and dismissing them when they disappointed. I'd had Sharon though, after everything happened. She had always welcomed me with a smile and asked about my day, her little boy on her hip. Tired but smiling. That was who I'd wanted to be.

Nina had been young, though. She'd been young when she had me. And some people weren't meant to be parents. Maybe she'd tried her best?

Dan had forgiven his imperfect parents, been welcomed back with their Sunday lunches and Christmas and birthdays. With their phone calls and in-jokes and get-togethers. He had people. History and blood ties.

If I didn't have Dan, I didn't have any family at all.

Mum used to play gin rummy with me some evenings, and she always beat me, every time. When I asked her how, she said, 'If it looks like you're going to be stuck with a pair, you change up your hand.'

If after all this I was going to be left alone, I would need to find family somewhere.

More importantly, it was action – changing up my hand would stop me from hanging around this house like a ghost, waiting for my husband to tell me he was done with me.

Maybe he would miss me. He'd realise there were no notes dotted around the flat to make him smile. No new pens on his desk to remind him to doodle and dream.

And I deserved answers, right? I deserved to know what made a woman abandon her child and then reach out twenty years later. To find out if she really was as cold and heartless as she seemed. A little spark of hope glimmered – maybe if she had a good reason for leaving, everything would be okay.

A smaller, more bitter part of me visualised how I would show off my perfect life to my mother, watching her withered and envious as I spoke of my rich husband and the fancy parties and the countries I'd been to. Taunt her with everything she had ever wanted. And then leave it all behind.

But I knew the truth behind all of my maybes.

It wasn't revenge or cruelty, or even hope.

I just wanted a reason to leave.

Chapter Three

Once I'd decided to go, I couldn't leave quickly enough. I packed a bag and was ready in twenty minutes. No worrying about what to wear, what to bring, what she'd think of me. I was methodical, sensible in my swiftness. If I took too long, I knew I'd chicken out, and the months and years would drag on like this, me waiting for him to leave, him not wanting to hurt me.

The only time I paused was to get the package from under my bed – a notebook I'd bought Dan, ready to give as a present. I'd been buying Dan notebooks ever since we moved in together. He'd told me all he wanted to do was draw, create something that mattered. So I made sure he did. Usually I gave them on his birthday, or the new year, whenever there was a new beginning.

I wasn't quite sure if that's what I was telling him by leaving him one now.

I made sure to leave it out on the kitchen counter where he would see it when he came home, and scribbled a quick note to leave next to it:

Dan,

I'm going away for a few days to see my mum in Scotland. (She got in touch, she's not well, it's a whole thing.) I thought I'd leave you this notebook. As always, you know the rules: fill it with things that matter.

See you soon,
Taz
x

I should have written that I loved him. We should have made up before I left, but if I did, he'd talk me out of going. And I *needed* to go, something in my gut was tugging at me, desperate to move, to be somewhere else.

After all that big talk I'd given Angie about not running away, I felt guilty. But I felt guilty about everything these days. Shame was like this twitch that I couldn't quite shake off. Sometimes there's simply no other way to break a stalemate.

The minute I got into the car and pulled out onto the road, my lungs seemed to expand. I knew, finally, that I'd made the right decision.

And if not, I'd have 500 miles of chances to change my mind.

I could have got the plane up to Scotland, but I didn't want to wait. I didn't want to be at the mercy of taxis and buses and plane timetables. I didn't want to sit in the airport departure lounge sipping on wine and watching the board, scratching my nails and thinking about my mother.

I made it most of the way to up to Liverpool before Daniel called me. I answered on the speaker system, wondering why he was calling in the afternoon.

'You're going to *Scotland,*' he exclaimed, 'and you left me a fucking *Post-it note*?'

'I waited up two nights and you weren't here, I couldn't wait any longer. I had to go.' I tried to stay calm.

'Bullshit, you're running away.'

'What are you even doing at home? I expected you'd find the note when you got home at midnight *again*.'

Dan exhaled, and I imagined him leaning on the breakfast bar, shaking his head, rubbing the back of his neck in exasperation.

'I brought coffee and cake. I felt bad. I missed you. And then you were gone and…'

'You thought I'd left for good.'

He paused, 'Haven't you?'

'I'm just going to see my mum. It's not a big deal.'

He laughed at that, and I couldn't blame him.

'Why would you want to see her, Taz? What good could it possibly bring? Or are you just looking for another way to make yourself miserable?'

I'd stopped mentioning things about my childhood a long time ago. Dan used to look at me with this bizarre mixture of pity and love, like he couldn't understand that I'd never ridden a bike, or been on a holiday, or been to the beach. Whenever I had that childlike joy at something he'd examine me, wondering if it was a new experience, or I was just excited. That look made me feel like a weirdo.

'Actually, I was hoping to make amends. Leave the past in the past. Forgive and move on.' I tried not to throw it in his face: *You told me I didn't forgive, you told me I wallowed. Here I am, facing things head on. Love me, love me again. I'm doing what you want.*

'She was a monster, Taz.'

'You never even met her.'

'You said the night she left she emptied out all your pocket money and took your hamster!'

'Well, I was a child, maybe Hammie died, or she left the cage open. It might have been a coincidence.'

I'd forgotten about the hamster. A kid on the estate was selling them for a fiver. I'd saved up all my pennies. I'd smuggled him in with a shoebox and Sharon next door gave me her old cage. I loved that hamster. It was weeks before Mum even noticed.

'A house full of vermin, excellent,' was all she said when she saw him. And once at night, 'You don't love that rat more than me, Tasha, do you? You love Mummy more than your rat?'

'He's a hamster, Mum.'

'That's not an answer, Natasha.'

She was holding me so tight, tucked up in bed, and yet I had this feeling that if she didn't like my answer, Hammie was going to disappear. She didn't like competition.

'I would have come with you, Taz,' Dan's voice cut through the memory. 'If you'd told me it was important, I would have come.'

I tried to find a way to say it without being accusatory. 'You've taken enough time off work already. It's clear they need you back there. And with these late nights I didn't know when you'd be free.'

He didn't say anything.

'I… it's best I deal with it myself, just get it sorted. I'll hear her out, let her say sorry. Ask about the hamster maybe.' I tried to laugh but it sounded choked. 'And I'll be home, all better.'

'All better,' Dan exhaled loudly. 'All better.'

If we were at home having this conversation, I'd have put my hand on his forearm, on that crappy compass tattoo he had done at nineteen, my touchstone. I'd have rested my forehead against his chest, and known without words that we'd get through this together. Without touch, it was hard to reach him.

We'd fought for a normal life for a long time, and we'd been happy for a good chunk of that. But maybe that was all we got.

The scariest thought of all was that sometimes love isn't enough, and it's no one's fault. So many of the people on the loss and grief forums I read were going through divorces and separations. Sometimes you just couldn't make it through together. You had to split up to survive.

But even the thought of that made me homesick for my husband.

'Taz, maybe when you get back we should… talk.'

'Talk.'

'About us. About everything. We can't keep going on like this, can we?'

And there it was.

In another life I slammed the brakes so hard I went flying through the windscreen and it was all over. But the traffic on the motorway crawled, and the sun shone, and the world didn't end.

'No,' I croaked, 'I suppose not.'

'I better get back to work,' he said quietly. 'I love you.'

'Love you too.'

The way I'd ended a hundred phone calls, maybe a

thousand. The idea that those might be limited was unbelievable.

He hadn't mentioned the notebook. The way I showed I still looked after his dreams, still pushed him to reach them. He'd be too busy to draw, he'd say, he was working flat out, he didn't have time for that silliness now.

His priorities had changed. And maybe mine should too.

To be fair, the fact that we'd even made it this far was a miracle. No one thought we'd survive. We were mismatched teenagers, drawn to each other through difference. Daniel transformed me. Before him, my job was to be invisible. Invisible on the estate, invisible at school, invisible at home. I had quiet dreams of university, and my teachers said I was smart enough, if I worked hard and didn't dream too big. All I had to do was survive.

Because of Daniel, I blossomed. I stopped hanging around with Jemma and Chelsea, the only people who used to talk to me before. They were racing to get knocked up to see who got the biggest flat off the council, and made fun of me for studying. Jemma said I always chose the harder way of doing things, that I wasn't being smart about it. I don't think they even noticed when I stopped smoking with them by the bins.

I took my hair out of that tight ponytail and I wore it

loose, softer. I nicked tinted lip-balms from Woolworths and pinched my cheeks to a blush.

He took me to the cinema, he held my hand like he wasn't ashamed, took me to parties like it wasn't completely ridiculous that someone like me was with someone like him. He said I knew him, really knew him, in a way no one else could. It was childish silliness, but it felt true.

He never took me home though, and actually, I was relieved. I knew I wasn't good enough for Daniel White. I didn't need to stand in the hallway of that giant house with two fancy cars on the drive and hear it from his mother.

We'd been dating for about six months when he started thinking about breaking up. I could just tell. He'd not been around much, and there were other girls on the scene now, pretty girls with swishy ponytails and houses like Daniel's. They went to the same parties and their parents knew each other. He was getting bored of slumming it, I was sure. I spent every moment together just looking at him, soaking it in so I could remember it all after he'd gone.

The idea of being alone again was unbearable.

And then everything changed. All I did was wince. One involuntary action, and there was no going back.

The thing is, people like Daniel, they're fixers. They believe in the system, they trust that everything works out the way it should. That there's good and there's bad and that's it. That the good guys win. People think everyone believes that as a kid, but it's a privilege. Some of us have always known better.

'The next time it happens, Taz, you need to call me, okay? Call me and I'll come get you.' He'd sounded so young when he said it, and I almost pitied him. I wanted to tell him this was the way the world was, this was how people were. That he didn't need to get upset, he just needed to get real.

But he was so attentive again suddenly, he wanted to be with me all the time, to protect me, to make me feel loved. And I knew I should have railed against the pity, pushed him away if he wanted to go, but I clung on, just a little longer.

If I'd been strong enough to set him free, it wouldn't have happened. I wouldn't have called him in a panic and he wouldn't have rushed over.

He wouldn't have stood up to my father, trying to reason with a drunken, staggering bear of a man who was accustomed to getting his own way.

He wouldn't have got in one decent punch, just one, and my dad wouldn't have fallen with a heavy thud, hitting his head on the back of the coffee table.

As easy as that.

Miranda said I'd ruined her son's life and it was true. But it was more than that. If not for me, my father would be alive. Daniel wouldn't have a criminal record. He never would have fallen out with his family, and most likely of all, he wouldn't be married to me.

I destroyed his life, and yet I had him. So how could I regret it?

There was more than enough to feel guilty about, but that was the main one. And maybe now he was finally realising what I'd known all along. He had stayed with me out of pity, out of obligation, because I had been so loyal and so grateful. Because his parents hadn't given him another option.

Daniel always said I was his compass. We both should have known I was an anchor when he deserved wings.

The grey skies and motorway gave way to vast greenery and I rolled down the window to let the crisp air in. The sun was watery, gentle, but she was there. It was so easy to get lost in the past these days. The guilt had been worse since we lost the baby.

The drive was exactly what I needed, to focus. The hours had crawled by on motorway after motorway, nothing changing until that last final push through Scotland, the Highlands proving themselves to be another world entirely.

Had Dan gone back to work, relieved to have finally said it? Had he already prepared for that conversation he wanted to have, his eyes resting on the rich, intelligent, *appropriate* women that his mother had been placing in his way for years? *Finally,* Miranda must be cackling, *finally I got him back.* She could have her version of him, without a reminder of all the things he went through, of her own failings as a mother.

As I followed the signs for the town, I focused on slowing my breathing. Being present. I wondered what my mother would think of my marriage, my life. She was always one for making the best of a bad situation, getting what you could before you moved on. It was easy to imagine her words in that smoky, rough voice, like a kernel of her was living in my head:

You shag him, keep him fed, make him feel clever. If he's looking elsewhere, babe, you better hurry up and pull another trick from somewhere. Get pregnant again, for God's sake. If you lose him you'll be all alone. You do what you can to survive. That mug loves you, somehow. So use it.

Or perhaps it would have been the other side of the coin. Divorce him, play the injured wife abandoned after the death of her baby. Get the money and start again somewhere new. Be someone completely different.

Either way, survival was her game. Smile and play nice, wink and tease and be perfect for as long as you can, then drop the act when you've got everything you want. Poverty could do that to you. Nina never stopped being disappointed with her life, angry that the world owed her more and it had never delivered.

I nurtured the smallest spark of hope that she'd changed, that whatever sickness she had, it had given her perspective. Maybe she'd met a man, the right man, maybe she'd softened. Maybe she finally found that thing she thought she deserved.

As I approached a roundabout, trying to shake her from my head, I noticed a man standing on the bridge that led over the main road. He looked down from the top of the stairs on one side, just watching the traffic, leaning against the railing. He was completely relaxed, dressed in a suit and he even had a trilby on. I slowed down in the traffic to look at him, intrigued. Who hangs out on a bridge in the middle of nowhere?

The traffic moved, sky darkening, and I was forced to look at the directions. I was only five minutes away. I still hadn't worked out what I would say to her. It was almost nineteen years. What do you say after nineteen years and a sad birthday card?

I pulled off the road down a dirt path, following it around until a house appeared.

It wasn't what I expected. A sweet chocolate-box cottage in the middle of nowhere, attached to a farm. The sun was setting behind it in a picture-perfect tableau, and suddenly I realised two things: travelling across the country to see a mother who had abandoned me decades ago was ridiculous, and I was so very, very tired.

A sign in the front garden said 'Any children found wandering will be sold to the circus!' There was a tractor parked around the corner of the cottage, and in the nearby fields there were hay bales. I couldn't imagine my mother in a place like this.

The Nina I knew before liked opulence. She liked impressive. She wanted everyone to know that our sad little life living off baked beans on toast wasn't good enough for her. She made up stories all the time, about wealthy men she'd known, places she'd been. She told me fairy stories about a man in the south of France who wanted to take her away from everything. Sometimes my dad hovered in the hallway during these stories, and snorted. 'When have *you* been to France? You haven't even been to Southend!'

There were good times though, too. I remember him reaching out and stroking her hair, or pulling her close to him, or tapping her bum as she walked past. He often looked around for her, as if when he couldn't see her he was afraid she'd left.

And clearly he was right to worry.

I parked up and turned off the engine, my hands shaking as I gripped the steering wheel until my knuckles turned white. I had planned to spend the journey working out what I'd say. How I'd be warm and kind, appealing. I'd stand there in my nice clothes, with a life that would make her jealous and I'd say, 'I'm fine, I did okay without you.' And yet suddenly I wanted to cry. To be a child again, diving beneath a duvet cover and refusing to come out into the real world.

What if she looked me up and down in that way she always had, and simply smirked? What if I was found wanting, the same way I was by Dan's mother? I had tried to grow into a decent sort of person. But what would impress a mother who once said, so matter-of-factly, that having you had ruined her life?

I couldn't get out of the car. I rested my head on the steering wheel and tried to breathe, tried to get myself together.

I needed to do this, for Dan. More than for her or for me, I needed to do this for my marriage. To show him I could be forgiving, I could let things go, that the past could stay the past.

The sharp rapping on the window scared the life out of me. When I looked up, a drawn woman in grey clothing glared at me, her lips a thin line and her eyes narrow.

'No loitering!' she mouthed, pointing at a sign at the end of the driveway. At least she wasn't pointing to the one about kids being sold to the circus.

I could barely lift my head from the steering wheel, and settled for tilting my face towards her instead. Her features seemed to change, briefly, and she beckoned me out of the car.

Oh God, it was going to be someone my mother had ripped off, wasn't it? There were enough of those times on the estate, people yelling after me, asking where my parents were. Mum always said to pretend I didn't understand, didn't speak English. How many times had she sent me to the window as a child, to shake my head at the big man knocking down our door, and say I didn't know a Nina?

But the woman didn't look angry, or upset, or any of the other emotions my mother used to leave in her wake. She looked concerned, and a quick look at myself in the rearview mirror told me I couldn't blame her.

I was a mess. I'd run my hands through my hair endlessly on the drive down, yanking at it in frustration. My lips were chapped from where I'd nibbled at the loose skin and torn it, and the eyes staring back at me were void of warmth or understanding. I looked like a runaway.

I got out of the car, breathing in the fresh air with a sort of relief. Yes, my lungs could still function, I was still here, still alive.

'Who are you?' I asked, then paused, rather shocked by my own forthrightness. I could hear the way my voice curved sharply around the vowels, so London. She raised an eyebrow as a warning and snorted.

'I'm the owner, who were you looking for?' The Scottish twang in her voice was soft, muffled by something else. I suddenly heard how demanding I was, so imperiously forward.

I ducked my head, 'Nina Clarke, is she still here?'

The woman's eyes widened, and a softness appeared

around her mouth. It couldn't be considered a smile, but it was an attempt.

'You'd better come in,' she turned on her heel and left, sprinting back to the house at a pace I had to jog to keep up with. She was in her mid-sixties, I'd say, and yet she looked solid and strong, with a fierce determination. And a flair for the mysterious, it seemed.

'I really don't need to…' I called after her, but she was already gone.

I had no choice but to follow.

The house was dark inside, but warm. The walls and ceilings seemed to slant slightly, as if they were drunk. I followed the woman through to the kitchen, where she filled an old-fashioned kettle and put it on the stove, gesturing for me to take a seat at the wooden bench by the kitchen table.

'Tea?' She tilted her head back towards me.

'Oh, um… sure?'

'That's the least sure a person has ever sounded,' her voice was sharp but when she turned she had a cheeky smile on her face. 'Would you like to try again?'

I half-smiled, amused despite the anticipation that had settled itself around my shoulders and in my jaw. 'Yes, tea sounds lovely. Please.'

'Good.'

I waited in silence, watching her fetch the cups, arrange a tray and put the teabags in the teapot, awaiting the water. It was only when I saw her add a stick of cinnamon to the pot that I started.

'Sorry, I forget it's not to everyone's taste… I'll take it out.'

'No… no, it's not that, it's fine… My mother made her tea like that, with cinnamon.'

The woman looked at me as if I should know better, but her voice was gentle. 'Of course she did, hen, it's the same way our mother made it.'

I looked at her again, trying to trace similarities in their features, looking for something that confirmed her story. The tilt of her head, or the narrowing of her eyes. But there was nothing.

'You're sisters.'

'Half,' she nodded, pouring the water into the teapot and letting the steam rise. 'Half sisters. I'm Kit.'

'Short for Katherine?'

'Short for Kitten,' she said, then snorted when I didn't respond. 'Of course it's short for Katherine. What does that have to do with anything?'

She put everything on a tray, brought it over and placed it carefully on the table. She busied herself pouring and stirring and then sat back, tapping her fingernails on the edge of her mug. 'You'll be Natasha, then.'

'Taz,' I shifted my weight uncomfortably, 'I go by Taz.'

Kit seemed to consider this, sipping at her tea, though

mine was too hot to even hold the mug. She seemed to be the sort of woman who was comfortable with silence. There was no rush to her movements, she was just considering her options.

I, on the other hand, felt this overwhelming panic that my mother was suddenly going to walk down the stairs and laugh at me.

Here goes nothing.

'So where the hell have you been all my life, then?' I had to stop myself from crossing my arms like a teenager, feeling ridiculous even as I said it. Kit guffawed, a brief flash of amusement on her face.

When Kit smiled the lines around her mouth became prominent. It was refreshing, to see someone touched by age and seeming not to care about it at all. The dark hair scraped back in a plait was streaked with grey and she wore muted colours, practical trousers and a thin, padded gilet. This was a woman who didn't care what you thought of her – she had a job to do.

'Honestly? I was hiding from your mother. Woman was a bloody banshee,' she crossed and uncrossed her legs, 'had to escape to the middle of nowhere, and she still found me. She's like a plague – she'll always get to you in the end.'

I laughed at that, an unexpected hiccup that seemed foreign to me. It was true. Mum always got what she wanted. Even now – I was here, wasn't I? She'd called and I'd come running.

'Why didn't she ever talk about you? I didn't even know she had a sister.'

Kit raised her hands, shrugging. 'We didn't always get on. I was the one from the previous marriage. Your ma was the golden child. She made my life a living hell growing up. It might sound awful but when she went off and got knocked up, I was relieved that she was somebody else's problem.'

I blinked. God, I couldn't remember the last time someone spoke so forthrightly. Kit grinned at me. 'Well, you're here for honesty, aren't you?'

'I am,' I laughed, 'I just never expect it. It's refreshing.'

'Ha!' she exclaimed, so loudly that I thought she'd hurt something. 'Refreshing! That's what they say when they think you're a barmy bobbin, but want to be polite. Refreshing! A breath of fresh air. What they mean is you're a mad old bag, but you've done them no harm and you give them a laugh every now and then.'

She twitched her lips at me.

'And you enjoy that?'

'Of course I do! If they're gonna talk, hen, I'd like them to have something interesting to say. So I'm that Mad Old Gal up at the farm, and I'll take that any day, please and thank you.'

I inhaled the scent of the cinnamon in the tea, it took me back in a way that wasn't completely unpleasant. Perhaps there had been good times. Happy times. So that the smell of my childhood wasn't some toxic scent that made me sick.

The reality of the situation suddenly hit me. I wasn't just having a snarky conversation with a funny older lady. I was speaking to a family member. Finally, there was someone else. I thought I'd had no one. Growing up, there'd been Mum and Dad, and that was it. No aunties or uncles or cousins. No siblings to play with, or fight with. No one to run to when life was a bit hard to understand.

Now I had kin. Another person who knew my mother. It was almost impossible to comprehend.

'So, why Taz?' Kit asked me, as if expecting some sort of story.

'What?'

'Why not Tasha?'

I shrugged, 'It's my name. I dunno.'

She nodded, watching me with a wariness I found appealing. Maybe she was looking for signs I was like Nina, liable to go off on something for no reason, to be crying one moment and laughing the next. To say what she needed to get what she wanted.

'Our mother's name was Natasha,' Kit cleared her throat and added an extra spoonful of sugar to her tea, stirring thoughtfully. 'I suppose she never told you about your granny?'

I shook my head, 'She didn't tell me much, to be honest. I wasn't high on her list of priorities.'

'When has anything been a priority to your mother, beyond getting what she wants?'

It was good to know she wasn't going to defend her. That she didn't even particularly like her very much. That was comforting. That someone else knew how she discarded people when they didn't sparkle the way she wanted. But… if she lived here, they must have made amends. I waited for some sort of explanation, some addendum to the story. *We didn't get along, but things are better now. She still drives me nuts, but we've grown up.* But there was nothing.

I wanted to ask where she was, but I was scared of the answer.

'Was my granny a nice woman?'

Kit paused, staring at the space on the wall behind me. 'Nice… is a difficult word.'

'Did you love her?'

'Of course I loved her, she was my ma!' Kit sounded surprised, but halfway through seemed to realise that wasn't a given. She bowed her head, as if embarrassed. 'Our mother was tough as nails. She was a survivor, but more than that, she was selfless. We had people visiting every hour, and there'd always be enough food for them. It's only when I look back now, I realise she went without. She ran her house like clockwork – cleaning, cooking, fixing. It was all about making sure we had everything we needed. Our school uniforms were always clean and pressed, our hair always neatly plaited. It mattered what other people thought.'

I didn't really know what to say, except that I felt an intense jealousy towards anyone whose mother bothered to iron their uniform or brush their hair before school. There was a time when I would have done anything for that attention.

I bet they were never bullied for having holey jumpers or greasy hair at school.

'Sounds like she looked after you.'

Kit nodded, 'Oh yes. All she wanted was for us to get an education and do better than she did. Every generation should have more opportunity than the last, that was what she thought.'

This made me feel such an abject sense of loss that I scratched my legs through my jeans in irritation.

'Her husband, my stepdad, he thought she was a soft touch. Always bringing strays home for dinner, looking out for everyone…' Kit trailed off, and I thought about how even speaking about this woman I didn't know felt like I'd lost the opportunity for something wonderful.

'Is she still alive?'

Kit shook her head, 'It's been a while without her now, although you never quite get over it.'

I thought about my dad. About having no one to walk me down the aisle, or anyone to give a shit about seeing me at Christmas. I conjured those good times, his hand around mine when I was a child, how he'd take me on the carousel at Christmas. There weren't many memories but I held them close. He was better before. After she left, he fell apart. I don't like to think about how he was after.

She did that to him.

'So... was my mum swapped at birth, or did something else go wrong? Because she certainly doesn't sound like your mother.' I snorted, then worried I'd gone too far. 'I mean, apart from the survival instinct, I guess.'

Kit smiled. 'Nina was a spoiled little girl, that was all. And when she felt she wasn't getting enough attention, she knew she could get into trouble to get it instead. She felt like the world owed her something.'

I could think of a few people like that. But usually they managed to make the world give them what they wanted. Dan's colleagues came to mind. They wanted it, they got it. Them's the rules, that's the world. *Why so glum, Taz babe, we're just making it happen. Everyone else could too if they tried hard enough.*

God, I hated them.

'Her da was just the same, always moaning about what everyone else had. Hateful little man, always concerned that someone got for free what he'd had to pay for.'

'So, why are you different?'

Kit laughed, 'I dunno, hen, different stock? We didn't have much before Ma married again. We were used to a life of hard work and getting by. A simple life. I never really felt comfortable with anything else.'

Something about that felt familiar, as I considered how awkward my expensive flat made me feel, with a thousand-pound sofa and the bottles of top-quality Champagne in the wine rack. I'd preferred our little rented flat with the condensation in the windows and the five-pound bottles of wine from the offie.

Kit looked around her at her home, and I could see her taking in how it must look to me. It was bare and simple, but there was warmth in unexpected places. The blue and white stripes of the mugs, the woven (and slightly wonky) table runner. The mustard cushion in the armchair and the irritable little ginger cat that pushed up against Kit's leg. It was simple, like she said, but it was beautiful in its own way.

'So, I assume Mum's not staying here?'

Kit chuckled, 'Not quite up to her highness' requirements, you mean? Aye, you may be right.'

She paused and sobered, 'She's in a facility about twenty minutes from here – St Michael's. They have nurses and activities and all that. It's *very* fancy, had some famous in-patients – in fact, they're not called in-patients, they're called guests!'

I pressed my lips together. 'So, what she said in the card was true, she's sick?'

Kit nodded, 'I'm afraid so, love. But not in the way you might think.'

Chapter Four

My mother had been diagnosed with early-onset Alzheimer's six months before. She'd ended up in a unit outside Glasgow, where she'd been living, and somehow they'd managed to track down Kit to take responsibility for her.

She was docile, most of the time, Kit said. In fact, Kit admitted, Nina was easier to deal with now. She seemed to have forgotten so much of what made her angry and jealous and vindictive. Her personality was sweet and childlike, and yet it was so hard not to expect that set jaw and imperious look to make an appearance. It did, every now and then, Kit said.

'Are you okay? You've gone pale. Paler.' I heard Kit get up, and watched as she brought a bottle of whisky and two glasses over to the table, pouring a healthy dram before clunking the glass down in front of me in a way that brooked no question.

I downed it, feeling the liquid burn my throat, and made a face.

'That's for *sipping,* not downing. And I gave you the good stuff!' Kit laughed. 'Serves me right for being a good hostess.' She topped up my glass and held hers up, '*Slainte.*'

I clinked my glass against hers and sipped, feeling the heat on my lips this time, a pleasant warmth that settled in my belly. It tasted a little like relief, a little like oblivion.

'So…' I took a breath, 'how bad is it?'

'Oh now, you were so fiery half an hour ago, don't tell me a little sickness makes you change your mind about your mother? She's been punished appropriately now, is that it?' Kit raised an eyebrow at me, mocking. 'Like how you don't speak ill of the dead?'

I shook my head, 'No, I just… I was expecting cancer… or liver failure. Or something where she might need a transplant from me.'

Kit snorted, 'Lord, my baby sister did a number on you, sweet girl, didn't she?'

I ignored that, however true it might be. 'Is she gone? Is there… nothing left of who she was?'

I'd never really understood Alzheimer's. It always seemed like something older people got as they gradually lost the memories they'd made in life. I saw it a bit like a spool unravelling, the thread fraying until it wasn't one thread at all anymore, just a mass of fluff and good intentions.

But my mother was young, and for all her faults she'd been vibrant, sharp as anything. She'd had… vivacity. Life. The idea of her being whitewashed was almost impossible to comprehend.

'Oh, she's there all right, she gets that look in her eye sometimes like she's the Queen of Sheba, demanding a royal greeting. The way she held out her hand to me once, like she expected me to kiss it…' Kit smiled, and tilted her glass towards mine, 'Have another sip, hen, it'll help, I promise.'

I did as she asked, closing my eyes briefly.

'I wondered what would happen when I sent the birthday card. If you'd come or if she'd burnt that bridge too badly.'

Kit's voice was so faint that I thought I'd imagined it. When I opened my eyes, she gave me a look of concern, almost guilt. 'She begged me to send it, convinced it was your birthday. The staff were getting worried about her, refusing to eat or drink. The only way she'd eat was if I wrote out a card for her. She said the exact words she wanted me to write.'

Kit gritted her teeth and shook her head, fingers tracing the rim of the glass. 'I was convinced she'd forget we'd written the card, that she'd wake up the next morning and insist again, refuse to eat until I'd written the same card every day… but she didn't. I went to see her, and she asked me how I was, and if I'd sent the card. She wondered whether you'd be eating chocolate cake for your birthday, as it was your favourite. I was shocked.'

I blinked.

'It wasn't.'

'Wasn't what?'

'Chocolate cake. It wasn't my favourite. It was Victoria sponge with strawberry jam. Sharon next door used to make me one on my birthday. Because Mum always forgot.' I gritted my teeth and pushed my tongue to the roof of my mouth.

I'd never really spoken about my mother with someone else. When I was a kid, admitting her faults felt shameful. I was always waiting for someone to say, 'Well of course she didn't get you a birthday cake, you're a bad kid and you don't deserve one.' The minute someone told me I deserved it, I knew I'd crumble. So I never spoke out.

When I reached my early twenties, I'd throw out the odd edge of a story with the insouciance of a well-trained liar, someone who was above such things. Unflappably cool, with her 'bad mum' stories and her dead father. The woman with the devoted husband at the age of twenty-two.

So I stopped talking about Nina. If I didn't think about her, or him, or any part of that life, then I could focus on my future, my own family. That had been the plan. And it had worked pretty well, until it hadn't.

'How did you find my address?'

Kit looked embarrassed, rubbing the back of her neck as she considered the grooves in the table. 'Ah, well, there are still some newspaper articles floating around from that time, it mentioned your boyfriend's name, and I took a chance that you'd married, and then there you were, this big shot at a charity! So I called your work and asked for you, and the wee lass on the phone said you were off on maternity, but she could tell me where to send the flowers.'

I growled, 'That'll be Simone, the number of bloody times I've told her about personal data and GDPR and staff security. Giving out my home address!'

'I know!' Kit agreed. 'I said to her, "Wee gal, what if I'm an axe murderer or something?" and she said, "Oh no, are you?" and I hung up! That'll teach her a lesson!'

Kit nodded, impressed with herself, as she waited for me to laugh. I did, but mainly from the earnest look on her face. And then once I started I couldn't stop, wiping tears from my eyes at the thought of twenty-year-old Simone's face as the axe-murdering Granny from Glasgow hung up on her.

'So, what did you have?' Kit asked and I stopped laughing. Damn.

'Um, I… didn't.' It was easier. Otherwise she'd ask what his name was, and we'd never given him one. It still didn't sit right with me. He was here, ever so briefly, he was real. But naming him felt like another loss. I think Dan had hoped that by not giving him a name, it would be like it had happened right at the start, before he'd even become a person. It didn't work.

'Ah, I see,' she nodded. 'I'm sorry to hear that.'

I nodded, staring at the table.

'Can I ask…'

Oh no, I thought, not more questions, not more prodding and poking and swimming around in my grief. *How far along were you? What happened, was it something you did?*

'Why did you come here? I would have bet a thousand pounds that you wouldn't have come.' Kit looked at me in disbelief. 'I know my sister, I knew what she could be like back then.'

'She could be kind sometimes. She had her moments.'

I kept those memories close, protected them. The days she'd do me up with her make-up, play with me like I was her little doll. She'd push me on the swings, so high I was sure I'd flip over the top of the railing, and in those brief months she worked at the bakery, she always brought me back an apple turnover because she knew I loved them.

I mean, I supposed I only loved them because she

brought them back for me, and she only brought them back because they were free. But I felt special. I'd never had a baked treat before then, not from a bakery, in a little paper bag! And my mum got it for me, especially!

You could destroy anything with enough hindsight and rationality, but it still made me feel cherished when I thought of that little brown paper bag clutched in my sticky fingers. Some things stayed despite the facts.

Kit's face softened, but she still looked unconvinced.

I didn't want to tell her that even bad family was better than none, when you'd built your life around someone. When you had kept secrets and told lies, and you figured your husband was going to leave you.

Nope, too much.

I shook my head, 'I guess I want to believe that people can change. That you're not the sum of the worst things that happened to you. I'd imagined her married to a nice man, maybe finally having what she wanted, and then maybe she'd be nice too. Maybe she'd be happy.'

'You want her to be happy?'

'I want to know that desperately unhappy people can be happy eventually, yeah. That people who make mistakes can find peace.'

Kit widened her eyes and shook her head, like she'd never heard such a crazy story in her life.

'And… and maybe I wanted to stand in front of her and tell her I was okay. Even though she left me in the shit, I survived and had a good life, a lovely husband and a beautiful home and a job I love…'

Even as I was saying it, I could hear myself and tried to stop. *You don't have those things, not really, Taz, they're a lie… this is all a lie… you tricked him and he picked you, and now you're getting what you deserve.*

I took a shaky breath. There was a kernel of the truth in there, though.

'… I wanted her to know I did well without her.'

Kit nodded, 'Well, *that* I can believe.'

'I know it sounds stupid, but—'

She held her hands up, 'Sounds like she got in your head and did a right number on you, hen, and you've a right to however you feel about it. But I'm telling you, that woman in the very expensive health facility has got no secrets left to keep. She hasn't got anywhere to hide them anymore.'

It was decided that I would stay at Kit's. I was dead on my feet, barely able to move, and she insisted. The roads through the Highlands could be treacherous for those who didn't know them, she said, and I honestly felt like I could sleep forever. It was unlike the bone-weary exhaustion that never ceased in the wake of grief. That, I had become used to. A tiredness you never seemed to sleep enough to wake from.

This was something different altogether. It felt like relief. Like suddenly I could sleep without a fear of monsters invading my dreams. I fetched my bag from the car, drowsily noticing how there were no lights in any direction for what seemed like miles, the flat land giving way to dark mountainous curves in the distance, the sky hovering grey.

There was no sound. No cars, no animals despite the farm behind us… There was the quiet chatter of the television Kit had put on for background noise, but then a big, wide nothing. An expanse that seemed to steal sounds with its vastness.

The room Kit led me to was much like the rest of the house: practical and sparse, with the odd flash of comfort. There was a whitewashed rocking chair in the room by the window, a blue cushion and a knitted grey throw hung over the arm. The bed was neat and small, and hanging from the window frame was a sprig of dried lavender.

'I hope this is okay for you, I'm sure you're used to…' Kit looked at me, her hands moving wildly, 'well, I don't know, but I imagine this isn't it.'

I suddenly realised how little I'd revealed of myself that afternoon. I had asked questions and Kit had offered answers, but she knew nothing about me at all.

'I… thank you, it's wonderful. I really appreciate it.'

Kit huffed like pleasantries annoyed her, 'It's family,

dunna fash. I'll be up early with the animals. I'll try not to disturb you. Sleep well.'

The last thing I remembered was noticing the fresh smell of linen, like it had dried in the sunshine, and then finally, for the first time in what felt like forever, I was asleep. Deeply, gloriously asleep.

'But Kitty, what if she's a charlatan, here to murder you and take your valuables?!' The voice that came from downstairs the next morning was high pitched and insistent. 'I know you're out to be a bloody saint, but do you have to take in every wretch you find along the way? How do you even know she's Nina's daughter?'

'There's a particular look of terror people have when they've dealt with my sister on a long-term basis,' Kit's voice was rich with humour, then softened, 'Dunna fash love, she's a good girl and she's been through a lot. She's the image of my mother too, it's unbelievable.'

'Well, I'll see it when I believe it,' the second voice came back, and I wondered if I'd misheard.

'I'm sure you will,' Kit's voice was mocking, and I could already hear the smile in it. 'But don't worry, I've already got a vial of her blood, ready to send off to the lab.'

'You're making jokes. A strange girl sleeping in your

house and you're making jokes. What if she *is* your sister's girl, have you thought of that?'

'Well, yes… that was the point, Effie.'

'I mean your sister was always a manipulative cow, God help her, so what if her wee girl's cut from the same cloth?'

I padded back to the bedroom, embarrassed at what I'd overheard. They thought I was here for Kit, for her money or anything else she had. Because that's just what my mother would have done.

I got dressed quickly, already making excuses and finding justifications to whoever this Effie was. I felt vulnerable, and angry and confused. I'd just wanted an escape, just for a little while.

Last night, softened by whisky and firelight, staying made sense. We were family, that's what Kit had said. Even I knew family put you up when you'd driven hundreds of miles and had two glasses of whisky after a shock. Whether you knew them or not, that was hospitality.

But this morning, even a look out of the window at the grey skies and muted greens showed me this was not my world to inhabit.

I held my head high as I came downstairs, but felt my eyes widen as I took in the breakfast on the table. It was a feast. My stomach rumbled at the sight of it. I'd survived on coffee most of the day before, too wound up and irritable to bother feeding myself.

'Well, good morning,' Kit smiled, widening her eyes at her companion in warning, 'sleep well?'

I nodded, tried for a toothy smile that was more a grimace, 'Yeah, thanks.'

'Well, sit down, help yourself. There's tea, coffee, toast, porridge, bacon and sausages. Eggs are on the way.'

Kit looked pleased as I sat at the table and looked around for the owner of the other voice, awaiting some kind of inquisition. She tilted her head.

'This is Effie McCabe... she helped me with the breakfast. Runs a café in town.'

Both Effie and I looked at Kit in surprise at the strange description.

'Oh aye, did I just wander in off the street to make your eggs?'

Effie was not what I was expecting from her voice. A small, round woman with short blonde hair that would have been a pixie cut if she knew how to style it. She looked at me, light blue eyes curious, seemingly taking in everything about me. I waited for the warnings and the snide comments. I'd had them most of my life, I was still used to them from Miranda. Dan's mum had never missed a chance to make a comment about which of her beloved china ornaments would fetch the best price if *someone* were to get a little light-fingered.

When you were born poor, people never expected

you to be good. Because, how could you be, if you never had enough?

I almost winced, waiting for it, but I met her eyes, willing her to see something decent, something real.

In that one moment, something seemed to switch, and Effie walked over and threw her arms around me.

I reached back automatically, patting her back, looking at Kit in surprise. Kit just shrugged and stole a piece of bacon. Effie smelled like cinnamon and brown sugar and butter, rather than the meats she had clearly just fried.

'Oh you poor wee lamb! With your mother how she is, it must be quite a shock!' Her accent was stronger than Kit's, which now barely seemed like a burr in the back of her throat. Effie let go of me, stepping back. 'And look at you! Skin and bones, you'll need feeding up while you're here. I'll bring the eggs.'

I looked at Kit, who shrugged again. 'Oh yes, she's to be feared, no doubt. Who's that dog at the gates of hell that sleeps if you play it the right lullaby? That's our Effie.'

'Excuse me, I'll be having none of your nonsense,' Effie replied with absolutely no offence taken. 'I just wanted to meet the lass, is all, and anyone who looks at her can see the goodness and pain pouring out. How many eggs, darling?'

This, it seemed, was aimed at me.

'Uh, one please.'

'Two it is.'

Of course.

There was something so delightful in this forceful caretaking. I had never known anyone beyond Dan who was so insistent that I eat, and sleep and drink enough water. It felt like I was special enough for someone to notice, and I loved Effie immediately. It took a special kind of person to boss you around and make you love them for it.

Kit smiled to herself and poured me some coffee from a cafetière. 'Oh yes, we can be fancy here too, you know. It's not just London where you've got all your whosits and doodads.'

I snorted, and Effie chuckled in the kitchen.

'Were you up very early?'

'Oh, the same as every morning. That's why a good hearty breakfast is so important. Keeps your energy up.'

I wanted to ask her a hundred things – how long she'd had the farm, if she'd always known how to do it, if she was from Scotland originally, if we had a family kilt. I suddenly wanted to know everything, and I had to curb myself, as if asking even one question would create an avalanche.

I probably should have been thinking about my mother, but the idea of knowing these people, *good people*, and being related to someone who seemed kind… it was more than I could have hoped for.

Effie brought over the eggs, and piled up my plate,

serving for everyone. We sat together, eating in a companionable silence that I was surprised by. No one seemed in a rush to speak, even Effie. The morning brought birdsong and breezes and the taste of bacon fresh from the pan. I felt like I could finally take a breath.

When everyone's immediate hunger was satiated, I decided to ask a question. Something to make conversation, something innocuous.

'Do you always have breakfast like this, every day?'

Oh, what a moron you are, Taz. For God's sake!

But I'd been thinking about my sad little pot of yoghurt, how I ate sat at the breakfast bar, hunched over my phone and never finishing it because the idea of sitting alone for that long felt like torture. This felt like an *event*.

'Most days,' Effie smiled, daubing her mouth delicately with a napkin. 'I like to know she's fed. And she wouldn't bother to do it herself.'

Kit rolled her eyes, but there was affection there. 'Oh yes, I'd die of starvation, sixty-five years old and I'd waste away surviving on biscuit crumbs and black coffee.'

Kit gestured at Effie next to her, 'Now the *real* story is that this one could be making decent money for her breakfasts in town, but no, she's here for the gossip. If there's something interesting going on, she's out here to natter to me about it, or find out what I know.'

'Not that Kitty is any good at detail!' Effie huffed.

'She may as well be a man for all the attention she pays. No mind for the juicy bits of a story.'

'No mind to be sticking my nose in other people's business, you mean?' Kit replied, a holier-than-thou look on her face. 'And I hold my head high for it, too.'

'Oh, you'd never guess,' Effie grinned at me, shaking her head.

I loved them. I loved their back and forth, and their warm way of teasing each other. No harm meant, no offence taken. Just comfortable.

I briefly closed my eyes as I chewed the last piece of bacon, savouring how delicious it was.

'So go on then,' I said when I'd finished chewing, rubbing my hands together, 'what's the latest gossip?'

Kit and Effie burst out laughing.

'You, of course!'

'What?' I could hear the disappointment in my own voice, and the two women fell over themselves to let me know they weren't laughing at me.

'Oh no, we didn't mean—'

'It's just—'

'We meant—'

I held up a hand.

'It's fine, honestly. It must seem strange, me appearing suddenly.'

'It's more me, hen.' Kit smiled softly. 'Made a bit of a name for myself as a hermit. To suddenly have a guest, to have family... well, that's a big bit of news for a town with a population under five hundred people.'

'If it helps, it's big news for me too. I didn't have any family. I mean, I didn't think I did.'

Effie's eyes went to my left hand, and she nodded at it, 'But you're married.'

I nodded, 'Nine years.'

'Lord, married young. It's nice when that works out. Everyone thinks it's so old fashioned to grow up as you grow old with someone.' Effie nodded at me with encouragement. 'So, go on then, what're they like, your person?'

My heart seemed to inflate and puncture at the thought of him. I suddenly missed him so fiercely that I wanted to rest my nose in the crescent of his neck and have his fingers wound through my hair like he'd never let go. I hadn't even called him to say I'd arrived safely.

'He's… the best person I know. My best friend. He's funny and kind and so talented. And he'd give anything to make me happy.'

I suddenly realised what a weird thing that was to say, but when you had our history, when he'd given up what he had to be with me, to keep me safe, there was no way to properly explain it without a big story.

'Isn't that what the people who love you are supposed to do, put your happiness first?' Kit asked gruffly, and I felt suddenly like a gushing teenager talking about her crush, diminished.

'Well, he was the first one who ever did,' I shrugged.

It's so easy to throw around those words. That you'd do anything, give anything, for someone you love. So few people follow it up.

'Any kids?' I heard Effie ask, pulling me from my musings.

Suddenly I wanted to throw up my breakfast.

You've got to get used to people asking, Taz. That's what they do, it's normal. It's a normal thing to ask. I conjured Dan's voice sometimes when I panicked about these things. My imaginary friend, a Dan from years past, gentler than the one I knew now. And more readily available.

'No,' I managed to choke out, and then busied myself with my coffee.

'Ah, there's plenty of time for all that yet, you're no wee lass but you're fine,' Effie smiled, as if she hadn't just kicked me in the teeth. Kit looked at her, eyebrows raised and lips pressed together.

'You're a nosey wee wench, Effie McCabe,' Kit said pointedly, but her Effie ignored her, looking at me for an answer.

'We… we're looking forward to having children some day.' I sounded strangely formal, the words sitting awkwardly in my mouth. It was my go-to phrase these days, a way to discount the past and focus on the future. If we had a future for me to go back to.

Kit tried to apologise with a look, and I shook my

head, smiled at her. Dan was right, I'd had enough time to get used to it, for it to feel less like a bruise or a burn mark, to let the question arise and disappear like a wave. People would ask, it was only natural.

'And you?' I asked Effie, more in a desperate need to redirect the conversation rather than actual interest. 'So you have kids?'

'Good lord, no. I'm far too selfish. And unfortunately not a maternal bone in my body,' Effie laughed, serving me another piece of bacon, straight to my plate without me saying anything.

I raised an eyebrow at Kit, who snorted, holding up her hands. 'If mothering was just bossing people around and being a feeder, Effie would take a title. However, it does involve screaming, crying and bodily fluids.'

Effie shook her head, 'No, not for me. I just about tolerate the cat.'

'The cat just about tolerates you!' Kit retorted.

Effie looked at me, tilting her head at Kit as if to say, *Can you believe this?*

'Says the woman who *voluntarily* has enough animals to start her own travelling circus. Do any of them say thank you? Ask you how your day is? Buy you a glass of Pinot Grigio at the pub on a Friday night? Do they hell!'

'Oh yes, selfish freeloaders, all of them,' Kit laughed, and I tried to think of a good 'horse walks into a bar' joke, but went blank.

'So, do you want to see the farm?' Kit's voice was

hopeful. She tapped her hands on the table and stood up. 'It'll be a bit different to what you're used to, I'd imagine. But it's interesting…'

I nodded, not really sure what else to do. We hadn't spoken about whether I'd visit Nina, whether we'd go together, but it seemed stupid to come all the way here and then not go through with it.

That was the point of it, right? To show Dan that I could forgive, I could move on, I could be that fun, loving, happy person I was in our twenties. I'd go say the magic words to my mother, and *boom*, I'd be better.

Except what if she didn't remember me? Was there even a point?

What I *did* know was that I already loved Kit. She was grouchy and sharp and funny. She absolutely didn't give a crap what people thought, and yet she clearly wanted to look after everyone.

The idea of family was intoxicating. I'd been focused on making one, a new generation, but discovering one existed, with history and stories to share? It was impossible to resist.

Kit's farm was not what I expected. Yes, there were the chubby pigs in their pens, and the few sheep that milled about. There were her chickens, and I liked the way she yelled 'Ladies!' as she approached, chucking seed every which way as they dived and scattered. She was a leader, weaving through her domain and being carefully watched by her subjects.

'Do you… is this a working farm?' I asked, trying to find a way to explain how little I knew.

'Ah, you mean how can a wee farm like this survive?' Kit raised an eyebrow, amused.

'No, I just… I don't know how farms work…' I paused, 'Do all the animals go off to be eaten?'

Kit shook her head, 'They're not the main event. Although the kids like to see them on their school trips.'

She led me round the back of the barn and I was surprised to find a stable, with six horses.

'Now these boys are my money makers, for the most part.'

I said nothing, and Kit whistled at them, leaning on the stable door. 'People pay to come and ride them around the land.'

'You teach them?'

'I used to, handed it over to one of the wee'uns I used to teach. She does a better job. In the summer we do fairs and fetes, and we take them around to the schools. The kids do their trips here to learn about farming and horses and the other animals.'

A young woman with red hair, brushing one of the huge horses down, smiled and waved at me. I actually stepped back in awe of her beauty, the natural freckles that kissed her cheeks and were scattered across her nose. She wore similar clothes to Kit, a practical gilet and dark jeans, but her shirt was a bold green that jumped out against the background.

'Speak of the devil,' Kit said by way of greeting.

'Ah you'll be the niece then?' the girl said, nodding as we approached, holding out her hand and shaking mine with authority.

'How…?'

She grinned at me, 'Oh this is a wee place, we've no secrets here. And we need a bit of excitement, don't we Kit? It's been far too long.'

Kit rolled her eyes, 'I dunno, sounds like that moron you're dating made enough excitement for everyone last night.'

'It wasn't Murray's fault, he was provoked!' the redhead argued, almost stamping her foot.

'Aye, by some truths he didn't like, I'm sure he's no fan of most of them.' Kit's accent became more pronounced as she spoke to the young woman, almost as if she was echoing her. A different person, a different life.

The redhead also rolled her eyes, sighing dramatically, then gave me a warm smile. 'I'm Sarah, by the way. I help with the horses from time to time.'

'Taz.'

She could only have been about nineteen, she had that look of not being entirely comfortable in her own skin. But she had a calmness that the horses seemed to pick up on. A warmth.

Was I ever that young? At nineteen I was working as a charity fundraiser on the street, and I *loved* it. It was a test in conjuring stories to get people's attention, to draw them in and tug their heartstrings. It was something that made me feel good, I was doing something *good*. And it reminded me that most people wanted to help, if they could. I was tenacious, Dan called me his little Jack Russell. He did his first mural that year, making a living making art. Nineteen was a good year.

'Don't listen to anything she says about me,' Sarah faux-whispered to me. 'I'm a great help to her, despite her moaning.'

'Oh I'm sure!' Kit laughed. 'A great help to clearing out my fridge and hearing the woes of young love because you waste yourself on a moron.'

'Kit… we said we wouldn't…' Sarah crossed her arms, as if she were the adult in the situation. As if she was disappointed.

Kit held up her hands in surrender, and tilted her head to suggest we continue with our tour.

'Nice to meet you!' Sarah called after me and I waved back.

'You too!'

Kit huffed as we walked further down the field, shaking her head. 'Wee girl's dating an absolute gobshite.'

I tried to hide a smile, 'So you mentioned.'

'Headful of bricks would be a gift to a lad like

Murray. He's got a mean streak I don't like. And a snaky look to him, like he's about to unhinge his jaw and eat a passing deer.'

'Well,' I replied seriously, 'Effie's *completely* wrong, you're *very good* at gossiping, when given the right subject.'

Kit laughed, a single, loud 'HA!' that seemed to shock even her. She nodded begrudgingly, 'Well, some things it pays to know about.'

She carried on with the tour, leading me down the track, pointing out things as she went, Sarah's horrible boyfriend now seemingly forgotten.

'There's old Millie and Mabel,' I looked at the beautiful Highland cows across the field, their blonde hair flicked over their faces like a shampoo advert. 'And the tours tend to stop off here to take photos and buy some authentic Scottish titbits, which gets me by.'

'What does that mean?'

'It means that Angus who runs the tours, and young Michael and all the others stop by with their buses full of tourists, and they pay me a pretty penny to bring out a tray of whisky and tea, and encourage the girls over for photos and to have their hair stroked.'

'Sounds like a sweet deal.'

She seemed proud of the life she'd built and I could understand why.

'Oh yes, and if I'm particularly well prepared, I'll have some little bits to sell. Scottish tablet, postcards and local artwork, some cakes for the rest of the trip. In the winter the cottage becomes almost an art exhibition. I bring them in for a portion of stew and bannock, put on a strong accent and tell a few depressing stories about *these here lands*, and they love it.'

We walked on, and I couldn't help but ask, 'So... are you actually Scottish?'

'Ah, the favourite question around here,' Kit grinned at me. 'My da was a Scotsman. He came to England and met my mother, and then when he died, we stayed there and that was that. He had the most beautiful voice when he sang, and told me stories about where he grew up. And when I was old enough to find my way in the world, I ended up here. I found an aunt, his sister, and even my grandmother, very briefly. This was her farm. Her legacy. I worked it with my aunt for a while, and then eventually it fell to me to keep it going. It certainly wasn't a tourist destination when she owned it, but I've made sure it survived this way, and I think she'd be happy.'

She rubbed one of the posts with her rough fingertips, sighing, and I wondered if she really believed that. Kit turned those eyes on me, a knowing smile on her face.

'So, to answer your question, I am a Scottish woman raised in England. And this lot have never let me forget it.'

She knew exactly who she was, and made no apologies, that much was clear. But I couldn't stamp down the slight disappointment that this came from her father's side of the family. There was no shared history for me, here. I wasn't Scottish in any way, there was nothing of my heritage in this land, as much as I wished there were.

I'd found blood, but no legacy. Not yet anyway.

'Come see my special weapons,' she patted my shoulder, heavy handed and unaware of her own strength, and then set off round a corner.

'Well, my granny would not be pleased about these two, I assure you, but they make me good money and they do make me smile, funny wee things.'

Kit put her fingers to her lips and whistled, loudly. I'd always wished I could do that, even though the noise cut right through me.

I looked around, and heard a steady gallop that gradually got louder. I turned, expecting horses, but instead I found two alpacas, their funny little faces cheerful as they bounded over and nudged Kit.

'This is Neville, and this is Hermione,' Kit plunged her fingers into their fluff and they stood there, vacant and cheery. 'We take these two to lots of events. They're big at weddings at the moment. Put some flower necklaces on them, or a little bow tie on Neville, and they're a hit! People love them.'

'I can see why!' I reached out tentatively and stroked a fluffy neck.

'People thought I was mad. They still do,' Kit

laughed, putting on a strong accent, *'Oh, you're knitting yourself a wee scarf with those two, are ye Kit? Sell yourself some jumpers, aye, become a fashion mogul?'*

I snorted, and Kit rolled her eyes, 'But it's good business, and these two are happy. And they just make me smile! We used to take Terry out to the weddings too, but he's a little grouchy in his old age.'

She pointed over to the next gated section, where a tiny spotted Shetland pony looked over his shoulder at us, audibly huffed, and then trotted to the far end of the enclosure.

Kit sighed, 'Just because he looks cute, doesn't mean he's not an arsehole.'

'A universal truth,' I laughed.

As we walked back to the house Kit said gently, 'You know, you don't have to decide right away about seeing Nina. You might stay a few days, see how you feel?'

I knew I should be confused, somehow, the same way I always was about my mother. Knowing she'd abandoned me, left me with a broken dad and a mountain of debt. Knowing what her leaving led to. And yet… it was so easy to remember how sweet she could be. How she'd wink and make a hand gesture in Woolworths to let me know when to stick a fistful of cola bottles into my pocket. How she'd make me into an Egyptian mummy using loo roll, telling me to hold my arms up and laughing, 'Twirl, Tashy, twirl my princess!'

I wanted to see her. I wanted to see who she was now.

The curiosity was killing me. But I didn't want Kit to see that, to think I was weak. She knew how vindictive my mother had been, possibly more than anyone else. How desperate was I for a mother, that I would forget all that?

But maybe, *just maybe,* there had been a reason she had to go. A really good reason.

'What would I do in the meantime?' I asked.

Kit shrugged, 'Stay with me, you can help out with the farm if you like. We always need an extra pair of hands.'

Her gruff demeanour might have put someone else off, but I understood it. When I didn't immediately respond, she added, 'Or go on holiday, explore the Highlands. Whatever.'

She wanted me there. She had people, clearly, Sarah and Effie proved that. But I liked the idea that she wanted family too.

'Thank you, I'd like that. Helping on the farm, I mean. Though I'll probably be crap. But… it'll be nice to get to know each other better.'

I stuttered a little, embarrassed, feeling my cheeks warm. I knew it was the answer Kit was hoping for, because her lips twitched briefly into a smile before she waved a hand.

'No need for all the hippie dippie feelings and kum bye ya yas. And no need to thank me either, there'll be 4 a.m. starts.'

'Ah, so it *was* just an attempt to get free labour. I should have known,' I grinned.

Somehow, Kit's varying degrees of vulnerability, grouchiness and snark were comforting. Whilst everything seemed incredibly strange, it was the closest I'd felt to normal in ages.

Chapter Five

'So, how is it?' Dan's voice was almost lost in the strong breeze as I stood at the back door. Kit's house was small and if people in the town already knew about me, I imagined they had their ears pressed up to my bedroom wall, concocting stories about the runaway niece with the awful mother.

Outside was better.

I stood looking at the grey, beautiful landscape, a cup of tea carefully placed on the windowsill for me by Kit, before she went back out to welcome the kids for their riding lessons. She was thoughtful.

'It's... weird. Beautiful though. Earlier on I helped muck out stables.'

'You! You get annoyed when there's mud on your running shoes!'

'I do not!'

I did. I was always cleaning my running shoes, mainly because I'd felt guilty spending so much money on them and wanted to keep them in good condition. A by-product of getting something you never got to have as a kid. I was the same with my bike too.

'And did you enjoy it? Shovelling shit?' Dan's voice was light, but I could tell he was distracted, far away. I could picture him at his desk, half a sandwich sitting untouched, papers everywhere, furrowing his brow at a screen. I heard a rumbling voice in the background and he said, 'I'm on my lunch David, come back in ten.'

'Do you need to go?' I asked, not sure if I felt relieved. I wasn't sure how to talk to my husband anymore, it seemed.

'No, I want to talk to you. These bastards just see work–life balance as a sign of weakness.' He ensured his voice was louder at the end of his sentence, and I could imagine whoever David was sticking up his middle finger. 'Mum asked how you were.'

'Really.' I did not believe that. 'And what did you say?'

'I said we were taking some time. That you were dealing with family stuff.'

'And how well did she hide her joy? Has she already sent you a list of potential second wives?'

'Taz, come on,' Dan sighed. 'Let's not.'

I nodded, taking a breath. 'Okay. Sorry.'

'So, are you going to see your mum?'

'Yeah, that's why I'm here.'

Dan let out a sigh, and I tried not to jump on him. 'What?'

'I just wish you'd let me in, let me help. You don't get points for doing it alone.'

'I've spent my whole life being saved by you…'

'And I was saved by you. We saved each other, that's what we do.'

It occurred to me that my husband had spent our life rewarding me for my loyalty. Because I loved him as a teenager, behind bars. That I was there, every moment I could be, every visiting hour, every week, painting a picture of our future together. Giving him something to look forward to. That hadn't been my role in a long time.

'What's your aunt like?' Dan was always good at finding ways to keep a conversation going. Being interested, coaxing people into talking until they didn't even realise they felt comfortable.

I felt that knot in my stomach start to unfurl.

'She's… grouchy, but I like her. There're no games. And she named her alpacas after *Harry Potter* characters.'

'Clearly a sign of a decent human being,' Dan's smile was audible. He paused, 'I'm sorry things are weird right now, babe. I miss you.'

I smiled in relief. It didn't make things less complicated, but I was glad he missed me. Glad that my stomach could still flip at the thought of him. In the good kind of way.

'Do you take husband classes or something? Is there an app you're using that tells you the right thing to say?'

'Nah, I've just loved you for over a decade,' he snorted, 'not a bad idea about that app though. I'll look into investors. Then maybe we can retire to that Caribbean island, what do you think?'

I heard more sounds in the background, and Daniel huffed, his softness and smile gone. 'I said ten *minutes*, David. If you can't count maybe you shouldn't be in banking, right?' His voice got louder again, directed at me, 'I'm sorry, I've got to go.'

'Okay, look after yourself.'

'Yeah you too,' he paused, 'Taz, only go see your mum if you really want to, okay? You don't need to punish yourself just because you think you should.'

God, if only he knew.

The farm was a little bit magical. I imagined what it would have been like to visit as a child, or even as a petulant teenager. I could see it, clear as day, Kit rousing me from my bed and shooing me out into the cold to help feed the chickens, or learning to ride horses.

Perhaps, in another life, I might have even lived with her, if I'd known who she was. If I'd known she'd existed. I'd be outdoorsy and ruddy-faced, a healthy complexion instead of that ghostly skin of mine, made worse by the dark circles under my eyes and the sharp angles of my face. It was a portal into another world, and I was enjoying imagining who I might have been.

Except there would be no Dan. There would have been no damp studio flat in Tufnell Park, no years spent as a barista/waitress/admin assistant/Saturday girl at the estate agent's. There would have been no weeks living off tuna pasta bake and no nights curled around each other for warmth, telling stories about our glorious future, until we could fall asleep.

There would be no me, no us, if Kit had come to save me.

She seemed to be the sort to collect lost causes. She had a constant stream of people turning up at the farm. Not just the kids to ride the horses, or the people who'd booked a 'take an alpaca for a walk' event. Not just Sarah with her boy trouble, but almost every tour group seemed to offer someone she could help, whether it was an older gent researching family history, or a child in need of a second slice of cake. She wanted to help. But she pretended she didn't.

Seeing Kit in full 'sales' mode when a tour bus arrived was something else. I stood there awkwardly, just watching. She looked ten years younger, suddenly vibrant and soft.

The visitors were delighted with her, expanding under her charm and warmth, accepting glasses of whisky from the tray that I held out. They tasted tablet and bought shortbread and took hundreds of selfies with the cows. I watched them enjoy themselves and somehow became part of it.

'And how old is this place?' a woman asked me, her American accent a slight surprise. 'Has it been here for centuries?'

I looked in panic at Kit, who just threw her hands up and then twirled them around, to indicate I should say *something, anything*.

'Oh yes, it's been in the family for generations. Did you know those beautiful cows are only that colour because the queen once pointed out she liked them?'

The woman looked at me with a slight disappointment, 'Oh, you're English.'

I saw Kit raise an eyebrow at me, as if to say, *Told you so. Give them a story.*

'Unfortunately so, but our family has lived here for a long time, from before it was a working farm,' I started, seeing Kit nod, then mouth *more*. 'And those cows the queen passed when she made that comment were *right here, on this land.*'

I watched the woman's eyes go wide, then turn to her husband, 'Jeff! Jeff, did you hear about *the queen and the cows*?'

These visitors were thrilled with it all, and it was only when they packed themselves up and the bus disappeared, Kit stopped waving and let out a deep sigh, seeming to become herself again. She rolled her eyes and muttered to herself as she collected up glasses or counted up the cash in her little tartan-covered tin.

That night she put down a simple dinner of beans on toast and grilled sausages, and two bottles of beer.

'Sorry, I… I tend not to bother much with dinner when it's just me.'

I shook my head, 'I'm the same. Most nights I'll have a piece of toast. This is a bit fancy by my standards, you need to use a fork and everything.'

Kit looked at me, as if checking to see I wasn't laughing at her. Then she raised her bottle to me, and I lifted mine in response.

'You did a good job today, I thought you'd be far too moral to spin a yarn for the tourists.'

I shook my head, 'People want a story, often doesn't matter if it's true.' I thought about the stories in the paper after Dan went to prison, the Romeo and Juliet angles they worked, the way they painted him and me until we were barely recognisable, either saints or sinners, depending on the rag. 'Of course, give me a couple of books and I'll find something true. Those are the best kind of stories anyway, the ones that have a little truth in them.'

'You know I don't do it to mock anyone, or take advantage,' Kit sighed into her meal. 'I give them the experience they want. They don't want the grouchy grey-haired woman talking about sustainable farming. They want wee Neville to nibble carrots and for me to talk about the clans and haggis and whether any of us met that handsome red-haired fella from *Outlander*.'

I snorted, 'And have you?'

Kit tapped her nose, 'Well, the best stories have a hint of truth, do they not?'

'Meaning you've watched a few episodes?'

'Or I may have driven past when they were filming at the castle.' Kit grinned at me, wrinkling her nose at her own hilarity. 'So you think you're up to helping me tomorrow? It's an early start.'

I shrugged, 'I like to be busy. To be useful. I have no experience at all, but I'll try hard.'

'Aye, I can tell that just from looking at you,' her eyes rested on me, searching for something. 'You're not like her at all.'

I shook my head, 'I am, more than I'd like to admit sometimes. She didn't mind telling people stories they liked to hear, either.'

We didn't say anything for a moment, and I tried to find the words.

'My husband says I could talk someone into giving me the coat off their back if I needed it enough.' I smiled, spearing a sausage with my fork. 'It was what made me good at fundraising. If there was an angle to work, I'd find it.'

'And do you think he's right?'

'I think if I had enough of a reason, I could make anyone do just about anything,' I said, trying not to think about how scary that was, and how many times I had walked that line before. How many times I'd crossed it.

Even in the ways Dan didn't know. Manipulation was sometimes like a muscle, you had to resist using it. But when you're a scared kid, afraid of losing the only good thing in your life… I didn't like being my mother's daughter. And I didn't like keeping secrets from my husband.

I shook the thought away and stood to clear the table, focusing on being a good house guest. I washed up the plates, and Kit dried them and put them away. It was comfortable, companionable, and I was relieved not to talk. After months of being on my own all day, all this talking felt almost overwhelming. When I bid Kit goodnight she handed me a book from her bureau, the local history of the area.

'See what stories you can spin tomorrow with a little truth,' she smiled. 'I'll wake you around 4:30.'

She was waiting for a horrified response and I just shrugged, 'Sounds good to me.' She couldn't have known how many times I woke at three in the morning and went for a run just to exhaust myself, to escape my thoughts. How often I'd wake and slip down to the shed in the garden to use Dan's punch bag. I was not delicate, I would not break. People thought I was made of glass when I was made of leather.

I waded through a few chapters of the book, curled up in that small bed, hearing the sounds of the television from downstairs. When I closed the book and turned out the light, I padded over to the window to look out at that view across the land, that pitch black sky offering stars like I'd never seen.

I was meant to be here. It felt like the best choice I'd made in years. Like an escape from Taz from the estate, or Taz the banker's wife, or Taz the disappointing daughter-in-law, or the not-quite mother. I was here and I was welcome.

I exhaled, a smile on my face as I crept back into bed. Family. I had family.

I was not feeling quite so warmly towards Kit in the morning. I had been so prepared to impress, when I jumped out of bed at the sound her sharp rap at the door, but I was blurry and sleep-drunk. It wasn't like at home, where I was wired and alert all the time, waiting for something to go wrong.

I thundered down the stairs, still bleary-eyed in my jeans and hoodie, feeling vaguely nostalgic for those early morning flights Dan and I used to take when we were saving. When we'd have done anything for a holiday, even if it meant getting to the airport for 3 a.m. and only spending twelve hours in the actual location.

Kit handed me a coffee, and I stifled a yawn. 'I'm

sorry, normally I'm better than this! I'm a morning person!'

'Well, you've had lots of news to take in. It's natural,' Kit shrugged, 'just try not to pour your coffee in the horse's food, or wash the alpacas with washing-up liquid, and you'll be fine.'

'It's that bed, it was too comfortable.'

Kit looked pleased, then paused, 'Oh, actually, I store those sheets with lavender when they're not on the bed, that might not be helping you.'

'So you want me too dopey to help.'

'I like my guests sleepy enough that they shut up. It's usually wee Sarah staying and she can talk like no one else.' Kit stood up, 'Speaking of, enough jibber jabber, let's get going.'

I honestly didn't know what to do, so I followed Kit closely, did what she asked and tried not to ask too many questions. We fed the animals, watching as they flocked (or waited irritably in the case of Terry the Tiny Pony) for their feed. We mucked stables and brushed horses, moved hay and bedding and refreshed water. By the time we'd done the rounds, more than two hours had passed and as we made it back to the cottage, the smell of bacon made my mouth water.

There was Effie, standing at the stove wearing that same smile and same 'kiss the chef' tartan apron I'd not even noticed yesterday. 'Ah she's roped you into helping her! Look at you, all ruddy from the fresh air, looking healthy, girl!'

I gave a little curtsey and sat down at the table, asking Effie how she was. She waved a hand and pursed her lips, as if she couldn't think of anything more boring than talking about herself. Which was lucky, because she had more than enough to say about everyone else in town.

'The latest theory, Kitty, is that Taz here is some wee love child from your past, back to claim her rightful inheritance.'

Kit snorted, sticking a cinnamon stick in the teapot, 'Inheritance? And what would she inherit, pray tell? A few pretty cows and an ageing pony with terrible flatulence?'

'Don't be mean to Terry, I'm sure he warms up when you get to know him.'

'Aye, warms up right in his belly and then lets you know how he feels to your face.' Kit snorted and Effie nodded.

'He is a wee smelly pony,' Effie laughed, then put her hand on Kit's shoulder, 'but I have a soft spot for old grouchy things.'

She served up the same huge breakfast as yesterday, but today I was ravenous, not even blinking as Effie piled my plate high. In fact, when both chewing and conversation slowed, I even snuck another pancake onto my plate.

Effie nodded at me with a sort of pride, and then suddenly stopped. 'Oh! So you will have met Scottie McTavish yesterday, the inn-keeper's wife?'

'What?' I blinked, looking to Kit, who rolled her eyes.

'It's what she calls my *work persona*, comedian that she is.'

'Well, can you blame me? She goes from being a regular sour puss who hates people and just wants to be alone with her animals, to *Helloo there dearies, welcome to my truly authentic Scoootish experience!*' Effie wiped her eyes as she laughed, 'So happy, so *amenable*! Anything you want, Scottie McTavish will get it for you with a smile on her face.'

'Ah yes, but she'll charge you for the privilege!' I laughed, and Kit pointed.

'See, the girl gets it.'

Effie shook her head, 'You can pretend it's business all you like, I don't believe it.' She turned to me, 'She loves it really, putting on her airs, I'll bet she's got a backstory and everything.'

Kit neither confirmed nor denied it, but picked up our dishes to take them to the sink without another word. Effie nodded at me as if to say, *Well, there you go*.

I loved having breakfast with them, hearing about people in town that I'd yet to meet. It felt like the kind of thing families would do. We used to do it, Dan and I, when we first got together. When we worked strange shifts and our mornings could start at any time of the day. We'd eat breakfast at four in the afternoon before I went off to my bar job and he went to load and unload lorries at one of the depots.

Since he'd started at his dad's firm, we didn't see each other in the mornings. He left me little notes by the coffee pot, or made me a cup of tea. Some days we nodded sleepily to each other, when I used to wake up early to go running. That was the first few months after the miscarriage, when I was so desperate just to run. To escape my own body. But Dan said it worried him, how far I ran, how much weight I lost, the damage I was doing to my joints. The pulled muscles and inflammation and shin splints.

He bought me a treadmill, and an exercise bike. They had both sat in the nursery, unopened.

Life was simple on the farm – an early start, a big breakfast and then there was time. The kids had their riding classes, Effie went to the café, and Kit baked her cakes, the smell of lavender and lemon permeating the cottage. And there I was, I curled up on the sofa with my book, breathing in the scent and warmth. Being looked after. It was what I imagined school trips were like, activities and learning and then free time to just be. An adventure holiday from my life.

I helped a little with the first tour group, but I was

strangely exhausted, unable to keep up the enthusiasm that 'Scottie' seemed to emanate. She was always busy, always saying something, laughing with someone, offering food or jokes or titbits. I sort of hovered there, and I knew Kit was looking to me to impress her, show her some of that 'selling magic' I said I'd had, but I could barely remember anything in the book she'd given me.

'Give yourself a break, girl.' Her lips were a thin line and told me she would not take any arguments. So I trudged back to the cottage, almost ready to collapse onto those sheets, pausing to take photos of the view and send them to Dan. I didn't know what to say to him, but I still wanted him to know I was there, to miss me.

When I let myself in, I was faced with a red-haired woman sat at the kitchen table. When she looked up I realised it was Sarah, her tear-streaked face so incredibly young compared to when I saw her yesterday. Then she'd looked confident and determined. Now she had the look of someone thrown headlong from childhood a little too quickly.

'Hello?' I let my voice float out before I appeared around the doorframe, so as not to spook her.

She wiped her eyes rapidly, and put a winning smile on her face.

'I didn't realise anyone was here, sorry Taz. How's it going?'

That smile killed me. I'd seen it in the mirror a hundred times.

She was holding a baby, a round-faced cheery little thing who didn't seem to notice her tears at all. He gripped her beautiful red hair in a chubby fist as she bounced him on her knee, an automatic motion.

'Fine, all fine... are you here to see Kit?' I asked gently, trying not to stare at her. Her eyes were an alarmingly bright blue, and she looked so very sad. I wanted to gather her up and hold her tight, she looked so drained of energy, like she was unspooling.

'She's usually the person to hear my troubles, and talk some sense into me,' Sarah laughed, sniffling a little and adjusting the baby. 'I know she's got the kids in for the horses about now, so I thought I'd wait inside.'

I wasn't sure whether to leave, or go get Kit, or whether I should leave her to herself, give her space to fall apart. And then I took a breath and remembered it wasn't about me.

'Would you like some tea?' I said, and immediately hated myself for my Englishness. Sarah didn't even pause, just looked grateful.

'Aye, that would be lovely,' she didn't make fun of me, 'this is Lachlan, by the way.'

'He's adorable,' I said. Not a lie, but an expected phrase. I tried not to look at babies too much these days. Dan once said there was a hungry look on my face, and I was horrified for others to see that weakness.

'Well, they make 'em that way so you can't throttle them when they won't stop screaming, don't they?' She smiled again, more natural but still tired and world-weary. There was something more than motherhood there. I put the water on to boil, got the teapot out the same way Kit had.

I smiled back at Sarah, but said nothing. I thought she might prefer the silence, her eyes closed in prayer or thought, I didn't know.

'Go on, say it,' she said suddenly.

'What?'

'I'm too young to have a bairn, and isn't this my younger brother, or nephew? How *did* I get myself in such a fine state, me so young with the world at my feet?'

I snorted, relaxing as I opened the pot of cinnamon sticks and inhaled that complicated scent of home.

'It's funny how people seem to think they have a right to comment on your life choices. But stranger still that they think you should care.' I smiled at her. 'He's beautiful. And you look like you know what you're doing, no problem.'

Sarah sighed a little at that, snorting, 'I'm pretty good at pretending most of the time. People keep saying it'll get easier. I'm waiting for that to be true. That's what Kit's for, I come to her when I need some sense talked into me. She'll be harsh, but it's for the best.'

'You've come for… a telling off?' I tried to keep the surprise out of my voice, but failed miserably.

'Aye, I've come for my penance. Better than church. Kit's always looked out for me, ever since I was one of those kids out there, desperately wanting to ride on the horses but no money to pay and no family to help me. She didn't have much family either, so we sort of… had each other.'

'I'm just visiting,' I said, inexplicably, as if I needed to convince her I wasn't there to steal her beloved mother figure.

'Well, good, I'll not be sharing her,' Sarah said, and when I looked up from filling the mugs, she grinned at me. It was impossible not to smile back. 'You'll be having your own dramas that need a little Kit magic, I'll imagine?'

'Something like that.'

I brought the tea over, and Sarah was delighted that I made it the same way as Kit, cinnamon in the pot. It seemed to mean something. It was a relief to talk to someone who didn't expect anything of me, didn't ask for reasons for my trip or want clear answers. Instead, we talked about what was on television, and how long Effie had run the café, and what people in town thought of the alpacas.

Lachlan fell asleep, and Sarah asked me to hold him while she ran to the toilet. Before I could make up an excuse, he was in my arms and I dared not move.

After a few seconds of fear, I looked at him, tracing his velvet soft skin with my fingertip. He was beautiful, so beautiful. I closed my eyes and put my nose to his head, taking a deep inhale of that baby smell.

Which of course, was when Kit walked in. I looked at her, like an addict caught in the act, heart thumping in my chest with guilt, but Kit saw nothing amiss. Just a woman holding a cute baby and having a cuddle. Which was exactly what it was.

'Ah, I see you've met the wee rascal,' she nodded at the baby as if he was another of her animals. A little affection, alongside a subtle belief that he'd probably shit on the carpet if given half a chance. 'How long has Sarah been gone?'

'A few seconds, she's just popped up to the loo.'

'Oh the loo, is it?' Kit snorted, then went to her purse, took out a twenty and slipped it into the front pocket of Sarah's handbag. She turned to me, raised an eyebrow and put her finger to her lips.

I made a sign as if I were locking my lips up, and she nodded, satisfied as she helped herself to a cup of tea from the pot. When Sarah returned, she gave Kit a hug. Kit, exactly as I expected, stood there and withstood it, patting her briefly on the back until she let go.

'What did the moron do this time?' Kit asked, not one for preliminaries.

'Lost his job,' Sarah pressed her lips together, reaching to stroke Lachlan's head but making no move to take him from me. 'But it wasn't his fault…'

'Oh aye? The boy seems to have terrible bad luck when it comes to staying employed, doesn't he?'

Sarah blushed a little, 'That fight the other night... it was with the boss's son.'

'Ah, an abundance of brains, that boy. And how does he plan to support you and his son now?' Kit's tone was harsh and I felt embarrassed for Sarah, but clearly this was what she'd come for. It had the feel of a conversation that had happened many times before.

'He'll find something. I just need to give him time to cool down. Do you think Fraser would—'

Kit shook her head, but did reach out a hand to pat Sarah's arm to soften the rejection, 'You know having Murray in a pub would not be good for anyone. I will do anything I can for you, hen, you know that. But I will not help that lad until he helps himself.'

'It's my fault, I got him all wound up and then he went to work and started trouble,' Sarah sighed, stirring her tea. Kit's mouth became a thin line, and I jumped in before she could say anything. I couldn't help myself.

'Um, I mean, it's none of my business, but... if he went and punched someone, it's his fault. His temper, his responsibility. Not yours.'

'Thank you!' Kit yelped. 'Someone who speaks sense. For the love of God, the women I've known who've thrown themselves away on worthless men. You see this girl, how smart and kind and funny she is? How she's a fine mother, even being so young? And still, she'll stay with a moron because no one told her she deserved better.'

Sarah frowned, 'I am here, you know.'

'Are you? Are you really, hen? Because we've been having this conversation from before the wee'un was even born, and we're still having it.' Kit bristled and I wasn't sure who I wanted to comfort. I just knew that I wanted to be out of that kitchen and away from whatever this was.

'Then I'll go, if it's such an inconvenience to you,' Sarah started noisily, ineffectively getting her things together, but still made no move to retrieve her baby. I could tell these were the moves of a well-trod dance, one they both knew the steps to well enough. It was better to wait until the music stopped, I suppose.

'Oh for goodness' sake,' Kit rolled her eyes, suddenly seeming like the young one in the argument. 'Everyone asks me why I never had children, and it's like I've got a teenage daughter on my hands without the labour!'

'I thought you were my friend,' Sarah said quietly, and with that, all the bluster seemed to dissipate. Kit sighed and closed her eyes, composing herself. Then she walked over to Sarah and took both her hands in hers, shaking them slightly as she spoke.

'My biggest fear is that I'm going to open the newspaper and read that he's killed you. That he was drunk driving with you in the car, or he brought some idiots back to party in your home, or he gets so angry one day that he doesn't take it out on the boss's son, or the wall, or the car door.'

'You're overreacting.'

Kit shook her head gravely, 'There are broken people who never learn enough to sort themselves, and there are wrong ones who never think they need to change. What about your son? What does he deserve?'

I held Lachlan a little tighter just hearing her say it. How awful could this boyfriend be? Sarah looked well enough. A little sad, a little weary. But she was young and a new mother and that was life. He sounded like an idiot, but how could Kit jump straight to the worst conclusion?

'He won't hurt Lachlan. He loves him.'

The way she said it, defensive and yet somehow slightly jealous, made something in my chest hurt. I wondered about my father, and if he'd ever even considered leaving my mother, starting a different life away from all the chaos and the trouble.

Yet, even when Mum had gone, he couldn't get his head round it. Couldn't conceive of the fact that she would dare to leave, that she wasn't coming back. Without her, he was nothing, I'd heard him say it. One night when they'd argued he'd threatened to kill himself if she left.

And still she went. Leaving me alone to look after a heartbroken man who hated himself and the world. She didn't care enough to stay, and now she got to forget that she'd ever done that. It didn't seem fair.

Holding the baby was starting to open this wound in

my chest, and the way Kit looked at Sarah, like she wanted to keep her close, keep her safe… it was something I'd never had. Except for Dan. Except for my beautiful, kind, considerate husband who never got into fights or left me making excuses. I missed him. I missed us. I wanted to conjure the image of that little flat in Tufnell Park, the damp on the walls and the towels that never dried, and us, curled around each other on a mattress on the floor, making up stories about the life we'd lead. I'd never needed anyone else to look at me like they couldn't bear to see me leave. I had that much, at least. And I should be grateful.

Kit and Sarah seemed to come to a truce over slices of gingerbread cake. I gave her child back and felt a relief that I was able. That I hadn't wanted to cradle him close and keep him for myself like a villainous fairytale character.

Sarah stayed for dinner, and I found myself relieved at their easy back and forth, watching how at home she seemed. Kit was the kind of woman who said her piece and then let things lie, and I could tell Sarah had got what she came for. I checked my phone for messages from Dan, but there were none. I missed him but I wasn't sure what to say, so I said nothing. I could imagine him in that big flat by himself, craned over his laptop, eating pasta at the breakfast bar. Flicking through TV channels before going out to the punchbag in the shed. Or maybe he wasn't home at all, still in the office proving his worth because he could, no broken wife to come home to and comfort.

I left Sarah and Kit to their evening, their time together, not wanting to intrude. They insisted I was welcome but it didn't feel right, like they needed their normal balance. And again, insanely, I just wanted to sleep.

I dreamed of all sorts of strange things. My mother's smirking face merging into Kit's concerned one, the long curls of Sarah's red hair unspooling, Dan's drawings walking off the page into reality. I dreamed of my father, those moments of kindness when I was a child, when he messed my hair up affectionately, his huge hands rough as he laughed. That look of adoration he gave my mother, like he was afraid she was going to leave, merging into one of their fights, ending with them cuddled on the sofa like nothing had happened. Then the bang as his head hit the coffee table, and the blood that soaked into the carpet.

When I woke with a jolt, I lay there for a few moments, trying to figure out where I was. The clock by the side of the bed glowed midnight, and my stomach growled. I wondered about Sarah and who she went home to. Whether she and Lachlan were safe. Whether Kit's instincts were right, or she was just an overprotective mother figure to someone who had never had that. Whose instinct were you meant to trust?

I tiptoed down the creaking stairs, hoping a glass of water (or perhaps a second slice of cake) would soothe me.

Kit was sitting at the kitchen table in her pyjamas, a big bobbly yellow jumper pulled over the top. Her nightwear always seemed so much more colourful than her practical green or brown clothes for the farm, and it made me smile.

'Aren't you meant to be up in a few hours?'

'Aye,' she nodded, stabbing a piece of cake with a fork, 'unfortunately, my brain doesn't seem to care. Or my stomach.'

She chewed messily, crumbs all over the table and herself.

'Thinking about Sarah?'

She nodded.

'Did you offer her the spare room? I'll be gone soon, she could stay there?'

'She won't take it, stubborn wee thing. She feels she's made her bed and has to lie there. As if sleeping with a moron means a life sentence! When she's ready, she'll come, I hope.'

I patted her arm, briefly. 'She's lucky to have you.'

'You seemed like a natural with her little one,' Kit smiled at me, and I inhaled sharply, trying to remind myself that she clearly wasn't trying to hurt me. She was trying to get me to open up. But I wasn't ready.

'Will Effie be here tomorrow?' It was like a game of topic tennis.

Kit noted the change of subject again, her eyebrows registering it as if to remind herself what was off limits.

'Aye, if you like.' She pulled open the drawer and got out a fork, offering it to me as she pushed the cake midway across the table.

I took a breath, not looking at her as I stabbed the piece of cake.

'I think I want to go see her… Nina.'

Kit said nothing, chewing for a moment. Then she sighed and nodded.

'I have to prepare you, love. She's not… you'll not find what you're looking for. She's not really in there, most of the time.'

'I don't know what I'm looking for,' I said.

Kit smiled sadly, 'Of course you do. You're looking for the nasty piece of work who left you, I'd wager,' Kit shook her head. 'The problem is, it's hard to blame someone who doesn't remember what they've done to you. Believe me, I've tried.'

I chewed slowly, savouring the taste of the cake, somehow better after midnight, in the quiet of that house, just me and Kit and the truth.

'Doesn't matter. Even if she doesn't remember, I do,' I said. 'What you said earlier about being too weak to change? She wasn't too weak. She knew the destruction she brought, she just didn't care.'

Kit pressed her lips together, pausing, and I shook my head at her.

'Oh, come on now, don't tell me you're holding back to spare my feelings? I thought you were all about the brutal honesty, *auntie*?' I smiled to take the sting out. I wanted the truth. I wanted someone who said what they meant and didn't hold back.

Before I'd got here, everything in my life had been a veneer, a lie with a shiny smooth surface. No one spoke about the son I'd lost hours after he was born, instead they talked about how well I'd lost the weight, or how I must be enjoying my time at home.

The same thing was true of our past, mine and Dan's: my dad had died, and Dan had gone to prison. Instead the polished surface told the story of a girl who overcame adversity and a boy who became a man. Skip the details and focus on the triumphs. Never let them see weakness.

But Kit wasn't like that. When she spoke it was like cauterising a wound – it might hurt, but it was better in the long run.

'I'll not lie to you hen, my sister was a piece of work. She was spiteful and manipulative. Some people grow up with little and it makes them grateful for what they've got, or it makes them work harder for their dreams. Nina was forever annoyed that whatever she felt she deserved had never turned up…'

I sensed a 'but' coming.

'But… I've noticed there's a tendency to blame women when their men do wrong.'

'She broke him and left me with the pieces.' I looked her straight in the eye, daring her to contradict me. And then I heard Dan's voice in my head, those sharp barbs he left me with before I came here: *unyielding, unforgiving, desperate for drama.*

'You won't be faced with that woman, in fact she'll probably have a completely different memory. For all she knows some days, your da's gone out to get milk and you're playing in the other room. You won't get closure. You won't get an apology. You need to come to terms with that before we go.'

I felt my hands tremble, and balled them together in my lap.

'It doesn't matter,' I said faintly. 'I came to say what I needed to say, to her face. Whether she can understand me doesn't matter at all.'

For the first time, Kit looked at me like I might be capable of more than she'd expected, like my spine was made of steel instead of silk, and like I wasn't someone to trifle with. That look made me feel powerful, and just the tiniest bit afraid of what I might do.

Chapter Six

The care facility was only forty-five minutes from Kit's.

I'd been fairly useless helping Kit that morning, seemingly robotic in following orders. My hands didn't seem to want to follow my instructions and I kept dropping everything. Eventually, Kit sent me back to help Effie in the kitchen with breakfast, but my stomach was a drum and even the smell of bacon made me feel slightly sick.

Effie made noises about the 'most important meal of the day' and 'everyone's a sour puss this morning' but she was kind about it. At Kit's request she settled for making bacon sandwiches instead of her usual spread. I could tell she was desperate to fry an egg or flip a pancake, she kept looking at me like she was afraid I'd fade away. So I made an effort, picking at the bread of the sandwich, chewing a few bites even though it felt impossible. I drank down my coffee and then a glass of orange juice, looking to Effie for approval.

As she put away the plates she paused and gave me a little smile, squeezing my arm briefly.

'You'll be fine. You're a bull terrier, like your aunt.' Effie gave Kit a look, but Kit wasn't playing along this morning.

We were both nervous, but her nervousness exhibited itself in irritability and grouchiness. I preferred silence. My stomach was in knots and all I could think was that I needed to breathe.

The countryside looked bleak and beautiful as we drove. The town we briefly went through was cheerful and busy, coaches pulling up through country lanes and letting out tourists who flocked to public toilets, pubs and shops selling tablet.

We dropped Effie off at work, the Cranachan Café. It had a bright red sign and little net curtains, with people moving in and out. Business was booming, it seemed. Effie waved as she jumped out from the car, and squeezed Kit's wrist, 'Be nice. She's a sensitive lass.'

Kit rolled her eyes, but she smiled for the first time that morning.

'She doesn't mean me?'

'She means you,' Kit confirmed, pulling the car out into traffic and weaving around the tourists. I snorted. It was hard to imagine me as sensitive, or at least, in need of protecting. I was a survivor. But maybe I could see why Effie might think that. I felt things deeply, I thought a little too much. She didn't know that I'd always been someone who just got their head down and did what they could do. It's why I was enjoying all the manual labour on the farm in the mornings – not enough time to think.

Kit gave a running commentary on goings-on in town, pointing out Sarah's flat above the butcher's, and the pub they all convened at on Friday nights. It was expected that I'd join them that evening, if I wanted.

We made it out onto the wide country lanes, and as we approached that same roundabout I noticed the same figure on the bridge, his flat cap and smart tweed suit standing out. As a passenger this time, I could focus on the details of him, the white hair and the kind face, the neat shining shoes that matched his suit. Standing on a crossing over a small roundabout in the middle of nowhere.

Wondering about the man in the tweed suit was a welcome distraction from thinking about my mother, and acting out a million different receptions from her when I arrived.

I'd heard people with Alzheimer's could be cruel, and last night when I lay in bed, struggling to sleep even with the lavender scent, exhaustion and fullness from the cake, I tried to prepare myself by imagining every awful thing she could say.

I saw her snarling, calling me a waste of space, a disappointment, a failure even with my fancy new life. I saw her screaming, crying with rage and jealousy, making pointed remarks about how I needed to help her after all she'd done for me.

It wasn't hard to conjure that version of Nina, I'd seen that side so many times before. Spitting with rage and injustice, so sure she was getting less than she deserved.

In the end, I couldn't have imagined it.

My mother didn't look like herself.

I'd expected that, of course, but when Kit gave that warning, I thought she meant she looked sick, frail. Instead Nina looked… soft. Her hair was a light brown, and her make-up was subtle. Gone were the days of silver eyeshadow and thick black kohl rimming her eyes, with her peroxide blonde hair scraped back in a tight bun. Instead, her cheeks were rouged gently, her eyeshadow a soft pink, her hair falling gently around her shoulders. She looked… harmless. Sweet and soft like candy-floss. A little old fashioned, perhaps, but healthy and vibrant. As if all the poison had been sucked out of her.

She sat in her room, watching television, and when we knocked on the door and went in, introduced by a soft-spoken nurse, she didn't look up.

I couldn't take my eyes off her. She was so small, so pretty. She sat there in her pastel twinset and her jeans, hands delicately folded in her lap. My mum had always wanted to be a queen, and here she was. Lording over everyone around her, people attending to her every whim.

'Hey Neen, how's it going?' Kit said awkwardly, hands in her pockets, the tote bag of treats and gifts falling from her shoulder.

My mother's eyes lit up as she saw her sister, somehow waking up, 'Oh Kitty! There you are! It's so good to see you!'

Kit nodded, uncomfortable as she walked into the room and started looking for things to fix, fluffing pillows, unpacking her bag and putting each item on the kitchenette sideboard.

'Oh jelly babies! My favourite!' Nina clapped her hands like a child as she got up, and I waited, fearful I was invisible, like she wouldn't notice me. 'And who have you bought to visit me, Kitty?'

My mother's eyes were curious and wide, like a child's. She took in my clothes carefully, her gaze tracing my features, meeting my eyes, searching for something. She stepped forward.

'I'm sorry, have we met? Everyone says I'm not very good at remembering things these days.'

It wasn't so much the voice that was strange, somehow so soft and welcoming and proper, compared to the sharp, twenty-fags-a-day rasp she'd had as she'd called out across the estate. She sounded like a forties film star, so incredibly posh in that way the past did.

But that wasn't what shocked me most, it was those words I'd never heard from her before: *I'm sorry*.

I felt like I might cry. This was all too much, standing there and watching her watch me like I might be someone important. Waiting for the moment she realised who I was, and dismissed me yet again.

'This is Natasha. Do you recognise her?'

My mother blinked, tilting her head as those light eyes flickered, 'God, she looks like Mum, doesn't she? Is she yours?'

Kit cringed a little, 'No, Neen, she's your girl, Natasha. Do you remember? You've got a little girl?'

My mother laughed, a bell-like sound that rang out. She held up a hand to hide it. 'Don't be silly, my Natasha is only eight!'

I didn't want to ruin it. I wanted to play along, protect her from the truth. Oh, how a moment's look and some soft make-up had swayed me from my purpose.

'I'm not, Mum. It's me,' I felt awful even as I said it. The pride I felt as she looked at me, that smile widening on her face, it physically hurt.

'Oh, but you're so *beautiful*. Isn't she beautiful, Kitty? Such a *lady*!'

I searched her features for the mother I remembered, the pinched looked, the sharp words. The face that would turn on you when you least expected it.

But the set of her mouth was different. It was like looking at a completely different person. Someone rounder, softer, happier. A fairground mirror or a child's portrait – the same, but different.

'Aye, she's a fine girl. Just had her thirtieth birthday,' Kit offered, looking at her sister to gauge her reaction. Time passing seemed to get to her, she'd said in the car. You had to be careful to establish not only who you were, but when you were.

'Oh how lovely! And did you have your chocolate cake? I know it's your favourite,' Nina smiled, so warm that I wanted to cry. 'Chocolate cake with rainbow sprinkles.'

Where on earth did she get that from? I'd never had a chocolate cake with rainbow sprinkles.

I smiled and ignored the question. 'How are you? Do you like it here?'

'Oh yes, they're lovely here, aren't they Kitty?' She reached out a hand for her sister, and Kit obliged, though clearly reluctant. 'My lovely Kitty is so good to me, she comes to visit and brings me sweeties. When we were kids I always wanted the cherry from the Chelsea buns Daddy bought on Sundays and she always gave hers to me. She's the perfect big sister. That's why Mama loved her best, because she was so very good.'

I looked for a sharpness in her features, but there was nothing but light. That same smile. But she gripped Kit's hand until her knuckles turned white.

'Tell me about you, Natasha. What is your life like, where do you live?' She settled back in her chair and gestured for me to sit opposite. She was queenlike in her approach, receiving visitors.

'London,' I said slowly, wary of giving too much away. 'North London. With my husband.'

'Married! My goodness! And how's your dad?' She tilted her head with a smile, 'Such a sweet man.'

She could have been talking about the postman. Did she even remember that she'd left him, abandoned us both?

I looked to Kit, who shrugged.

'Um, actually he died, quite a few years ago.'

She raised a hand to her chest, and shook her bowed head. 'Oh, how very sad. I always said to him, "John, heart disease runs in your family, and if you don't stop with the smoking or the drinking, you're going to find yourself in trouble." Terribly sad.'

I raised an eyebrow at Kit, almost shaking my head in disbelief. My mother, the patron saint of healthy living? She'd smoked like a chimney when I was growing up, and she was no stranger to a drink either.

Kit's lips quirked and she seemed to tell me to take it easy.

'He was a good man,' Nina said solemnly, bowing her head as if in prayer. Then she clapped her hands together, 'Well, we all get what we deserve. Shall we have some tea, I think you brought cake, didn't you Kitty?'

The minute I slid into the car, I felt a wave of exhaustion overcome me.

'It's hard, isn't it? When you want to be angry with someone and she doesn't remember anything she's done?' Kit said, eyes on the road, hands gripping the wheel. 'The thing is, that disease is nasty. I never gave her the cherries on those pastries. Never. They were my favourite bit. And she'd eat hers and then demand mine, and cry when I didn't give it to her. And yet that brain of hers focuses on that, rewriting history… to tell me I'm a good sister!'

'It's a peculiar kind of torture,' I said, unthinking.

'For her, maybe. For us, definitely. Since I saw her again, she's been sweetness and light most of the time. But those odd moments where her mind flutters to the past… it's like the Alzheimer's is punishing me for everything she thinks I wronged her for at sixteen.'

'That's tough.'

Kit shrugged, 'We all have our lots to bear. I'm sure I must have done something to deserve my sister.'

I snorted, and Kit's mouth twitched.

'So… did I do something to deserve her as a mother?'

Kit looked at me and shook her head.

'No, kids don't count. I'm sure you're being punished for something else.'

Her voice was so deadpan that I couldn't help but laugh.

'The staff must *love* you visiting her. You're such a sensitive soul,' I teased.

'Oh yes, they want me to come in and teach some classes.'

Kit took the opportunity to take me sightseeing, as if I was a child who needed distracting. Or maybe she wanted the distraction herself, I don't know. But it was welcome. We drove around and stopped at a little restaurant for lunch, Kit chatting away about how she first moved up here and how she'd felt so alone.

It was like she felt the need to make up for Nina, undo the harm she feared she'd caused by taking me to see my mum. But I didn't mind, listening to her chat away about learning about the farm, travelling around the Highlands with her granny, learning the history of the lands.

There was always a shame, at being not quite Scottish enough. That much was clear. But we ate stew and sipped whisky and looked out at the lush green that surrounded us, and I remembered to breathe.

'It's okay, Kit,' I said when she'd seemingly run out of things to say.

'Could you not have said that twenty minutes ago? I don't think I've spoken that much all year.'

I laughed, and shook my head. 'I like quiet. My idea

of heaven is a library where anyone who tries to talk to you gets shushed and escorted out by security.'

It was Kit's turn to laugh, 'You're a strange wee thing. Not like Nina at all. Was your da a quiet man?'

I tried to search through my memories for what he used to be like. When you're a kid you feel about your parents how they feel about you, and it was hard to remember spending any time with Dad. He was the back of the head that I used to see watching TV when I sat on the stairs and peeked through the bannister.

There were a few times he'd pat the sofa next to him and let me sit there, but I knew I had to say nothing, barely move so I didn't distract him.

Occasionally when I was older, he'd touch my face and his eyes would get watery, 'God, you look just like her,' he'd say. Even though I knew it caused him pain, I cherished the moment, because it was a flash of reality before he disappeared back inside a bottle.

I pressed my lips together, 'You know, it's hard to remember what he was like before Mum left. I think he was quiet. He worked a lot. He loved her in this way… he was always looking at her like he was starving but she refused to feed him.'

I paused.

'What was Nina like, when you were growing up?' I asked, wanting to shift the subject. I didn't like thinking about Dad. The guilt sat like a creature around my neck, and the tail always fluttered when my father was mentioned. No one should have to die like that. The paramedics tried to comfort us that it was the alcohol that killed him, he bled out because his blood was so thin. If he'd been sober he might have survived.

But if I hadn't called Daniel, he definitely would have survived.

'She was spoilt, mostly,' Kit shrugged. 'I mean, she had a sweetness about her, but she'd use it, given half a chance.'

'So she was manipulative?'

Kit paused, and I knew she was looking for a softer way to put it. 'She was desperate to be adored.'

I waited, and Kit put her glass down.

'She'd play this game where she'd say, "Would you drink this whole glass of water for me, because you love me?" and I'd say yes, and she'd say, "What if it was poison?" She'd list all these things and ask if you'd do them for her.' Kit shook her head and started shovelling again. 'Very strange, always gave me the creeps. And her father, to whom words meant absolutely nothing, used to always say yes. He was that sort of man, "I'd take a bullet for you darling, I'd eat shit for you, I'd crawl along the floor for weeks." She wanted people to prove their loyalty, I guess.'

'Do you think she's still like that?'

Kit looked at me, eyebrow raised. 'Everyone wants to be loved, hen. There's no shame in that.'

'There is if you make them stay out of obligation.'

My aunt paused, and didn't look at me as she replied, 'Are we still talking about your mother?'

'Of course,' I looked past her to the window, focusing on that beautiful view, 'who else would we be talking about?'

Kit told stories as well as any tour guide, epic tales of clan warfare and the English as we drove through the countryside. When we finally arrived back at the farm, I went up to my bed and passed out for a couple of hours, completely exhausted.

I had strange dreams, ones where I felt afraid, where I curled up as small as I could, or ran as fast as I could, but I still woke with that feeling of dread. There were no people, no stories, no monsters under the bed. Just the image of my mother, looking like she had that day, stroking my face, calling me her good, beautiful girl. She told me I could have the day off school, and gave me a doughnut. Jam went everywhere, making my fingers sticky. And still the dread remained.

When I awoke, Kit said we'd have dinner down at the pub.

'Sorry, I should have realised you'd need to rest. Effie told me off,' she said.

I waved away her concern.

'When I first visited your mother I came home and

slept like the dead. Right through to the morning. The chickens were angry at me and that bastarding little pony definitely wanted me dead.'

I laughed and sipped at the cup of tea she'd made me. I hovered, unsure if I should change, but Kit shook her head and told me to hurry up. She had fish and chips on a Friday and she didn't want to be late. I was told Sarah would be there, which was the only thing that allayed my nervousness.

Explaining who I was, why I was there... the thought of it made me sick. But Kit didn't seem like the type of person who shared of herself and her history. So hopefully her friends would be much the same. Taciturn and unlikely to probe, that's what I wanted. Except... Effie. Effie was the sort of woman who coaxed gossip from you before you even realised what was happening. And yet, I didn't mind at all.

Kit drove us into town, explaining that normally she'd walk or cycle, but she couldn't quite face it. I was relieved, I still felt exhausted. The pub was called The Thistle. It hadn't quite reached the gastro-pub levels of double-digit gin offerings and fancy high tables, but it had charm. The long, dark wooden bar was not particularly busy just yet, and the banquette seating had a dark tartan pattern. The wooden beams of the ceiling had a wobbly effect, making me slightly fear that the roof might cave in at any minute. Maybe it stopped people from getting too drunk. One look at that ceiling and you'd be convinced you'd had enough.

'Fraser, this is my niece, Na… Taz. My niece, Taz.' Kit gave me a look to tell me she was trying, and I snorted, nodding my appreciation.

The man behind the bar looked familiar, like a good elf or kindly wizard, with more white hair coming out of his ears than on top of his head. He wore a white shirt rolled up at the arms, and a tweed waistcoat. Fraser's face looked like it had been carved out of wax, shiny, smooth and red. He had a lovely smile, and kind eyes. It was impossible for me to know him, but I immediately felt like I did.

He nodded at me, and gestured between the two of us, tilting his hand in the universal symbol for 'Drink?'

We ordered two pints of bitter, and Kit told him we'd both have fish and chips when the others arrived. We settled ourselves at a table, clearly Kit's usual, and I asked the obvious question.

'Can Fraser speak?'

Kit shrugged, 'He can, when he has something to say. He's just not much for the chit chat.'

'Doesn't that get a bit difficult, running a pub?'

Kit thought about it, 'Folk round here love him. He's the kindest, gentlest man I know. Whether he speaks or not.'

'Yes, of course,' I paused, 'but on a *practical* level, running a pub…'

Kit just raised an eyebrow at me. 'You'd be surprised how little people are listening. Why waste words that go unheeded?'

'That's very mystical.'

'Well, wait until Sarah arrives and we'll have ourselves a fun game of *Who can talk and be ignored the most?* Usually, it's me.' Kit sipped her pint.

'But you won't give up.'

'I most certainly will not. I just might try to be a little more patient with the poor girl. Who isn't a fool when in love?'

I made a face in agreement.

'Right? Everyone's a damned fool. Best to let the madness pass and talk sense then.'

'Who's talking sense and how many drinks will it take to get them to stop?' Effie appeared at the table, smiling at me. She gave me a once over, and then seeing that I apparently had no visible injuries, sat herself down and gestured behind her. 'Taz, this is Jakob. Jakob, sit down love, for God's sake.'

The tall, dark-haired man seemed a little shy, smiling from under dark eyelashes and clutching a small lemonade in his large hand. He nodded at me and sat down next to his boss, who immediately launched into a story about a wayward group of tourists who were outraged she didn't have any vegan sausage rolls.

'And so...' Effie gestured between me and Kit, 'how is her highness?'

'Good, well in herself. Taz was surprised to see her so well, I think?' Kit turned her question to me, those little lines appearing around her mouth.

I tried to find the words, and seemed to become very formal.

'I was surprised to find her so… amiable.'

'Oh, aye, *amiable*,' Effie rolled her eyes at me, 'we speak as we find, hen. You might want to try doing the same.'

How to sum up coming face-to-face with the woman who left without a word one day when I was a kid, and now wanted to know me? How to explain that I came here for a fight that I wouldn't get to have, and I'd just have to make peace with it?

Or worse, how to share the horrible truth: I had liked that woman I met today. I had missed the idea of a mother, and her compliments had warmed something in me.

'She wasn't as much of a bitch as she used to be,' I said, then made a face. 'Was that better?'

'Aye, hen, much better,' Effie laughed, raising her gin and bitter lemon in a salute. 'So you'll be seeing her again?'

'It would be nice to learn a bit more about her, to see who this new version of her is,' I said, trying to sound casual. I wanted to go back with a fierceness. I wanted to just keep looking at her and tracing those features for a sign of that harsh, spiteful woman I knew. And I didn't want to find her. I wanted this new, lovely version of a mother, twenty years too late.

'I know I won't get the answers I need, but… I may as well, whilst I'm here.'

'And you'll be helping your aunt out with the cost of your mother's care, now you know what's going on?' Effie said it as innocently as if she was asking my views on the latest cinema release, or how I was planning to spend my weekend.

'I… uh, I didn't realise, I mean… of course, I should have—'

Kit was clearly furious, her lips pressed together as if to stop herself saying anything. The look she gave Effie was enough to make her put her hands up, and declare she'd leave us to talk in private. Poor Jakob was stuck in the middle, deer in headlights, smiling awkwardly at me as he followed Effie to the bar, greeting Sarah as she walked in. I watched as he lit up, smiling as he took hold of the baby and jiggled him gently.

I turned back to Kit.

'I do not require any help ensuring my sister gets the care she needs.' My aunt's voice was proud and she didn't look me in the eye. Instead, she focused on Effie, standing at the bar, resolutely avoiding her gaze.

'It must be quite expensive, and Effie's right, it's not just your responsibility. I didn't know before, but now I do, so…'

Kit looked up, meeting my eyes. 'I do not require any

help, financial or otherwise. I will take care of Nina. It is not Effie's concern what I do with my money, much as she thinks she has leave to share her opinions on everyone's activities. I will not accept anything, and Natasha, I do not want you to offer again. I mean it.'

There was a graveness in her tone that almost frightened me. 'Maybe she doesn't deserve your help?'

'Maybe not, but I'm her sister and she needs me. That's what family means.'

'Sacrifice?'

'Being a fool. That's love, right?' Kit offered me a small smile and I felt the tension drain away. 'Don't fuss. I appreciate it, but I'm serious. This is my burden and I claim it. I will not share it, do you understand?'

I nodded.

'Good, let's get the rest of them back, I'm starving.'

And that was that.

Sarah slipped into the seat next to me, whilst Jakob kept hold of Lachlan, seemingly very comfortable. Effie and Kit seemed to exchange a few whispered words and looks which suggested there would be some further conversation, but Kit put an arm around her so all seemed to be well.

'And how are you finding our fair town, Mrs White?' Sarah laughed, so different to the anxious, exhausted woman I only saw the night before. She looked older now, wearing an invisible armour. I saw it though, how you could sit and smile and take up space to hide the worries. The only polite thing to do was play along.

'I'm impressed, and I get an Effie breakfast every morning, so I'm more than spoilt.'

There was a brief look around the table, and I wondered what I'd said, but before I could ask, the food was brought over and everyone began talking in earnest about sauces and cutlery and everything else. Fraser sat down to eat with us, his staff taking over from him behind the bar, and I found I didn't notice his silence after a while. He nodded and made eye contact and smiled. He listened actively, not as someone waiting for their turn to talk, and something about him comforted me.

'So, when are we going to get you out on a horse then?' Sarah asked me, taking her son back from Jakob, who smiled at her with such frank affection that I was a little embarrassed for him. Kit raised an eyebrow at me and nodded. Poor guy.

'Um… I mean, I fall over when I'm not even off the ground and those horses look pretty high up, so…'

'Oh, don't be a wee wimp! There's nothing to be afraid of! They're just animals!' Sarah laughed, her face bright, hair flapping over her shoulders. Lachlan whimpered at the sound, and she tried to hush him. 'Oh sorry, love.'

'It's good, you should try,' Jakob nodded, smiling at

me. 'Sarah is a good teacher. Very calm, unlike the rest of the time.'

'Hey, quiet you! You're not helping.' Sarah grinned at us both, rocking her son automatically. 'Jake was already good with horses, I'd have nicked him to help me teach, but Effie can't spare him. No one makes a fry-up like Jakob.'

'Or puff pastry,' Effie added.

'Or bread!' Kit chipped in, nodding at Jakob in appreciation. He ducked his head, embarrassed by the attention.

'I should even say, and I am ashamed, Jakob makes better neeps and tatties than any Scotsman I've met,' Sarah was defiant, holding a hand up, 'and I stand by it, you shall not convince me otherwise.'

'Goodness, Sarah, are you trying to get the boy killed?!' Effie faux-whispered. 'I cannot lose him, I've no other staff worth anything!'

A voice from the bar yelled over, 'Thanks very much, Effie!'

She made a face, and called back to the young fair-haired boy scowling at her, 'Och, not *you* Carl, you know you're a keeper!'

She turned back to us, exasperated. 'Wee lad's got bricks for brains, but he's very sweet. Yesterday he put salt in someone's coffee instead of sugar, but I don't have the heart to fire him.'

Jakob assumed a long-suffering look and shrugged, 'He tries, very hard.'

'But?' I asked.

'It seems to make no difference,' he sighed, 'the people still get the wrong order, they still yell, and there's still food sitting cold on the side.'

'Och, calm down love, he'll get there. It's hard for the kids round here. He's a boy without a dream or a purpose. And I'd rather him waiting tables than signing up to the army like his brother. Even if he does a terrible job.'

'As you can see,' Kit nudged her, 'Effie is not only our town gossip, but our town busybody and saviour.'

'I would not be here, if not for Effie,' Jakob smiled at her.

'And I would not have high cholesterol,' Fraser said suddenly, his voice lyrical and his cheeky wink making me hoot with surprise. He gave a little bow, and started clearing the plates. Jakob jumped up to help but he waved him off.

'Saves the speech for moments of maximum effect,' Effie said wryly, 'makes him seem more clever than he is!' she yelled after him, and Fraser blew her a kiss from the bar, where he stayed for the rest of the night.

The evening passed more quickly than I would have liked, mainly because it felt so easy. It was people who knew and cared about each other, making conversation, catching up. There was no competition, no showing off.

No one mentioned how much anything cost, or talked about holidays or investments or Instagram followers. Instead, they spoke about the land, the town, the animals, the people. Stories from long ago, and books they were reading.

Kit and I didn't speak about Nina, Sarah didn't speak about her boyfriend and Jakob said nothing about the very clear crush he had on Sarah. Effie spoke about everything, of course, but always with such kindness and heart that you couldn't help forgiving her gossiping, because she just wanted to help.

As we drove back home, I looked down at my phone to see a message from Dan. It was a picture, a sketch in the notebook. It was simple, a copy of an old photo of me in a summer dress, twirling. I must have been about eighteen. It was during that time we spent our weekends walking London for free and doing very little at all. It was a beautiful drawing, but it wasn't about that. It was him showing he still cared.

It might not be enough to save our marriage, but it was enough to make me feel loved. I smiled, stroking the phone with my thumb.

'It's good that he makes you smile,' Kit said as she pulled the car up in front of the barn.

I showed her the photo of the drawing, and she squinted as she moved it further away from her face. 'Wow, he's talented. Is that you?'

I nodded, 'A long time ago.'

'You don't act like a woman whose husband draws portraits of her.'

'How do those sort of women act?'

Kit frowned, 'Well, happy, I'd imagine. I'm not one for all that adoring lark, sounds a bit exhausting personally, but… you walk around with a sign above your head that says how unhappy you are.'

'He's going to leave me soon,' I said, and as soon as I said it out loud, the fear of how huge it was lessened. 'Nobody's fault. We got married too young. He sacrificed too much for me, and it probably wasn't worth it. He wants a different sort of life with a perfect wife, and I got tired of pretending to be perfect.'

Kit raised an eyebrow, 'I have a feeling if I asked the boy what he thinks about it, he'd have something different to say.'

'Sometimes love isn't enough.'

'And sometimes things take time.'

'Who knew you were such a romantic?' I laughed, as I unbuckled my seatbelt.

'And who knew the woman with the husband sending her portraits was a pessimist?' Kit replied, and got out of the car. I followed suit and as she closed the door she leaned on the car roof. 'Taz, do you ever think that maybe your problem is you just think about things too much?'

I laughed.

'It's one of the things I spend too long thinking about.'

'You should bring him here, your fella. Let him be part of all this.'

'He's got work. He's always got work. Fancy clients and parties and doing X, Y and Z to get a promotion and get closer to the top.' I shook my head, 'Besides, this is my mess.'

'It's not mess, it's family.'

'Says the woman who won't let me help.' I knew I was pushing it, but I couldn't help it. Here she was, telling me to share my woes and she wasn't playing fair.

'Good point. But I'm older and wiser, and have much more right to make stupid decisions. Like a glass of whisky before bed.' She walked towards the front door and I followed, trailing behind her in the darkness. 'I will say this though, love, and you can take it or ignore it as you see fit: you cannot be responsible for other people's choices. Much as you might like to think you have control, you don't. Your husband wants to protect you from every bad thing in the world, to be a shining white knight because it makes him feel good.'

I thought of those months of despair, of being unable to enter that room at the end of the hallway. Of how my husband wiped my tears and stroked my hair and never once said the wrong thing. Never tried to tell me we'd try again and get it right. He was there with me, my Daniel, every step of the way. Protecting me from the outside world.

'What if I need protecting?'

Kit flicked on the light and turned back to smile at me, 'Well it's very lucky we're getting you up on that horse tomorrow then, isn't it? We'll make you into a knight in no time.'

Chapter Seven

I woke up from a dream where I was being swaddled. At first it was comforting, I felt safe and warm. But the blankets got tighter and the more I wriggled, the less I could move. When I finally woke, to the sound of my phone ringing, I had tangled myself in the sheets.

I looked down at my phone and jolted at the name: Miranda.

Immediately, my heart leapt into my throat. Dan's mother never called me. I literally only had her details in my phone because she'd insisted on arranging a fancy baby shower for me last year and she needed contact numbers. I'd told her I didn't want a party, that it felt like tempting fate. Dan told me his parents were trying and I needed to try too.

I still blamed her a little, as unfair as that was.

The clock on the wall said it was 6 a.m., I'd already slept through my morning duties with Kit, but surely she wouldn't be calling me unless something terrible had happened?

'Miranda? Is Dan okay, has something happened?'

'Yes, something's *happened,* Natasha,' her voice dripped with disdain, but not panic. I sighed, placing by hand on my chest and trying to slow my breathing. 'You've abandoned my son and gone off to Scotland of all places, and he deserves better!'

'I'm very aware of your feelings on that matter, Miranda, thank you. Now I've really got to go—'

Miranda huffed and I felt her vitriol flowing down the phone lines.

'Look, I know I wasn't exactly *thrilled* when Daniel chose you, especially after everything that happened, but I have gone above and beyond in welcoming you to our family! I planned your proper wedding—'

Because ours wasn't good enough.

'I planned your baby shower, I helped Daniel with your birthday party, which you *completely* threw back in our faces. And now you've disappeared and left your husband when he needs you!'

I took a breath. She wasn't wrong. I mean, the second wedding was vile and she was bossy and got in any possible jibe at my expense, but I could understand her wanting to be there at her son's wedding, wanting to be *involved.* It was just that her involvement seemed to eradicate so much of what made us *us*.

I adopted a kinder tone.

'What's happened, Miranda? What has Dan said?'

'He doesn't need to *say* anything, he's my son!'

Yeah, when it's convenient for you. It was easy enough to cut him out of your life for a decade.

'Then when he does say something, he'll probably explain that I'm up here visiting my mother, who is unwell, and I'll be home soon.'

'A mother who left when you were a child, who you have no loyalties to?'

God, the woman couldn't see the irony. I bit my tongue, the same way I had every day since she'd come back into our lives.

It was different before. During the months Dan was incarcerated, I went every week to her house. I knocked on the door and begged her, *begged* her to see her son. I told her he was sad, he was struggling to survive, he needed to know he had his family's support. She listened to me and turned me away every time. By the second month she stopped answering the door. The last time I went, I called out from the front door up to her window, knowing it would embarrass her in front of her neighbours. It was the only way to get her attention, shame her into talking to me.

She came down, opened the door and said, 'None of

this would have happened if not for your fucked-up family,' and shut the door in my face.

She was right.

But as much as Dan judged my mother for leaving, I judged his more.

'Miranda, Dan is a very capable man. There are dinners in the freezer and he knows how to order a takeaway. He has a cleaner come to the flat once a week. We are talking on the phone. He wanted more time for his work, and now he can focus. I know how much he wants to impress Tim, and this way he can put the hours in.'

'That's a pathetic excuse.'

I snorted, pacing my room, looking out of the window at the landscape and focusing on how peaceful it was. She couldn't take it from me, she couldn't take me back to being sixteen.

'I would have thought you'd be pleased I was away – more time to parade Citronella and Margot in front of him, tempt Dan with a better life?'

'It's *Petronella* and she's a friend's daughter from the club, they have a lot in common. They knew each other as children. There's no need to be sensitive about it. I suppose that's always your first instinct, to attack.'

I took a breath, closed my eyes, and thought of Dan. And then I thought of Kit, and what she'd say. I thought of what Angela would say. I thought of how many times I'd bitten my tongue, when she told me the wedding dress she'd chosen for me wasn't flattering, when she suggested that my miscarriage was 'for the best'.

Every Sunday dinner when she suggested I might be more comfortable with chicken nuggets or Lambrini. When she slowly offered extra descriptions for common facts – 'Paris, that's in *France*, Natasha dear' – I had held my tongue. But no more.

'Yes, that's what we did on the estate. Fight to the death. With rocks. The only way to settle things.'

Miranda huffed and said nothing. There was a moment of quiet.

'Can I ask a question? If my dad hadn't died, if Dan hadn't gone away and everything hadn't happened. If I'd just been a girl from the estate who loved your son… would you have accepted me, eventually?'

She paused, and I readied myself for one of two options: complete denial or a painful dismissal.

'If you'd been on board with his life, with helping him achieve his potential? Yes, I would have accepted you. But you insist on trying to make him someone he's not!'

I settled back into an argument I knew well enough.

'He's a talented artist, Miranda.'

'And he's going to be a talented investment banker. I doubt an artist would be able to afford that flat you've got.'

'It isn't what he wants.'

'And if that's true, I'm sure he's capable of telling his father. He's not a child.'

No, he's just desperate to please you. To make up for everything. To make you proud.

I blew out a deep breath, 'Miranda, this isn't the best use of either of our time. We both love Daniel. I'll be home soon. I don't really know why you felt the need to call.'

'I called because my son is hurting and I don't like it.'

You called because I put myself first for once.

'Neither do I.'

'Could've fooled me,' she snorted, and I wondered how much longer I cared to put up with this woman. How much longer I could try to be reasonable, to feel guilty for the years I 'stole her son from her' when it was her choice to abandon him all along.

'And what is that supposed to mean?' I kept my voice low and controlled.

'It means you've bided your time and stuck with him like a limpet, and now you're being rewarded. You've got the beautiful home, and you had the perfect wedding, and a husband who brings home a good salary, and you act like it's worthless.'

'Because it *is* worthless to me! I was happy before! When we lived in a shitty flat and we had jobs we loved and we were happy!'

'Before we got involved? Before we plucked our son out of the squalor you led him into?' Miranda was about to let her unbridled rage loose, I could feel it. When she worked herself up like this there was no talking with her. No reasoning. Dan said you just had to let it pass, like a storm or a steamroller. 'I *saw* that flat you lived in, he brought us back once when you were working and it was disgusting. The damp and the drug dealers downstairs and the kebab shop. You made him into a criminal and then you made sure he stayed as low as he could. You didn't want him to have a good life. You wanted him to suffer because you'd suffered!'

Wow, someone had been watching a lot of daytime television, or reading a lot of crappy psychobabble. I wondered if Miranda had a therapist. Surely someone that rich just paid someone to listen to them and agree with whatever they said? I couldn't imagine Miranda allowing anyone to tell her she was wrong, especially someone who 'worked for her'.

I didn't have time for this, that anxious tightness in my chest was creeping back in, the one that had disappeared in the wake of highland breezes and alpacas and laughing over whisky and lavender lemon cake.

'We wouldn't have been living in that situation if you hadn't abandoned your son when he needed you. Blame me all you want, but you made a choice, and we had to survive any way we could.'

'He could have apologised, he could have come home if he'd just…'

I smiled, knowing the end of the sentence before she'd even finished.

'If he'd just left me behind.'

He'd never said it. I'd guessed, of course, told him to go, told him I'd be fine. I didn't need pity or a protector. I was the savvy one now, the one who looked after us. But I was fine with the life we had. At first, I spent so much time worrying that he was unhappy, that it wasn't enough for him. But he was as happy as I was.

It was impossible for Miranda to comprehend, that two teenagers could be happy in a small, damp room living off noodles and dented beer cans, as long as they could curl around each other at night. I imagine Miranda had never loved anyone enough to lower her standards.

'Why would you call me to come back? You get everything you've ever wanted if I disappear.'

Miranda laughed, a dry hiccup of embarrassment, 'Believe me, I'm as shocked as you are. I spent the last ten years thinking my son would be better off without you.'

I said nothing, waiting for some sort of reasoning. This was the most honest we'd ever been, and even though the dislike was palpable, it was *real*. It wasn't hidden barbs and misdirection and her passive aggression and Dan making excuses and thinking me paranoid. It was clear down the line: her vs me.

'I still think that. I still think he would have been better off if he'd never met you,' she said, her voice trembling just a little. 'But he's in pain, and I'd rather he wasn't.'

It would have been so easy to return to the status quo, to throw in her face that she didn't care when he was in pain before. She didn't care when he was behind bars and had no one else to talk to but me, when he thought he'd disgraced his family. When he had no one to invite to his art show, or call on a Sunday afternoon. When his siblings had kids and he only found out through social media. It would be the easiest thing in the world to remind this woman that she gave up any right to her son the day she failed him.

But what did that mean for Nina, and what would it mean for me?

'Thank you for calling, Miranda,' I said gently, and hung up the phone.

An honest conversation between me and the wicked witch. Who would have guessed?

I ran out to join Kit for the remainder of the morning round, apologising. 'I overslept,' I said, and she gave me a look like she didn't believe me, but said nothing. I chucked my energy into every activity, every stab of the fork into the hay.

When we got back to the kitchen, it was clear Kit had something to say.

'Where are you this morning?' Kit said over coffee after our work on the farm, and I focused on her.

'Nothing, what? I thought you were happy with companionable silence?' I sounded like a teenager.

Kit's lips twitched, 'Oh aye, but usually my own. You're usually a chatty one in the mornings.'

I shook my head, 'Chatty?'

'Well, by comparison,' she refilled my cup, 'so what's up?'

I ignored the question, looking out of the window. 'No Effie this morning?'

Kit raised an eyebrow, as if acknowledging the change of subject, but humouring me. 'She's busy at the café, one of the girls called in sick. Is that what it is, you're missing a decent breakfast? I'd attempt to make something but I think the best I can do is toast and jam. Maybe some porridge?'

'I'm fine, really.'

Kit frowned at me, 'Are you nervous about the horse riding?'

Oh god, I had forgotten about the horse riding. Sarah had convinced me last night, and I'd agreed.

I gritted my teeth in a fake smile, 'Well… I'm more of a fan of staying on the ground. Or away from things that could trample me.'

'You just helped feed them!' Kit hooted.

'And I did that very well from a distance.'

Kit looked at me; that lined, reserved face that had become so familiar was unsure of what to do with me.

'Kit, when you're feeling out of sorts, do you like to be questioned about it? Or do you prefer people leave you be until you're ready to be a bit better?'

She held her hands up, but didn't look happy about it.

'All I'll say is that if it *is* about the horses, tell Sarah you don't want to do it.'

Of course, after that, I was left with a choice. Back out and hope Kit left my bad mood alone, or be honest. Because it wasn't just the bad dreams and the fact that the very large horses on her farm were measured in hand-spans. It was the niggling feeling hidden very deep down, an itch that demanded scratching.

I wanted to see my mother again.

I wanted to know this woman who was without all the memories and the bitterness. A woman who might stroke my hair and tell me I was beautiful and be impressed at what my life looked like now. Something had been unleashed and it was like an addiction. And I hated myself for it.

I wanted her to be proud of me.

But first, horses.

'Your face! Come on, I'll show you the ropes. You'll be jumping in no time.'

Sarah was in a good mood. She seemed more at ease with animals than people, and Lachlan was safe in Kit's care so she could focus on the task at hand.

'I sincerely doubt that.'

'Well if you doubt it, I'm sure that's true.' She gave me a look before leading me into the stables.

She tugged at her ponytail and laughed, raising an eyebrow. She looked so comfortable in her boots and padded gilet over her fitted jumper. I felt like a child playing dress-up with the stupid helmet on my head.

Sarah was an optimist. Kit described optimism as 'never learning your bloody lesson' but I liked it. She kept that thing that kids have, where their imagination is unlimited by hardship. Why shouldn't you go to the moon, if you want? Why shouldn't your dreams come true, if you work hard enough?

I was never like that, even as a kid, but in Sarah I loved it. I wanted to protect her, this girl who must have been about ten years younger than me, but had already made being a mother her main identity and priority.

She was patient with me and the horses, speaking softly but firmly.

'What's the problem here? You're afraid of the beasts?'

'Not in general. It's just… very high up. And I can't see it's very nice for him to have someone sitting on his back and telling him where to go. Maybe he'd just like to wander about on his own without some dumb human demanding things!'

Sarah rolled her eyes. 'He's a *horse*, Taz. Winston likes a good adventure, don't you lad?' She ruffled his mane affectionately. 'Give me a chance, hey? What's the worst that could happen?'

'That is *never* a good argument.'

Eventually, she managed to get me onto Winston, and whilst I didn't exactly take to it naturally, I did enjoy myself. Sort of. As much as awkwardly squeezing your thighs together and hoping for the best could be enjoyable.

'Taz! Relax, would you? You're sitting like you've got a stick up your arse!' Sarah called from below as she led us around the space in a circle. He was a good horse, I'd give him that. Very patient and took care of everything.

'You're so passive! You're letting him decide everything Taz – that's your job! Take the reins isn't just a saying, you know!'

I gripped the reins tighter and glared at her.

'You know, Winston has riders who can't see, kids with accessibility issues… he's not going to freak out because an English woman with an attitude problem tells him what to do.'

'Well he should, where's his national pride?' I laughed, and relaxed. We got as far as gently trotting before Sarah said we could go out on the land. She pulled a helmet on, jumped up on the other horse and told me to follow her. I desperately wanted her to keep hold of that rope attached to Winston's harness, but she said she trusted him (and me).

Once I stopped panicking, it was perfect. A wonderful way to see the lush green surroundings of the farm, and to talk to Sarah.

'I didn't realise this was a thing normal people could do,' I said suddenly, as our horses walked side by side.

'What does that mean?'

'Just… when I've met people with horses, they always were…. well, rich. Posh. Spent hundreds on outfits and making their horse do that funny dance and wear ribbons or watching polo matches. Horses are fancy!'

'Aye, and you're not fancy, with the expensive car parked outside Kit's house, or that huge diamond ring on your finger?' Sarah's voice wasn't judgemental, she was just trying to understand.

'I… it's kind of hard to explain. It's like skiing.'

She just waited for me to continue.

'Like, people who ski don't just go because it's a hobby they have, it's this whole *thing* with expensive resorts and *après ski* and hundreds of pounds in kit and clothing, and the food is insane, and they drink wine that costs eighty euros a bottle, and it's a rich people thing.'

Sarah sighed. 'You know you can go skiing here? About an hour away. Cost you about thirty quid for the day. Sometimes a sport is just a sport. A horse is just a horse.'

'So you're saying my whole concept of class and privilege is based on an Englishness that I don't really understand?' I thought about it.

Sarah laughed so hard and so long she had to wipe tears from her eyes. I thought she was going to fall off the horse.

'I'm saying… if you like skiing, go fucking skiing. Sweet Jesus.'

And with that, it seemed, I'd made a friend.

'So how's it all going with your ma? I get the sense she was a bit of a troublemaker?' Sarah's voice took on a gentle tone.

'Oh, she was a piece of work. But she doesn't remember any of it, and maybe it's better that way.' I paused, then realised what I'd said. 'Not that I want her to be ill, obviously, that's horrible. I just mean… without any of those memories… she's a different person. The woman in that room wasn't my mother, but she was the mum I might have had.'

'Well, who wouldn't want that?' Sarah nodded at me, 'My mum was a trainwreck. Always putting on airs and graces, wanted everyone to think well of her. So if I wasn't perfect, I wasn't good enough.'

'What happened?'

'I moved out when I was a teenager, and she found other things to fuss over and eventually married a man with two boys she could mother half to death. I think she's happy. Still see her around from time to time.'

I couldn't stop myself squawking, 'She still lives here?'

Sarah shook her head, 'One town over.'

'Has she met her grandson?'

Sarah shrugged, 'She knows he exists. I think she wants to, but if she asks me for anything she's got to apologise, and that's not her way.'

I nodded, and we plodded along in silence for a bit, taking in the scenery and just breathing. This so was so different to home, where everything seemed fast and pointed. If you stopped, even for a minute, you'd be behind. Left behind. If you weren't paying into your pension or investing, or saving for a bigger house. If you weren't getting higher in your careers or making a jump or taking the next step. Standing still was the most terrifying thing back home. And here it felt like just breathing was important enough.

'How's things with your... erm... with Lachlan's father?'

'Murray,' she said darkly. 'I'm sure Kit has given you no end of bad stories about him. Much as she says she's not a gossip, she doesn't forget a damn thing.'

I shook my head, 'She made it clear she didn't like him, and she thought you deserved better, but there was no big list of things he's done. And if I listened to things people used to say about me and my husband, I'd be a crumpled mess by now.'

'Murray's not a bad man. He's just a screw-up,' she smiled at me. 'Sometimes you've gotta give people a chance to grow up, right?'

'Sure,' I nodded. That was all we'd done, me and Dan. Grown up together. Sometimes quickly, sometimes more slowly. He taught me how to act at those fancy parties, he'd taken me on my first trip abroad and gripped my hand when the plane took off and I almost threw up. And I'd taught him things. Harder things, about being savvy with money, making things last, looking over your shoulder. He expected the best and I expected the worst, and between the two of us we survived.

Maybe Kit was being a little hard on Murray. After all, they were still only nineteen. Girls matured faster, and Sarah had motherhood to contend with. She was amazing.

'Is this your job, teaching people?' I suddenly realised I'd never asked.

She shook her head, 'I help out, but with Lachlan being so young… Murray doesn't like it. He says I should focus on our family, him and the baby, not doing so much and wearing myself out.'

'And what do you think?'

She looked skyward as if looking for answer. 'Most days I think it's not worth an argument. But when

Lachlan's older I'll probably ask Kit if I can do something more full on. She's been pushing for it. Wants to *get me out of the house* as if I'm a ninety-year-old in a relationship with the shopping channel!'

'I'm sure Kit will come around,' I said, knowing full well that was unlikely.

Sarah laughed, and shook her head. 'Come on, let's get back. You're gonna be sore tomorrow. And the wee fella will be wanting a feed.'

Sarah was still so young in many ways. She laughed freely, was easily delighted by things we saw as we travelled about, pointing out rocks in funny shapes or a particularly beautiful plant, or clouds that looked like doughnuts. Something about her seemed to soften the sharp feeling in my chest.

We laughed and chatted as we walked back to the main house, and I was surprised by how achy I felt already, how much I felt energised by exerting myself. The mixture of fresh air, hard work and Kit's dram of whisky each night doing their job. Making me strong.

'So what about your fella?' she asked me.

'What about him?'

'What's he like? What does he *do*?' She made a motion with her hand as if to suggest all the usual questions people asked.

'He's… I've loved him since we were teenagers. He's loyal and funny and gentle. He's an artist. Draws everywhere, scribbling on bits of paper. But… he wanted to please his parents so he got a fancy job, and hangs out with arseholes and I'm wondering if I can still love him if he becomes one of them.'

God, it sounded so simple when you put it like that. And so incredibly stupid. But every time he laughed along with the lads, or corrected something someone said, or even, once, clicked his fingers at a waitress (I didn't talk to him for two weeks after that), he stopped being *my* Daniel and got closer to being his father.

'You're the sum of the five people you spend the most time with, isn't that what they say?' Sarah offered. 'Is that what it is?'

'Yeah, maybe.' *Or we thought a baby would fix everything and instead it's broken us.*

'Maybe you need a holiday.'

I nodded, said something noncommittal. The nineteen-year-old with the baby and the unemployed boyfriend, making ends meet giving riding lessons, was telling me I needed a holiday. The woman who rolled around her huge flat all day doing nothing? I was embarrassed by her kindness.

When we walked to the door, we saw Kit bouncing Lachlan around, a smile on her face. Her eyes were soft and warm, her voice sweet as she sang some nonsense song that sounded all the prettier for meaning so little.

'She pretends to be this tough, crotchety old meanie, and she can be, but she's this softie underneath it all.' Sarah nudged me, smiling. 'She's struggled with your ma, these last few months. She feels like she's got to look after her, just because she never liked her very much when they were kids. As if that's what caused her illness!'

'Guilt is a special kind of prison.' I shrugged. 'Doesn't have to make sense.'

Suddenly, Kit's voice barked from inside the house. 'Well, are you gonna gossip out there all night like old women, or are you coming in for something to eat and to take this irritable lad off my hands?'

Sarah's face turned to guilt, 'Oh! Was he fussing?'

Kit waved it away, 'He was a sweetling. And you have excellent timing, his highness is in need of a bit of a clean-up.' She handed him straight back to Sarah, and looked at me, 'Feeling better?'

I nodded, not wanting to get into it. 'It was fun. I think I'm gonna go out for a drive, do some exploring. That okay?'

Kit paused, looking at me as though trying to decipher what I was saying. But I knew she understood the irritation of constantly being asked if you were alright, what you were feeling and how it was going.

'There's some maps and guidebooks on the side by the door if you want any inspiration,' she said, and left me to it.

Of course, I wasn't going to explore. At least, not the Scottish landscape. I was going straight back to that facility to see Nina. There were too many questions I had to ask, and I was sure if I just asked the right thing, scratched away at the veneer, she'd still be there underneath, rotten and bitter and ready to be honest.

As I drove, I looked up at the crossing over the roundabout for the man in the trilby, but he wasn't there. On the passenger seat I had two bags of jelly babies and some shortbread. What could I take to an estranged, sick mother, who most likely wouldn't remember me without Kit there?

I turned my focus back to the road, wondering what it was I was looking for. I could make excuses and justifications all day, but the truth was, I just wanted to see her. I wanted to hear her talk and see her eyes light up when she looked at me. I wanted to feel like a child again, just for a little while.

The staff were happy that I was there, they made a big fuss of *Nina's daughter from England* coming back again. Their voices cooed and were jolly, giving me updates on her health, her eating, her weekly activities. There were no whispers or warnings. She was a pleasant lady, they said, always polite, always asking about their day and their families. She remembered as much as she could.

'Miss Nina, you've got a special visitor!' the nurse introduced me, and there she was, sitting with a book in her lap, staring out of the window. She looked at me with a vacant politeness.

'Hi Mum...' it seemed too strange to ask if she

remembered me, so I just waited to see if her face changed.

She narrowed her eyes as if looking through a fog, trying to place me.

'Natasha. My daughter Natasha.'

'Right!' *Ding ding ding, you win the prize.* 'How are you, Mum?'

'I don't know, how do the nurses say I am?' There was a stubbornness akin to Kit's in the set of her mouth.

'They say you're good. They say you're a little ray of sunshine, a model patient.' I had stubbornness of my own. I tried to keep the bite out of my voice.

'Well, if that's what they say…' she smiled and shrugged. 'Are you enjoying time with your Auntie Kit? I bet you like her more than me.'

'Why would you say that?'

'Everyone likes Kit more. Perfect Kit,' Nina arranged her features into a smile, but there was a hint of something else there that I wanted to tease out. *Let's see who you really are, Mum.*

'What's perfect about her?'

'Mummy always loved her more. She was so kind and selfless and did what she was told. She was boring and that made people like her. Is that what you're like, Natasha? Are you a goody goody like your aunt?'

Her tone was still light, her head cocked to the side as she smiled at me, but there was something there, that steel spine, that bitterness. *Now we're on to something.*

'I guess… I just focus on surviving, mostly.'

Nina's face erupted into a smile, 'Ah you're like me, like your mum. Sometimes things have to be done to survive, sometimes you have to make hard choices to get what you want. What you deserve.'

'Sometimes that means leaving people behind,' I said innocently, and she went along with it.

'Oh yes, you can't take everyone. It's like swimming with stones in your pockets.' She stood up, 'Shall we have some tea?'

She walked over to the kitchenette, clearly she could be trusted to have her own kettle and bits and bobs. She picked up the box of shortbread I'd brought, and put a stick of cinnamon in the teapot.

'Where did you go when you left us?' I asked, and wondered how she'd react. Whether she'd forget, make excuses, apologise.

'Oh, lots of places. I met a man who was a film producer, or he said he was… or was it theatre? Something *glamorous*. And after London, we went to France somewhere. Then I met an older lady in need of a companion. She couldn't get around much, but very wealthy and lonely. So I stayed there for a few years until she passed away.'

'Sounds like you had some adventures.' *Sounds like you killed an old rich bird for her jewellery collection.*

'Oh yes, it was all such a wonderful time,' she spoke like something from a movie, and I wondered whether any of this was the truth. My mother in France? My mother thought chocolate chip brioche was 'up itself'. I'd once bought a pack of pain au chocolat on sale at the end of the day for 17p and she said it should have been written in English.

'I lived in Birmingham for a while with a young man,' she carried on without hesitation. 'But he was into a bit of trouble, imports and exports and all that, so I moved on.'

Drugs, of course. Or stuff off the back of a lorry.

She brought the cups of tea over to the coffee table and went back for the shortbread.

'I shouldn't, really, watching my figure, but I suppose it doesn't matter now,' she said sweetly, reaching for a biscuit. 'I can let myself go. No one to impress anymore. No need to survive if I've lost my marbles, is there?'

'You haven't lost your marbles, Mum.'

'I've lost something.'

Yeah, your personality.

She paused and then narrowed her eyes. 'I was young when I had you, you know?'

'I do know.'

'Too young to know better.' She nodded at me, with a smile.

'I'm not really sure how to take that…'

Nina froze, holding up her hands, 'Oh, no, no. I meant… I was young and overwhelmed and didn't know how to handle it. And I'm glad for this chance to get to know you.'

I pressed my lips together, 'Is that what we're doing here?'

'I hope so. It's hard, Natasha. People tell you it's hard but you never really *know*, you know?'

I nodded, not really sure where she was going with this.

'Do you have kids?'

And there it was. I was getting better, though. It was true, every time you said it, it hurt a little less.

'No, not yet.'

'When you do, you'll understand.'

'How easy it is to leave them?' I replied sharply, then clenched my jaw. I didn't want to ruin this.

She tilted her head at me, as if she'd misheard me. 'What were we talking about? I'm losing it, Kit, honestly. As if you'd ever have children!'

'Natasha,' I corrected her, 'I'm Natasha.'

'Of course you are. And how's your dad?'

I sighed. Of course, I was torturing myself with this. Answering the same painful questions every time I came, I was asking for it. But perhaps I didn't have to, if she didn't remember anyway.

Was it really so bad, to tell a small lie?

'He's good, still lives in Luton.'

'Oh, that's nice, good for him.' Nina was thoughtful,

frowning slightly as she stared into the distance. 'I thought he'd died. Hmm, must have been someone else.'

She was clearly used to being corrected, and had stopped fighting the answers she was given.

The rest of the visit was easier, when I stopped looking for the old version of her, stopped digging for something that seemed to only appear in flashes and then be gone again. People said Alzheimer's often took their family members away from them, made them cruel, frustrated, lost.

My mother seemed to have gone the other way; free from the consistency of her memories, she was more detached. She seemed to remember parts of the story, but they sat alongside my own, in parallel rather than matching. Her version of events was nothing like mine, but hers sounded nicer, so I let her believe it.

If I could have believed it, I would. Apparently we were very understanding about her leaving. She'd sat us down and explained she wasn't happy. She'd sent me postcards every week, and come back for visits. She'd been sad not to make it to my wedding, but she'd appreciated the invitation.

She had in-depth details for each story. How I'd gripped her hand when she told me she was leaving, that I was wearing that oversized one-shouldered purple jumper I had (non-existent) and I'd told her I understood that she had to go. She'd peppered these memories with unbelievable detail, always culminating in her being accepted, and there never being a bad guy. A happy ending, always.

It's amazing what the mind can do.

On the drive back I let myself become lost in her false history, I gave it space to breathe and develop. I imagined her at my wedding, this version of Nina. How she'd be polite but then bitch about Miranda and make faces behind her back. How she'd place her hand on my father's arm, though separated, brought together by pride in their child. Perhaps they would have confirmed that at least *one* good thing came out of their marriage – me.

I imagined those postcards from exotic places, always signed, *Love, Mum x*. Phone calls where I would have shared my big news, my raises at work, buying our flat.

If she'd left in the way she remembered, Dad would still be alive. Maybe he would have been kind, been good again. Would have found another job and a new partner and a new meaning in life.

And Dan… Dan wouldn't have been there.

He wouldn't have stayed with me. He would have gone off with one of those other girls, because poor broken little Taz didn't need to be saved.

And so the story fell apart before it even became possible. A family life less fucked up, and a world without Dan, without my Daniel. Without us. I would have met someone on the estate who'd bothered to look at me, gone along with what they wanted. Convinced myself it was enough.

Still, it was a nice daydream. One I could so clearly imagine now my mother was this other woman with the kind eyes, who gave me compliments and asked about my life. It felt dangerous, like the stoking of an addiction.

On the way back I saw the man on the overpass again, but this time I recognised his face – Fraser, from the pub. I knew he'd looked familiar. His hat hid the explosion of white hair that had been visible last night. I hesitated, not sure whether to pull over. He looked relaxed, his hands resting on the railing. He certainly wasn't going to jump.

Standing on bridges when you had no need to cross was not normal behaviour… but what did I know of normal here?

So I drove on, even though I doubted myself, because I was a Londoner and the first rule is that you mind your own goddamn business.

I called Dan on the speaker system in the car, because I was lost in the past and my past was his. I still hoped my future was too.

'Hello my beautiful wife,' his voice sounded tired, but I could hear the smile.

'Hello my wonderful husband,' I replied, glad that we still had a language we shared, rituals. 'How are you?'

'Same old bullshit, different day,' I could imagine him loosening his tie and rolling up his shirt sleeves. I wanted to place my fingertips on his skin, feel the warmth. 'Dad wants me to take on a different clientèle, more B2B portfolios.'

'I don't know what that means.'

'Nothing interesting. Same shit, just for businesses instead of individuals.'

'You think you'll do it?'

Dan sighed and didn't speak for a moment. He was preparing for a story, I could tell.

'Remember when we lived in Tufnell Park and that restaurant owner paid me two hundred quid to paint a mural during his refurb?'

'Yes,' I smiled, 'it was brilliant.'

'And we went out and bought a bottle of Cava because I'd made my first money as an artist and life was finally going in the right direction?'

We drank it from tea-stained mugs and shared a portion of late-night cod and chips from the chippie on our road. The guy even threw in an extra half portion of chips and a saveloy for free, because we were celebrating. Everything had seemed so perfect. No parents, no family to tell us we were wrong to dream, no one but the two of us, doing what made us happy.

'I remember.'

'I was just thinking about that today. About how happy I was to be paid a couple of hundred quid for three days of hard graft, and how every time we walked past the restaurant I would smile.' Dan paused, 'I went past it on the way home today. That whole block is flats. The restaurant is now a coffee shop that sells the best arancini in London, according to TimeOut. The mural is gone.'

'It's still there, though, under the paint, isn't it? It still exists, you just can't see it.'

Dan laughed, a little hollow, 'But seeing it's kinda the point, babe, isn't it?'

'What made you think about that today?'

'Guess just remembering the last time I was proud of the work I did.'

'Oh, baby.' It was a sad admission from a man who had made it his mission to make his parents proud. To be the financial whizz kid they had expected. To make it right.

'I guess it'll be easier when you're home again. When I have something good to make the bad worth it.' He paused, 'Not that I'm rushing you… or expecting you back, or… anything. You know. I just miss you, I guess.'

'I miss you too. And I miss those days. That was a good mural.'

'The best damn mural you'd ever seen, if I remember correctly.'

I grinned, 'Well, I'd just become your fiancée, I was pretty easily impressed in those days.'

'So all those lovely things you said about me being

the next big thing were just to get into my pants. The horror!' Dan's voice was so warm I wanted to curl up in it and never leave. I wanted to live in this state of nostalgia, in the safe parts of the past. The ones we had both loved.

'God, I love you,' I said, feeling it so much it was almost painful.

'I love you too, even though you lied about my mural,' his voice was soft. 'I was thinking about getting a cat to keep me company, what do you think?'

'I think you know damn well we're dog people, Daniel White.'

He burst out laughing, which had been my intention all along. 'How are the alpacas? And the irritable pony, and the other creatures that make me think you're living in a kid's storybook?'

'They're good, in fact, I've had my first horse-riding lesson… aren't I fancy? I'll have something to chime in with when we go to all those dreadful investor dinner parties.'

'Telling a story about the time you fell off a horse, sure…'

'I didn't fall off once! In fact, it might be my calling in life! I may have an affinity with the wild beasts and they'll heal my tattered soul,' I said dramatically, but Dan didn't really laugh at that. Perhaps 'tattered soul' was a little too close to the truth.

'I've been thinking I don't want to go to any more of

those stupid parties anyway. What do they achieve except making us both feel like shit?'

'Um, excuse me, Mr Director of something something, since when have they made you feel like shit?'

'Always'

'Bullshit.'

Why did everyone keep rewriting time on me? My mother denying all the things she'd done, and my husband suddenly hating the world he'd inhabited quite happily for the last few years? How was I meant to know what was real?

'Taz, you have to deal with those guys for an *evening*. Can you imagine what my days are like?'

'I thought it was a necessary evil to get to where you needed to be?'

'It is. But I'm starting to think I was wrong about where I needed to be.'

'You wanna go and paint murals?' I asked, suddenly hopeful.

'I want… I don't know what I want, except you. I want you, Taz. I want me and you and no one else.' He sounded like he was bone weary, burnt out and desperate for some sort of answer.

'You have me, you always have me. I'm just… figuring shit out. My shit.'

He took a breath and let the silence sit for a moment.

'I'm sorry,' I said. 'I'm trying to sort it out, honestly. I went to see my mum again today… I don't know what

I'm searching for but I'm feeling better,' I offered, somehow feeling the need to keep apologising. I'd run away from our life and I wouldn't let him come.

'Maybe it's being away from me,' he said sullenly and I huffed.

'It's not being away from *you*, moron. You're pretty much the only person I like.'

He was silent for a moment, and I felt him organising his thoughts, preparing a statement and a series of compromises and addendums. Dan was good like that, always thinking it through to the end. Problem solver.

'You remember when we decided to move to London, how we put all those cities we might go to in a hat and picked one out?'

'You mean where I picked out Istanbul and you vetoed it, so we ended up in London?' I laughed. 'Yes, I remember, scaredy cat.'

'I sometimes imagine us in other cities, the other versions of us, and I wonder what they're doing, wonder if they're happy.'

'You wanna move to Barcelona, baby?' I asked gently.

'Maybe.'

There was nothing to say to that, so I said nothing, just listening to the sound of my husband's breathing as I pulled the car onto Kit's driveway and sat there, staring at the cottage, an unexpected warmth in my chest at arriving 'home'.

'You just spin the globe, I'm always up for an

adventure,' I said lightly, segueing into my goodbyes. It sounded like something was going on with Dan too, he was taking his own journey and it was best I left him to it. His version of the past belonged to him alone. Just as mine did to me.

Sarah was still there when I got back, stirring something in a pot on the hob that smelled delicious, Lachlan resting on her hip.

'And how was your mother?' Kit asked me, eyebrow raised and a smile hovering.

I just looked at her, wondering whether to be annoyed.

'Did someone activate that village phone tree? Or is Effie secretly living in the boot of my car as a stowaway?'

Kit laughed, setting the table. 'Perhaps, hen, it's just that we are more similar than you'd like to admit. The only time I get as grouchy as you were this morning is when I'm annoyed at myself. And I imagined seeing your mother as a brighter, shinier version of herself has got to be tempting.'

I nodded, accepting defeat.

'So, how was she?' she repeated.

'Cheerful,' I sighed, 'completely retold her life, expunged her sins.'

'Ah, a regular Florence Nightingale, I'm aware. Did she talk about all her charity work this time?'

I shook my head, 'Good God, no. But… it was nice,

even though it was a lie. Which is a horrible thing to say about an illness like that, I'm sorry.'

Sarah waved it away and Kit rolled her eyes.

'No one's saying it's not a nightmare, a terrible disease that robs you of who you are and those you love. And I pray my sister isn't struggling, isn't frustrated or lost or hurting. And I don't believe she is. She's living a make-believe that's better than the life she had. There's no pain or shame in that.'

Kit was grave, the lines in her furrowed brow distinctive and solemn. Sarah looked at her in shock, Lachlan's chubby hand grabbing a fistful of her red hair.

'Bloody hell, Kit. I don't think I've heard you say so many words in one go.'

'Well, at least you know I'm capable,' she smiled at me. 'I don't want you worrying, hen. It's complicated, it's always complicated with Nina. But she's well cared for.'

'I know,' I said, focusing on Lachlan's bright eyes as he followed my face, breaking out into a smile. 'Oh hello, someone's happy to see me.'

'Oh aye, you're a favourite I think,' Sarah said, handing him over. I cuddled him close, that sharp need and grief dissipating a little more each time he smiled at me. 'He's a little demon sometimes, but I wouldn't change anything.'

'Maybe you should change a *few* things,' Kit huffed, and Sarah gave her a sharp look.

'I'll admit,' she said to me, resolutely ignoring Kit, 'I

had no idea I was pregnant, obviously. It wasn't exactly planned. Looking back now, it was clear. That tiredness, that sudden feeling that something was different… the way my face puffed up, it all made sense. And I just *knew*, before I even took the test, I knew.'

I thought back to when I first realised I was pregnant. I'd been so tired, so bone weary that I fell asleep heavily every night. I remembered telling Dan I'd never slept so well in my life. It was always easy to look back with hindsight, the sore boobs and heartburn were so distinct.

I wanted to join in the conversation with Sarah, but it felt too much like a long story. Explaining a pregnancy without a baby was exhausting, managing other people's feelings of guilt and awkwardness. It was better to sit and nod and pretend I had no idea. People always asked, 'So where's the baby?' and I had to say, 'Oh, it didn't work out' like it was a dress I'd bought in the wrong size and returned, or a restaurant reservation I hadn't managed to keep.

No, these were good people, but they knew enough of my trauma. I didn't want to share any more.

So I nodded along and asked questions about Sarah's pregnancy and it didn't kill me as much as I thought it would. It didn't hurt in the same way it might have a few weeks ago, and that realisation was a relief. Finally, it was starting to sting less like a war wound and more like alcohol on a papercut. One day, it might just be scar tissue. A memory and nothing more.

It was only when I was on the edge of sleep that night, snuggling down in that comfortable bed, that I thought about how well I'd been sleeping the last few days. How I'd been bone weary with what I'd thought was early mornings and Highland air.

I scanned my body, tried to do the maths in my head, barely able to consider the possibility.

When I closed my eyes, I allowed myself a smile.

Hope bloomed.

Chapter Eight

I'd created a comfortable routine now. I got up early to help Kit with the animals, working in companionable silence. We sat and had a huge breakfast with Effie, listening to her chatter about what was going on with the café (Jakob was definitely hung up on a completely clueless Sarah) and the pub (Fraser was considering adding a quiz night). Then I'd go and see Nina. I felt less guilty about it now. We were building something, and as much as I remembered the bad times, it was nice to ignore them for a little while.

I got to correct the past, live in the alternative history Nina had concocted and find the slivers of truth in there. The nuggets of reality, the memories I remembered, but had never had context for.

Every time I got back, Kit gave me this look like she was waiting for the shit to hit the fan.

I knew what it was. I hadn't asked the important questions. The ones I had held on to for years. I was too scared to finally get answers. To break this peace I'd found. Asking your mother why she left you is never going to go well. There's never a right answer. And unlike Nina, I wouldn't be able to forget and start again. I just wanted us to stay happy – what was so wrong with that?

So I took sweeties, and biscuits and we drank cinnamon tea and played cards and laughed. And we didn't talk about the things that hurt.

Until my mother iooked at me, that sweet smile on her face, and I knew the same question was coming. The question I'd choked on yesterday, and the day before that, and if I was honest, any time anyone had asked me it in the last six months.

'And do you have any children, Natasha?'

She was sat there, queenlike, her head tilted in expectation of an answer. She wanted to know if she was a grandmother, that's what she'd said yesterday. And when I'd told her 'no' with an attempt at a smile, she said what everyone says: *Oh, lots of time yet.* Like parenthood is something to be ticked off a list.

I'd already told a lie, about Dad. Why not do it again, just to make my time here less painful? Just to have one moment where I said the thing I wanted to be true?

'Yes,' I heard myself saying, and my heart almost

broke as I watched her face light up. She clapped her hands together.

'I'm a grandmother! Tell me, tell me!'

'I have a son,' I felt my chest tightening, painful with the half-lie. 'He's six months old, almost to the day. He's with his father right now.' *God, how had it been six months already?*

'Wow, a hands-on daddy, how wonderful. You must be missing him! It's so hard to leave them at that age,' a shadow briefly crossed her face, 'at any age.'

That touched me, that acknowledgement. She knew she was wrong, on some level *she knew*.

'Well, I'll be back home soon,' I said, and pressed my lips together. I shouldn't have done it, this was a path I wasn't ready for. It had felt easier, somehow, to pretend he was still here. But now I was a sad woman telling stories, just like that sixteen-year-old girl pretending to be a delicate flower so Daniel White would save her.

'Do you have any photos with you?' Nina asked, leaning forward, her hands clasped as if she worried they'd grab or reach beyond her control.

'I'll bring some tomorrow for you Mum,' I said, desperately hoping that tomorrow she would ask the same question again and I could divert it the way I always did. What if she remembered this? What if it got stuck in her head as the truth, the same way that she thought chocolate cake was my favourite?

'Oh god, I'm so silly!' She laughed at herself daintily, hand over her mouth.

When I was a kid she always laughed loudly, mouth wide open until I could see the metal fillings in the back. Her laugh had been obnoxious; I used to cringe and look around when she laughed in public in case she caught someone's attention. She'd always tell me she didn't care if people looked, let them fucking look if they wanted, they had boring, small lives anyway.

And here she was now, so demure, so gentle. I wondered how much of it was the Alzheimer's and how much of it was life. Had she been sanded down and softened in the years since she left? She had still told me so little of what she'd done, where she'd been.

'What? What's funny?' I felt my lips twitch in response, even under the circumstances.

'I've asked you a hundred questions and I didn't even ask his name! What's my grandson called, Natasha?'

I pressed my lips together to keep from crying. I didn't know his name. Naming him made it real and we didn't want that. We wanted to say goodbye and pretend it had never happened.

I took a breath, and thankfully a staff member came in to tell Mum she had a doctor's appointment, and to lead her over. I made my excuses, marched out to the car and sat there for twenty minutes wondering why the hell I was so stupid. What had possessed me to lie?

I wanted the daydream, more than anything. I

wanted to say out loud that I was a mother, that I had a son. That I had grown this perfect little person within me. But all of that was tarnished by the fact that he wasn't here anymore.

I called Dan, unsure of anything beyond the fact that I wanted my husband. He was the only person who understood. Except he'd never wanted to talk about the baby. About what happened. And I went along with it, because if he was fine I needed to be fine too.

'Hey, Taz, you okay?' He was concerned already, just from a call in the middle of the day.

'Why didn't we name him?' I said, hand across my forehead like I was trying to keep every single memory in there. 'Why didn't we do a service, or acknowledge he existed? He was *here* Dan, he was here and he was ours, and we threw him away…'

I heard him sigh, and then nothing. The click that might have been a closing door, the softness of his voice as he replied.

'I thought it was what you wanted. A way to keep the pain at bay.'

I shook my head to myself, 'We should have given him a name. Everyone deserves a name. Proof that they were here once.'

'What do you want to call him, Taz?' Dan was using the voice he had when he 'handled' me. I'd accused him of it years before, like I was a spooked horse about to bolt, but honestly that voice was the only thing that held me together some days. A low, quiet voice saying that everything would be okay again.

'Something angelic, something peaceful.'

Dan went quiet and then cleared his throat, 'I had a name, in my head at the time. Callum. It means "dove" and I thought you'd like that. I'd kind of had all these images of us arguing over different names, compromising eventually, and we never got a chance to do that.'

'I like it,' I said gently, echoing the name, rolling it around my mouth like I was trying it out. 'Callum White.'

I stopped, then laughed, 'Oh God.'

'What?'

'Callum means dove. White. White dove.' I snorted, 'Good thing we didn't burden him with a name like that in life. In death, it's probably okay.'

I wiped my eyes, taking a few deep breaths. Somehow, now that he had a name, the panic had eased. I could talk to him, I could remember he existed. Callum. My son, Callum. He had been real.

Dan cleared his throat, 'It broke me too, Taz. I was trying to be strong, but I almost lost you too. I don't think you realised how close it was. *I almost lost you too.* And ever since, it's like I have. Like you're not really here.'

'I've been at every event, every family meal. I haven't missed a dinner party or hair appointment or gym class!'

I reeled them off as if I'd known this argument was coming.

'You know I don't mean that stuff. I mean you're not really *here*.'

I paused, 'I know.'

'So will you think about what I said, about the therapy?' Dan's voice had changed to his bargaining one. I heard this when he was on his work calls, his I'm-so-reasonable-and-I-care-about-what's-best-for-you spiel.

Therapy rankled. I'd seen enough school counsellors as a kid to know how much power people had over your life, how much someone with a couple of degrees and problems of their own got to decide what you did. They'd all been so quick to tell me I wasn't a problem child, that I wasn't in trouble, they just wanted to be there to support me. And yet if I kept my head down and did my school work, they left me alone. As long as I looked like I was alright, as long as everything seemed perfectly normal, I could get along without their interference.

Looking alright and being alright were different things. And the minute I went home, they didn't care what kind of mess their interference meant for me – counsellors could send you away, land you in foster care, leave you completely alone. They were the bad guys, Mum always said, always prying into people's business, playing God like they didn't have any skeletons in their closets.

It all seemed so middle class, though, therapy, so self-indulgent. Like a form of self care all these early-twenties banker wives had as part of their routine; yoga class, therapy, hair appointment, nails. People who have to listen to you because you're paying them, but at least your hairdresser isn't going to tell you to leave your marriage or that you're inherently unlovable.

I didn't want someone telling me how to live my life. I'd been looking after myself for most of my childhood, and I looked after Dan from the moment we started our life together. I just needed time to recalibrate. To give myself a break from pretending to be okay. A holiday from being me, that's what this was. And then I'd go back and be the perfect wife again. I could do it.

'Taz?' Dan prompted.

'I'll think about it.' *Would I hell.*

I remembered those counsellors jumping all over me after Dad died. God, they were desperate for a bit of drama, foaming at the mouth to deal with poor little Natasha, suddenly an orphan, with her boyfriend in prison. All alone again.

And before that, when they called my mum into school to talk about my dirty clothes, and how she ranted and raved at me that she'd been embarrassed, that those people thought she was a bad mother, that they could all go to hell. She said they'd try to take me away if my uniform wasn't clean, because they'd think I'd been bad. She said I needed to do better, I didn't want to disappoint her, did I? Didn't want them to say bad things about my mum?

I took to washing my uniform in the bathroom sink after that, tried to look as neat as possible, but the material never dried properly and I always felt slightly damp. They never did take me away though, moved on to other kids with bigger problems.

'I've got to go, I've got a meeting,' he said gently, and I could hear the regret.

'Right, of course.'

'I'm glad you called, though.'

Hope bloomed. 'I could call you again later, around dinner time?'

'Ah,' he paused, awkward, 'the lads are taking me out for dinner, because they know I'm on my own.'

Poor Daniel, with his embarrassing wife, who shat all over the birthday party he threw for her and ran off to Scotland.

'Right, of course. That's nice. Strip clubs and lines of coke?'

'Steaks and beer,' he sighed, irritated with me. 'Anyway—'

'You've got a meeting, right. Speak soon, bye.' I hung up before he could say anything else, before he could justify, or make me feel guilty for being annoyed. Yes, of course, I'd abandoned him and he could hang out with his friends.

It was just that I hated those banker boys more than anything. I hated how he was with them, how he snorted and yelled and joined in with their crude jokes and Peter Pan energy. Like money didn't matter and decisions never had consequences.

I closed my eyes and took a deep breath, sighing. I conjured the sight of my husband all those years ago, walking out of that prison and seeing me, looking at me like I'd been worth it. And then I smiled. Callum. Callum White. At least something made sense.

'Love, would you mind visiting your mum later in the afternoon? I've got a big group coming in now, could do with the help?' Kit seemed angry at having to ask, as if it was weakness. She was so grouchy about it I almost laughed.

'Sure, what do you need?'

We worked together well, regimented but rushed, cutting cake and finding display boxes, getting change for the tin. She got the big coffee urn out and dragged it outside, before I chased after and insisted I help. How had Kit managed this long on her own? It was a small farm, sure, but between the animals and the riding lessons, and the events she had booked in, it was busy. Even before the tour buses that stopped by twice a day.

'Are you okay?' I asked, and Kit pressed her lips together, switching her little neck scarf from a dull grey one to a tartan one. Scottie McTavish, preparing herself for her time on stage.

'Don't fret yourself, I'm just tired. Wondering what I'm going to do with this place when my bones are too creaky to get down those stairs of a morning.'

I shook my head, 'Do you want me to do the heavy lifting today?'

'And what about when you're gone, hen? Back away to London?'

I nodded, rolling my eyes sarcastically, 'You're right. No point getting dependent on me if I'm not going to be here.'

'I'm not dependent on anyone.'

Even though she wasn't offering, the idea of staying was tempting. Already a week had flown by, and I felt better than I had in years. My arms felt strong from all the lifting, my thighs were sore from the second riding lesson on Winston, which was marginally less terrifying. I had put on weight, really tasting my food, and my face looked less drawn. When I saw myself in the mirror every morning, I marvelled at how healthy I looked, how my skin looked ruddy and tanned. There was dirt under my fingernails and more than anything else, it was the fact I could *breathe*. I could stand outside the cottage, looking out at those miles and miles of land, the sun hazy behind clouds and I could take deep lungfuls of air. There was no weight on my chest, no worry.

Only the guilt that I was happier without my husband

was getting to me, and the sneaky suspicion that we may be better off without each other. That everything he'd been through, we'd been through, was for nothing, because we weren't actually right for each other.

But I could see my life up here, passing the days in this way. Helping Kit, seeing my mother, laughing with Kit's friends on Friday nights at the pub. Living a better, simpler life. One without fancy parties or expectation or an insane dedication to money and status.

I was thirty years old and I'd never been alone. I'd fallen in love at sixteen and been with Dan. I'd built homes with him, learnt to cook with him, forgotten to put money on the electric meter, and got stung with bills and learnt to drive, all with him. The idea of starting over on my own was like a flutter, though whether it was excitement or fear, I couldn't tell.

I could recreate my life to be happier.

But I'd have to do it without my husband.

And that idea felt like something was being ripped from me, like someone taking a liver or a spleen. Something essential.

'Here they are,' Kit said, and her voice trembled a little.

'Are you okay?'

'I wish people would stop asking me that,' she rolled her eyes, and charged off to greet the bus, waving her arms wildly with that big grin on her face.

Everyone pretends when they need to.

I milled about, supporting Kit, listening to her stories, directing people to the toilets, explaining what went into the cake and selling little trinkets, tying them in to the stories Kit told. A little girl tugged at my leg and pointed at the alpacas, and I smiled at her, before trying my best to whistle the same way Kit had. It was a little weaker, but Hermione and Neville's heads turned, and they galloped over to us. I could have sworn I saw pride on Kit's face, if only for a second, before she turned back to her captive audience.

The girl's parents thanked me, and I told them all about the alpacas, listened as they talked about how it was their dream to come back to Scotland, how they'd wanted to show their daughter where they met.

The little girl didn't seem to care much, beyond feeding the alpacas carrots and giggling as they honked their appreciation. Just watching her joy made me feel good.

When the big group left, Kit seemed exhausted, but I felt elevated, energised.

'You're good at this, you know,' she said as we carried the urn back inside and set about cleaning up. 'You listen to people.'

I shrugged, 'I didn't do anything.'

'That wee girl had been crying before she headed over to you. You made her feel better.'

'Neville and Hermione made her feel better. She's a kid. They don't need much.'

Kit sighed, 'You're terrible at taking a compliment, you know?'

'And you're the mad old bag from the farm with the wee crazy beasties,' I replied, in my best attempt at a Scottish accent. Kit guffawed, almost dropping the tray she was cleaning.

'I'll miss you when you're gone, girl.'

'I'm not heading anywhere yet,' I said, 'although maybe Sarah's closer to accepting the spare room now?'

Kit shrugged, handing me the tray to wash. 'Sometimes you've got to let people hit rock bottom before they climb back up.'

'A bit like Mum?'

She considered me, frowning slightly. 'I don't know hen, we don't know anything about Nina's life before she came here. She's still stuck in the past. Prefers it to now.'

I knew the feeling.

But maybe Kit was right. I'd been enjoying living in Nina's memories, but I'd been too scared to ask real questions. Every kid wants a great excuse, a reason their parent had to leave them. But there are so few reasons that are good enough.

Some days I asked the same questions and the answers were different. Sometimes they were the same, but I listened to the story again just because I was so pleased to hear it. It was like panning for gold, shaking out the dirt and confusion until I was left with only truth.

There were so many big important questions that I didn't know how to ask, so I started with the easiest one: what happened to Hammie the hamster?

The first few times I asked she had no idea what I was talking about, couldn't recall a hamster at all. She got irritable with me, and as I left the nurses were all smiles and sympathy, explaining that this disease robbed people of themselves so gradually, that a few things might fall through the cracks and my mother was dealing with it gracefully.

Most of the time.

I would try to be softer, I promised myself, try not to prod so much.

The next time I acted like I was writing her life story, rather than interviewing for her part in mine. On that visit, she remembered Hammie.

'Oh, my, the little hamster! I remember when your dad bought him for you, you were so excited!'

I shook my head, about to correct her, but I didn't. I was sure I'd snuck him home, I remembered picking up the cage from Sharon, who found it at the charity shop for me. But I could have been wrong, I was just a kid.

Some memories were just feelings, foreboding, guilt, excitement, not attached to anything in particular.

'So… what happened to him?'

'Oh! Yes!' She clapped her hands as if it had just occurred to her, 'I took him with me, wee thing. I thought he'd keep me company!'

I'd kind of expected her to say he'd died. Or maybe that his death had started her spiral – kills her kid's pet, thinks she's not good enough to be a mother, disappears into the night, that sort of thing.

I didn't think she'd kidnapped my rodent.

'Right… but you didn't take the cage?'

'Oh no, that would have made a lot of noise and was very bulky. I just stuck him in my pocket, took a sandwich bag of food for him. He was a sweetie, wasn't he?'

I paused, taking a breath. 'Sorry, you didn't take the time to write your eleven-year-old daughter a note, but you had time to get a sandwich bag of food prepared so you could steal my hamster?'

Mum tilted her head, 'Oh, don't be upset with me sweetie, I didn't think you'd remember to feed him, so it was better to take him with me.'

'You didn't even remember to feed *me* most of the time!' I squawked, trying not to laugh madly at the situation. 'You left, and you thought it was okay to leave your kid, with no word of warning, no kiss goodbye or explanation, but it was *absolutely not* okay to abandon the hamster? Because *that* would have been irresponsible?!'

Her eyes widened, and she clasped her hands together, 'Oh dear, I've upset you.'

Why would I be upset, I wanted to pout, *my mother preferred the hamster to me.*

We'd missed the teenage years, the fights and screaming and what I imagined other people had with their mothers, usually based on what I'd seen in movies. But I didn't want to have that, I wanted to come to this relationship as a grown-up.

I wanted to pretend it was harmless – this *need* to show her what I'd achieved, for her to be proud of me. But it wasn't that. It was that part of me capable of great cruelty, dipping the tip of the arrow in poison. Back then she had raged on about how little we had, how poor we were. How we never got to go anywhere or do anything. How Dad didn't make enough money, didn't buy her jewellery or take her away for the weekend.

Our home was a disappointment, and so she never bothered trying to make it nice. We had ruined things for her. We had run her chances down to none, that's what she used to say. I never knew what that meant, only that it was bad. *'I'll give you a chance, Mum!'* I used to say, a moronic child with good intentions.

'What happened to Hammie, Mum?'

She frowned, staring into space as she tried to recall. 'You know, I don't know? I got on a train to Manchester, and I had my coat hanging over a chair. When I got off, I don't think he was with me any more. Perhaps he found a nice little family as he wandered the train? An adventure of his own! It would be a good children's book, wouldn't it?'

She tried to jolly me along, but I didn't want to play.

'I cried for a week when you left,' I said.

'Yeah, probably more for the hamster than for me!' she bit back, that tone so incredibly familiar, and I raised an eyebrow. Yes, perhaps I had cried for my poor little pet, who had loved me unconditionally, and had been someone I could cuddle when I hadn't touched another person in days. Not a hand on the shoulder, or a hug or a kiss.

'I lost a mother and a pet in one day, you can give me a break, can't you?'

She huffed, 'Look, everything is very fuzzy for me, and I can't always remember what I did, and I don't think it's fair to be angry at me about it. I can't change it.'

I blinked, watching the change. I had been warned.

'I'm sure it's not fair to be angry about a lot of things, but it's not really about fair. It's an emotion, it appears as and when it sees fit. I don't think telling you that abandoning your kid made her upset is particularly surprising.'

'Well, why do you have to mention it, what does it achieve? Nothing can be undone! We just sit in the past and fester, like all these other nutcases slowly losing their marbles, trapped in their histories, reliving them forever.'

I averted my eyes, feeling that familiar shame. *Be invisible. Be quiet. Don't make eye contact. Find your chance to leave. It's better when they don't remember you're here.*

'Oh look, I've said I'm sorry, let's not argue. Shall I make us some tea and we'll share a doughnut?' She was hopeful and I looked up at the warmth in her voice.

She still didn't look like my mum, the one with the pulled-back hair and the bright lipstick, the frown lines at her lips and that haggard, severe look of someone who was afraid to eat. This woman was soft, warm, gentle. The good twin.

'That would be nice. I don't want to argue either.' She nodded and jumped up, heading over to the kettle. 'But we still haven't talked about why you left.'

She paused only for a moment with her back to me, and when she turned, it was like the clouds had rolled in. 'What? Kit, what were you saying?'

I wouldn't lie again, not after last time. It was tempting, especially as her forgetful moments were starting to be incredibly convenient. But I wanted answers and I wasn't going to stop until I had them.

'No, Mum. I'm your daughter Natasha, remember?' I said, and we began the dance again.

I made her lunch, and we sat out on the little patio, eating sandwiches. She had enough freedom here. The staff clearly weren't worried about her having access to knives or glasses, or her own little back door that led out to the communal gardens.

I made a note to do some more research, to learn more about what the future looked like for Nina. At the moment, it was easy to pretend she was in a nice enough hotel, the pretence only broken by the occasional nurse visiting to check on her, or the porters taking her to appointments.

'What are you talking about?' she had a smile on her face, like she was humouring me. 'Your dad wasn't a drinker! He never touched the stuff! His father drank like a fish and gambled away most of their money. He hated it.'

I looked at her, her pink lips and perfect hair and tried to think back. Wasn't he wandering through my childhood with a beer bottle hanging between his fingers? Or was I just visualising every other dad I knew?

It was hard to picture him now, actually, beyond being tall and big and dark haired. He had a tattoo on one of his arms, a lion or a tiger, something jumping out, because sometimes he'd turn and 'rawr!' at me, his hands like claws, chasing me into my room.

'He was a smoker though, right?' I asked, suddenly unsure.

Mum nodded, 'Yes, me too. Bad habits, but couldn't

be helped. I did quit but I still sneak one with the old dear next door. Good way of making friends.'

My mother paused, tilting her head, as if she was concerned.

'Sweetheart, you know we were happy, right?' She pressed her lips together, searching for the words, speaking slowly as if she was scared of picking the wrong one and messing it all up. 'I know… I know I left. I was weak and unwell, I had a lot of issues I didn't deal with and I ran, but… we were happy, once. The three of us. A little family. We used to go to the fair, do you remember? Every bank holiday we went to the fair and you carried around your huge candy-floss, trying to make it last, until it got sticky and dissolved all over your hands. Do you remember that?'

I tried searching for that memory, but I couldn't find it. It was nice to hear though. Nice to imagine.

'What else?'

She blinked back tears, 'Oh sweetheart, I'm so sorry I left. And more sorry I didn't leave you with any good memories.'

'It was a long time ago,' I shrugged. 'I have some good memories. When we made the blanket fort? And you always used to share a KitKat with me. And sometimes on Fridays we'd get fish and chips from the chippie.'

She snorted at me, 'So all about the food, then?'

I didn't want to tell her that when I tried to conjure a

memory or a feeling from childhood, hunger was the main one. Hunger, and this desperate need to be invisible. That being silent was the best thing I could do for myself. But how could that be true? Why had I spent my childhood sneaking across the landing on tiptoe so I wouldn't irritate anyone, if everything was fine?

'You know how your dad asked me to marry him?' my mother asked, a cheeky smile on her face. 'It's a good story!'

I blinked, 'I didn't think you were married.'

She didn't miss a beat, 'No, we never did in the end, never got around to it. But he asked me. Right before we found out you were coming along! He jumped on the carousel at the fair, that's why we always went every year. He came right over to my horse and held out this ring and said, "How about it Nina, we getting married or what?" and I said, "Or what!" and we laughed.'

I looked to her left hand, where she wore a ring. 'Was that… or did you get married to someone else?'

My mother shook her head, 'No, there was no one else for me. No other life or other family. I left my first, I didn't deserve a second.'

Well, that self-judgement sounded familiar.

'What about Kit? Did you come and stay with Kit when you left… Luton?' I'd gone to say 'us' and stopped myself.

'No… I knew my sister would judge me for what I'd done. She wouldn't have welcomed me. I was her annoying half-sister after all, she never wanted to be around me. Our mum used to force her into taking care of me when we were kids. And then as soon as she was old enough, off she went! Disappeared. She sent the odd Christmas card out of obligation, but…'

'Well, at least you're getting that time together now?' I offered, smiling, and she narrowed her eyes at me, as if I'd said something wrong.

'You really like her, don't you?'

I nodded, 'She's… honest. There's no games, no ego. She says what she thinks, if it's necessary. She doesn't hurt people but she doesn't sugar-coat it either. It's just… easy. Life everywhere else seems so complicated. Here it seems simple.'

'I'd be careful, love. Kit's got secrets of her own too. And how honest is she when she's pretending to be Scottish and selling her bits and bobs to tourists?' My mother offered a raised eyebrow and knowing smile. 'I came up once, wanted to see her but bottled it, so I joined a tour I knew was going through. It was a shock to see her that way, all cheer and silly stories and that over-the-top accent. Everyone's a liar if the pay-off is big enough.'

It was those words that went round and round in my head as I lay in bed that night. *Everyone's a liar if the pay-off's big enough.* It was true, obviously. We all had lengths we'd go to, lines we'd cross. Reasons we'd lie, so it could be justified. A job, a living, a loved one. Safety, security, fear of losing someone. Lies were a part of life, but I had the terrible feeling that my mother had seen right through me.

She'd looked at me and told me I was a survivor, that she knew I'd do anything to get what I wanted, and even more to keep it. That I was just like her. She patted my hand and smiled, this peculiar, unwavering smile, like she knew just who I was.

Like she knew what I'd done.

As if she could know that fourteen years ago my perfect boyfriend had started looking elsewhere, stopped holding my hand. Hadn't met me in the library after school, the text messages fewer in number and syllables. That there were suddenly endless shiny-haired girls who didn't wear their brokenness so openly.

So I did what I had to do to keep him.

Later I dreamed of candy-floss, melting as it touched my grubby little hands, how I clenched the stick and refused to let it go. How I let the tiniest bit dissolve on my tongue, but the rest I would save. I would have candy-floss for days! I'd ration it out and eat pink clouds for ever, even as it made me sick.

I was on my father's shoulders, high above the crowd, looking down at everyone. He patted my knee, 'You alright up there Tashy?'

I patted his head in response, with my sticky fingers and he didn't get cross or say anything at all. He just carried me through the crowd so I could see, the queen of all I surveyed.

'What did you do, Tashy?' my father's voice asked me, but I wouldn't answer, stuffing more and more candy-floss into my mouth so they couldn't make me talk.

'She did what had to be done!' my mother's voice called out, and I saw her swinging from the horses on the carousel, all brightness and joy. I kicked and wriggled and made my dad put me down so I could run to her, but by the time I reached the carousel, she had disappeared. And when I turned back to see my dad, he was gone too.

I clung to the wooden horse on the carousel as it started moving, and it was only when I read the name on the painted armour said 'Winston' that I jolted awake, gasping for breath.

Chapter Nine

The memories haunted me, things I hadn't remembered suddenly too real. That ache in my chest where I missed my dad, or missed who he might have been, entangled with the guilt of his death. I could still feel the candy-floss on my fingers from that dream, and I kept wiping my palms on my pyjama bottoms, but the feeling wouldn't leave.

I woke to a message from Dan, another photo of a drawing. It was a cartoon of three men sat at their desks in the office. They all had thought bubbles above their heads. One was thinking about money, one was thinking about a stripper, and the one that was clearly Dan was thinking about me. He'd drawn me in the thought bubble, and labelled himself 'Dan' below, just in case I hadn't realised. I snorted.

He was trying. We had both been trying to find our way back to each other through this.

But it was never really his choice.

I burst into tears, snotty, loud wails that I tried to muffle with my hands. Oh God. I'd done this. Everything that had happened, everything that brought us to this moment was because of me. Because I was a scared, unloved teenager who thought her perfect boyfriend was going to leave her.

Some people will do anything not to be alone. To be loved.

You're a survivor, just like me. You do what needs to be done to get what you want. That's what Nina had said, and she was right. I was just like her. Twisting things, making it so I got what I wanted. And I had wanted Daniel.

So I lied.

I had lied and he had believed me. He had stayed with me, so desperate to save poor little Taz from the estate, with her big bully of a father and those bruises on her wrist.

But my dad was a good man. He'd always been a good man. He'd loved me, he'd loved Mum. He would have done anything for us. It was clear now.

She'd made me remember just how much I'd twisted it all in my mind. I had lied to keep a boy's attention, and my dad had ended up dead. Daniel had gone to prison, estranged from his parents, and he'd turned to me, he'd loved me and depended on me and made me feel like I would never be alone. He'd never leave me, because he needed me.

A girl who bruised easily and a boy who wanted to save her.

I needed air, I couldn't breathe. Couldn't think. Nothing but the same words over and over again on repeat. *You lied, you tricked him, he never picked you.*

I pulled on my clothes and headed out to the farm, marching past people with a determination. I wasn't sure where I was going until I got to the stables and saw Winston. Winston, the friendly giant of a horse, who had protected me and kept me safe. Who could get me away from everything. I headed straight into the stables and led him out, struggling to get up on his back until he dropped down to help me.

And then we were off, walking, then trotting, then galloping.

He didn't choose you, you tricked him.

Your selfishness killed a man.

Daniel would never forgive you. You made him stay. Made him lose his freedom.

Your poor father, judged and dismissed. You're scum.

You're worse than your mother.

I galloped faster, kicking my heels into the horse's muscled torso to speed him up. I tried to keep my legs strong, move with him, but all I could think about was that horizon, going as far and as fast as I could. Outrunning the voice with the sound of the wind.

I heard yelling from behind me but I ignored it, desperate to get away. And then I felt the saddle slip. I felt myself sliding even as Winston tried to slow down, even as I clenched my thighs and tried to stay upright.

When I fell I hit my head. It was more the 'thunk' noise than the pain. And then everything was quietly, gloriously black.

'Well hello there,' a soft voice said as I opened my eyes. Sarah's red hair was the first thing I noticed, and she raised an eyebrow. 'And how are we today, Lady Godiva?'

'Is Winston okay?'

'Aye, he's a big boy. Well used to chucking wee beasties off his back,' Sarah smiled, patting my hand. 'Do you want some water?'

I shook my head. 'What happened?'

'You stole a horse like a mad woman, didn't check his saddle, or sit on him properly, and then disappeared into the distance like a very badly organised bandit.' She shook her head. 'So go on then. Tell me.'

I looked around the room, 'Where's Kit?'

'Looking after Lachlan. Probably using him to sell a few titbits to the tourists, no doubt. I've told her I expect a commission.' Sarah smiled at me again, that gentle smile. 'It's just us here. I've never seen someone move like that before.'

Sarah sat on the edge of the bed, handing me a glass of water even after I said I didn't want it. She had a little tray with a cup of tea and a few biscuits. She sat, just watching me. It reminded me of all those school counsellors, who just sat and watched, waiting for you to make the first move, like it was a battle of wills.

'Did your husband leave you?' she suddenly asked, point blank, and I blinked in surprise.

'No. But he should.'

I didn't know where to start, but somehow, I told her.

Honestly and simply, I told her our story. Right from the beginning, leaving nothing out, twisting nothing to make me sympathetic. Offering no excuses. Let her hear it and make her decision.

I had loved a boy, I had wanted an escape, I had told a lie. When you took away the consequences, that was all it was.

I hadn't meant to lie, I don't even remember doing it. All I remember is that *fear*, that he would go and I would be alone again. I'd be at home with Dad and everyone else would get their escape, but not me. Dan would date the kind of girl he was meant to be with, with the swishy hair and the nice clothes, who could afford to go to the cinema and had the right outfits to wear to parties.

I remember the moment it happened – we were sitting on the picnic tables on the grass, and he kept telling me I should take my jumper off, but I didn't want to.

'You must be hot, Taz. You look uncomfortable.'

'Look, just leave it, it's fine.'

'What's wrong?'

'Nothing!'

I'd been unfairly grouchy, I knew. I could sense he was about to leave, and it was easier to push him away than it was to try to convince him to stay. And yet… life had been better since Dan had chosen me. Getting up in the morning was about more than going to school and doing well so I could get out. My evenings and weekends were full with text messages and phone calls, someone who cared what I had to say. Before him I'd spent most of the time studying and staying out of Dad's way when he came back from the pub.

Life had become technicolour and it would go back to grey. It was heartbreaking.

'Babe, come on, what's up?'

He'd reached for me, knocking my wrist and I'd winced.

'Taz, you're hurt. What's wrong?'

I didn't say the words, exactly, I didn't say anything. I just let him gently push my jumper sleeves up, one then the other, and inspect the bruises. The purple circles around my wrists, the thumbprints against my pale skin.

I didn't meet his eyes, even as he tried to tilt my head. I looked past him.

'What do you want to do, Taz? Do you want to go talk to someone?'

I shook my head.

'Do you want me to do anything?'

I shook my head again.

'So I'm just supposed to forget this?'

I sighed, closing my eyes. The truth sat on my lips, the fact that I was just clumsy, that my Dad hadn't meant to, that he'd never done it before. But I didn't say that.

I'd fucked up. I'd meant to iron Dad's clothes for his interview, his first in ages. He wanted to work, to provide for his family, and I'd been too busy mooning over my boyfriend to help him. He'd been drinking and he'd been upset. It wasn't a pattern. It was a one-off.

But Daniel looked at me like he wanted to save me, like he wanted to protect me. He wouldn't leave me if he thought I needed him.

And so I didn't say anything. I let him think it had been going on for ages, that it was a regular thing, that I hadn't mentioned it because I was used to it.

I let him want to save me.

If I hadn't, if I'd corrected him, or if I'd never let him push up my sleeves in the first place, when I called him to help me that weekend, when I cried incoherently and asked him to pick me up, he might have waited for me in the car. Everything might have been different, if I'd been selfless.

I tricked my husband into staying with me, and if I

hadn't, he might have had an entirely different life. One where he didn't feel the need to reward me for my loyalty.

But I'd tried, I'd tried so hard to make it worth it. To be the best girlfriend, the best wife he could have ever had. To support his dreams, lift him up. He wanted to be an artist and I worked two jobs so he could do that. I never said a word when his parents came back into our life. I smiled and nodded and gushed my appreciation when they wanted to give us money for a deposit, when they wanted to redo our wedding so we could get married 'properly'.

Before we lost Callum, I never said a word back to Miranda. I withstood the barbs and the comments and the parade of better suited women. The suggestions that I was a gold digger who'd done well out of everything in the end.

I had tried so hard to make it worth it. To be worth those months he'd spent behind bars, the uni experience he never had, the family who didn't want to know him.

I hadn't lied, technically. But I'd let him think something untrue. I'd spent over a decade trying to be perfect, but I lost my son and it was like I couldn't do it anymore. I was grateful and guilty and in love with my husband.

But that wasn't enough, was it? We'd reached one of those crossroads, and I had to let Daniel choose.

'But he did hurt you, he hurt your hand,' Sarah said, in confusion. 'You didn't lie.'

'It was an accident. He wasn't like that normally,' I clasped my hands, 'I let everyone think he was a monster. He died a monster. They wrote about him in the papers, and people were so nice to me.'

'So it was all an accident. Him hurting you was an accident, him dying was an accident. Love, you were sixteen. He was an adult.' Sarah swallowed as she said the words, and I wondered how many times she'd heard the same things she was saying to me. As people told her it wasn't her fault when Murray drank and fought and yelled.

And yet she had stayed.

And I was the bad guy.

'You know, my mother had a little bird in a cage,' Sarah said, and I frowned at her in confusion. She continued without pausing, holding up her hands as if to reassure me that this was relevant. 'A beautiful little budgerigar with a yellow and white body. She sang and trilled and seemed happy enough. My ma left the door open for her, tried to get her to fly. But no matter how we coaxed her, she would not leave that cage. Curiosity and treats couldn't tempt her. It wasn't that she loved her mirror, or her toys. She just didn't know how to be outside.'

'She loved her cage,' I said, suddenly realising what she meant.

Sarah nodded, pleased. 'Aye, and so when some bastards broke into the house and trashed the place, she didn't fly out, she didn't try to save herself. She just waited. They reached in and snapped her neck. Just because they could.'

There was a sick feeling in my stomach.

'We all get used to our cages, Taz.'

'But I lied.'

'You were still a child, for chrissakes!' She huffed, 'This was the man who went on to be your husband, your soul mate. Do you not think that perhaps that has something to do with it? That perhaps this all played out exactly as it needed to?'

'That my Dad died because of *fate*? That I lied because it was *fate*?' I scoffed.

'Your da was drunk and aggressive and took a tumble. And I'm sure that's something your husband has had to deal with for the rest of his waking hours. No matter that it was an accident. No matter that he was protecting you.'

I nodded, 'But it was my fault.'

Sarah narrowed her eyes at me, 'I've never met someone more willing to be blamed for something and honestly, it's pissing me off.'

I recoiled, a little surprised.

'I see why, honestly, I understand that you'll carry that doubt and your guilt with you. But why do you want to be judged so much? Why do you seem to *want* to be told how awful you are?'

'Because then maybe it's karma,' I said quietly, not sure she heard me at all. 'Maybe I've deserved everything.'

'What was your punishment, Taz?' she asked me, and I took a breath.

'I lost my baby.'

How strange that I hadn't said it before. I'd practised it, preparing myself for the questions, but there had been none. Daniel had dealt with it. I hadn't gone back to work, hadn't faced those eyes, that pity. I had always hated the phrase. *Lost.* I didn't lose him. I didn't lose anything. It was taken, he was taken and I did everything I could to keep him. I remembered pleading with Daniel that if there was a choice, he should let me die, let me go.

But there wasn't a choice. And Daniel had spent his life saving me, I didn't trust him to make the one I wanted anyway.

'And you think it's punishment? You lost your baby because you told a lie when you were sixteen?' Sarah's voice held no judgement, just clarity.

Of course I couldn't think that, of course that didn't make sense. The world didn't follow clear rules, right and wrong. Bad things happened to good people and wonderful people suffered and everything was a mess.

But I had escaped the darkness once, and I was sure it meant to claim me.

In a way, it had.

'Sweetheart, you understand that isn't true, don't you?'

I knew, I knew logically that it wasn't true. That something I did fourteen years ago hadn't created a debt. That I didn't have to pay for the trauma I'd caused.

But something deep in my gut told me what I knew to be true: I didn't deserve to be happy, and there was a price to pay. There would always be a price to pay.

I nodded, lips pressed together.

'Do I deserve the things Murray does? The drinking, the gambling? The way he talks to me like I'm a silly wee woman who knows nothing? How rough he gets when he's had a drink and I've annoyed him?'

'No, of course not!' *Oh God, Kit was right about him.*

'But I'm no saint, Taz. I stole when I was a wee'un. I wasn't hungry or poor, necessarily. No more than anyone else. I just wanted things. Lipsticks, CDs. I wanted what everyone else had.'

I shook my head.

'I did a hundred other awful things. I was cruel, I was unfair, I started fights. I never visited my old granny even though she was lonely and wanted company. Do I deserve it, Taz? Did the actions of a child decide what my life was going to be?'

I resisted, but shook my head again, feeling the tears building.

'Why do you stay?'

'You get used to living for scraps when they're all you're given,' she said as she looked down at the bed, ashamed. I forgot how young she was, how incredibly young, how much life she had left to live. 'I'm going to leave, though. I've decided. No more. Not for Lachlan, not for me.'

I nodded, and she reached across to take my hand. 'I'm so sorry about your baby.'

'Me too,' I said, my lip trembling.

'So what are you going to do now?' she asked, and that, at least, I had already decided.

'I'm going to tell him the truth, let him make his choice with all the information.'

'And if he leaves?'

'Then it'll be his choice, and I will have been honest. That's what matters.'

Sarah helped me downstairs for a cup of tea, and we didn't talk again about what we'd mentioned. It was like those secrets sat in that room, in that moment, and each of us was working out what we needed to do. I could see her working things out in her head. Where would she live, who would look after Lachlan, how would Murray react? These things had to be carefully planned when you didn't know what people were like, how they reacted to things. When to be invisible and when to be adoring. Those were the only two options. I remembered those feelings.

And for me? I had to tell Dan. That was the only thing that mattered. Let him know the truth. Let him pick me for real, or leave to start life on his own terms.

When I walked back upstairs, Sarah gave me a nod, as if to say I wouldn't be disturbed. How funny to share such secrets with strangers.

When Dan answered the phone he was so happy to hear from me, chattering away in that childlike way he had.

'Did you like the drawing? I haven't done that style in so long! It was fun, just playing around, did you like it?'

'Yeah,' I said softly, 'I liked it. It was beautiful, it's just…'

'Oh.' I heard the click of a door as he closed it. 'I thought we were going to talk properly when you got back? In person?'

'It's not that. I just… I've been thinking a lot about everything, about the past and us, and I need to tell you now, because if I don't do it now, I won't ever.' I heard myself saying the words, somehow pulled along on a current. 'And you might hate me, and that's okay because I hate myself and…'

Dan's voice was small, 'Did… did you cheat on me?'

'No! God, never! This is something from… from when we were younger.'

He hated talking about the past, reliving everything

he'd been through. He never talked about juvy or what went on inside. It was a part of his life even I knew nothing about. During those visits he'd only wanted news from me, from the outside world. He hadn't wanted to share his experiences. He wanted to protect me, yet again.

'The reason you came to my home that night… the reason I gave to make you come…' I took a breath. 'It wasn't true.'

I waited, but there was no sound, so I continued.

'I lied. About my dad. He didn't hurt me, I was just a clumsy kid, and I saw you were losing interest in me. And remember that girl Lauren had joined our year and she really liked you…' I could hear myself speeding up, filling the air with unneeded words, stupid details. 'I lied. I tricked you into loving me. And then everything happened and you were stuck with me.'

There was a sharp, loud noise and I realised Dan was sobbing.

I could picture him in his office, facing the window so no one could see him, caved in on himself. Why did I do this now? Why didn't I wait? Why was my need to be free from this more important than treating him kindly?

'I'm sorry, I'm so sorry. I know it's unforgivable, I just didn't want to lose you. I couldn't. I was a dumb teenager and I've felt guilty for so long… After everything we've been through and I tricked you into it.

I've tried to make up for it, to be good, to be what you deserve but…'

I wanted to throw myself at his feet and cry. I didn't deserve forgiveness, I knew that. I must seem like a stranger to my husband, someone who'd snuck her way into his life for all these years. An interloper.

When Dan finally calmed his breathing, I heard him sniff and take a deep breath. If I had waited I could have comforted him, wiped away the tears the same way I had always done. The way I did after the judge's ruling, on our wedding day, after the death of our son.

'Taz,' his voice was croaky and he rubbed his forehead, 'sweetheart, you didn't lie.'

Oh god, he didn't believe me. Of course he didn't. He didn't believe I was capable.

'I'm sorry, but I did.'

'I saw the bruises, Taz. There's no way you were that clumsy. And you stood up in court, do you remember?' He was grasping at straws now, desperate to convince me. 'You told everyone why everything had happened. You gave a statement.'

'It wasn't true.'

'You didn't lie in court, Taz, you couldn't have.' He sounded exhausted. 'You think that big scary lawyer wouldn't have picked up on it? I was *there*, baby, I was there for our history. You think it's just you all alone but I was there too. I saw everything too.'

We sat in silence, at an impasse. I couldn't convince

him, and he couldn't convince me. Two versions of the truth. It would be easy enough, I suppose, to live as this woman he thought I was. The honest, moral wife he was sure he had, back up on the pedestal.

'Taz,' Dan paused, and I wondered what on earth he could say after that. I'd told him the truth and he'd rejected it. 'There's been a lot going on, okay, a lot of trauma. With your mum and everything on top of that… I really think you need to speak to someone. I'll come too, if you want. Whatever you need.'

'So now you think I'm crazy?' I felt my hands start to shake, the fear intermingling with a rage in the base of my stomach. 'I'm broken?'

'I think my wife is hurting, and I should have done something a long time ago,' Dan said, 'please? We'll get this sorted.'

I really wanted to believe him. But he needed to believe me first.

Chapter Ten

'Hello there, you,' I made kissy noises at Terry The Angry Pony in the hopes he'd show a little softness. Kit called him an arsehole, but I thought he just liked to make people work for it. Or maybe to make sure you were going to stick around before getting attached. He trotted over carefully, then turned his back to me, giving me a front row seat as he released his bowels.

Maybe he was just a bastarding little pony. Tiny horse syndrome.

'Well, bollocks to you then,' I said, laughing.

After my phone call with Dan, I had wandered most of the afternoon. Kit took one look at me and said I should take myself off into the wilderness, that I needed some rambling.

'Really exhaust yourself, a good Jane Eyre sort of wander, if you get my drift?'

I looked at her, 'Am I gonna need rescuing?'

She stared straight back at me, 'You tell me.'

I'd rolled my eyes, stuffed a few essentials in my backpack and off I'd gone, crossing kissing fences, nodding hello to the cows. I felt like I was off on an adventure to anywhere, and for a few glorious hours, I hadn't thought about anything.

That weight of guilt that sat in my chest had lightened though, and I knew there was only one thing left to release it completely.

I had to tell Mum. I'd spent so many years blaming her for everything. If she hadn't left, none of it would have happened. He wouldn't have been sad, I wouldn't have messed up his outfit for the interview… I'd spent years rationalising, sourcing everything in my life back to that moment.

But she was a kind woman now, and I had a second chance.

When I got back that night, Kit said very little, but we ate in companionable silence, the TV in the background.

'You'll go to see your mother tomorrow?'

I nodded.

'And how are the two of you getting on?'

I thought about it, 'Well, I think I'm… I'm a bit more understanding than I was. About her leaving.'

Kit frowned, 'Did she say why she left?'

'Just that she was young and overwhelmed, and that she was sorry. Even just an apology goes a long way.'

God, would she even want to see me after she heard what I had to say?

'And what are your plans long term?'

I snorted, 'I feel like I'm in an interview. I can clear out if you need the room for Sarah.'

'Sarah's got a flat,' Kit looked at me in confusion, then raised an eyebrow. 'You two have been scheming, and I don't need someone to look after me.'

I shook my head, 'It's nothing to do with that. Sarah's going to be making some changes, hopefully. And I know she'll want you there when that happens. But also there's no harm in having people want to help you and look after you.'

'Sure, stick me in that home with my sister and we'll live together like a kooky TV show, slowly going mad.'

I frowned at my aunt, her prickly temperament getting to me more than usual, 'What's up, Kit?'

'People say to forgive and forget, and I just worry about the forgetting part, that's all.' She focused on cutting her food up, aggressive and resolute.

'You think I'm getting too close?'

'I think you came here wanting to say something to her, and you're too scared to do it. Because you want her to love you. You want her to make up for all the times she wasn't there because she's harmless now. She's a pretty lady who doesn't have to remember all the horrible things she did.'

'So, what? I'm meant to remind her? I'm meant to be

angry every time I see her? Have an argument and tell her off for leaving every day? Why can't I just have a mum for a bit? Just enjoy having someone love me and call me special and tell me they love me? Why is it so wrong for me to want that?'

I could feel myself getting teary and to my shame, my voice broke. I coughed to try and cover it up, taking my food to the bin and scraping the remains before washing up.

'There's nothing wrong with that, hen. I'm just afraid for what it means when you don't get a do-over every day. When you've got to go back into the real world.' Kit brought her plate to the side and stood next to me, 'I just don't want you to get hurt, that's all.'

I pressed my lips together and said nothing. I nodded, and let her pat me on the shoulder as she started washing up. It occurred to me that she was jealous. That I got to have the mum I'd always wanted, finally, and she was still holding on to old grudges.

As I headed up to my room I felt that familiar tightness in my lower abdomen, like a clenched fist. My period. Of course. I almost laughed to myself as I stomped up the stairs.

That tiny bud of hope extinguished. Probably for the best.

So much for new beginnings.

I didn't hear from Dan, and I didn't expect to. I carried out my normal morning routine with Kit, working well together even as the silence felt more taut than usual. And then I jumped in the car and headed over to my mother, ready to tell the truth.

Of course, with Nina, there was the option that she might not remember it. She tended to cling to particular nuggets of information with certainty, and others she let slip away. The ones that reinforced what she already believed, that fitted in with the existing narrative – they got to stay. The ones that made no sense, that were unpleasant or unbelievable, they didn't tend to make it through the weeks.

She seemed to want to talk about Dad anyway, it was like I couldn't stop her.

'Well you know how much he adored you, he'd have done anything for you,' Mum said, patting my clasped hands as she sat down opposite me. 'I remember when you were born he cried. Didn't want to put you down.'

These memories had seemed so at odds with what I'd remembered. I only remembered the end of his life, the way he'd been after she left.

A man who disappeared to the pub for hours on end, came back stumbling and loud, swore when there was nothing in the fridge or when he saw me studying. My priorities were elsewhere and that always upset him. The best thing I could do to keep my dad sweet was leave him a portion of dinner out on the side, take time to smile and ask about his day, and then disappear.

So that was what I did, for years, with the skill of a royal servant. Knowing when to fade into the background at exactly the right moment. And as long as I jammed a chair under my door handle at night, the bad moods didn't matter.

'I always wondered what might have happened if I'd come back, you know? If I'd sorted myself out sooner, I could have come back and looked after you all, made everything better.'

I took a sharp breath, wondering why that comment felt like a knife to the chest. I didn't like what ifs – I'd been punishing myself with mine for years. And now I'd finally come clean to my husband, he didn't believe me. I'd created a perfect persona over the years, and now he didn't believe me capable.

But my mother knew me, knew how much like her I really was. She would believe that I was capable of causing a man's death. And I deserved to be punished.

I wanted to throw myself at her mercy. Make her punish me, make *someone* punish me. I had taken away this man, I'd been responsible for destroying him. This man she had wonderful memories of, a loving partner who had adored her.

'Mum, I've got to tell you something.'

Something behind her eyes flickered, as if she knew

what I was going to say, and was preparing herself. As if she'd been expecting it.

'You spoke to the doctors, didn't you?' she said, that throaty edge back to her voice.

'What? No. It's about Dad. All these lovely memories you've shared, and how much you loved him… it's… I'm glad I got to see a different side of who he was. Because later on, he was… more difficult.'

She frowned at me, waiting for me to finish.

'You know he died when I was a teenager.'

'Yes, you said it was an accident.'

I took a deep breath, scared to meet her eyes. 'It was, it was an accident. But it was also my fault.'

I told her everything. I told her how Dan made me feel, how alone I'd been, how scared I'd been to lose that. How Dad had been so sad and volatile, but how I'd let everyone think he was a monster. And how that had killed him.

'But all these beautiful memories you had, who he was… I've been carrying this guilt for years, and Dan doesn't believe me because he thinks I'm perfect. But *you know*, you know what I was capable of. You always said I was a survivor, and I would do anything to get what I wanted, just like you. And you were right.'

My voice cracked as I looked at her, waiting. I expected judgement, pity, anger. My old, volatile version of Nina to reappear, perhaps. Or the new softer version to gather me up and tell me everything was okay.

Instead she nodded, her mouth a thin line as got up and walked into her bedroom. She was gone for a few minutes, I wasn't sure if she'd return or if I should go. But she came back holding a box, clutching it tightly. It was well worn, the edges fluffy with age, and she carefully plucked out two pieces of paper, folded neatly. She thrust her hand out and forced me to take them, her face still blank.

The first was a newspaper cutting from when Dad died. I hadn't looked at any of them during that time, any mention of reporters just brought back that moment, that horrible clunk as his head hit the table, the sight of his open eyes staring past me.

I scanned the article:

Jonathan Donnolly, 43, died this week after an altercation on a council estate in Luton, Hertfordshire. Donnolly died of a head wound at the hands of his daughter's boyfriend, Daniel White, 17. White insisted he was coming to collect his girlfriend and was scared for her safety. Donnolly was drunk and a brawl ensued. He was known to the police for multiple drunk and disorderlies. A neighbour said they had often been concerned for his daughter, Natasha. An eye-witness said, 'He was always drunk, abusive. Yelled at me about my dog barking, threatened to poison her. That boy did nothing wrong trying to help the young girl.'

Despite potentially saving his girlfriend's life, Daniel White will be charged at Luton Crown Court for manslaughter. His family did not make a statement.

I looked up, but Mum was looking out of the window, wringing her fingers.

The next piece of paper was jagged and old, ripped from a kid's lined school book.

I recognised the handwriting, loud swirls in smudgy black ink. The same as the only birthday cards I'd had for years.

Dear Nina,

I know this ain't what people do and I'm sorry. But I know what you're going through, I lived it myself. And Tasha is a good girl. She deserves more. So do you.

I called the police last night. I'm sorry if I made it worse. I thought he was going to kill you this time.

If you need help getting out, come to me. I did it, you can do it too. For now, if it gets too much, send Tasha round to me, I'll keep her looked after.

Always here if you want a cuppa (or something stronger).
Sharon (no.12)

Fuck.

I watched as my hands started trembling, until I had to drop the pieces of paper on the coffee table.

As I looked at my mother, the years stripped away. That soft pink lipstick and chocolate brown hair changed and she looked the way she used to, bleached blonde, red lips, dark kohl eyeliner. The pinched look around her lips, constantly pursed around a cigarette.

'The day we made a pillow fort and watched movies all day, eating biscuits,' I said, and she refused to look at me.

It was my favourite memory of my mother, the one I got out and walked into whenever I missed her, whenever I wanted to remember she had loved me, once.

But suddenly I remembered why she'd let me have the day off, creating a magical fort out of pillows and sheets, watching Disney movies cuddled up together. I had a split lip and a bloody nose and Nina had said, 'Best stay home today sweetpea, we don't want your teachers to get upset, do we?'

I felt the tears threaten, pressed my lips together. There was a photo of me in that newspaper article, and seeing myself as a teenager, so small, so fragile, it was hard not to pity that little girl. I didn't remember being that small. I'd always felt so strong, so tough. I was good at surviving, that's what Mum had said. I had to be good at surviving.

'You knew. You knew and you left me behind,' I said. I swallowed, trying not to be sick.

Nina looked at me, shaking her head.

'Oh, *now* you've got nothing to say? All these stories about how much he loved me? How much you loved him? When you knew what he was?' I tried to calm myself, tried to remind myself she wasn't well, she couldn't remember, she got easily confused. But this scrappy bit of paper proved one thing: my mother had known her kid was being hurt, and she left her anyway. She saved herself.

'Are those memories even true?' I asked her. 'Look at me!'

Nina turned to face me, twisting her fingers over and over. 'What's true, really?'

'Oh, fuck off.' I stood up, gathering my things.

'You lived for years with the guilt of killing your dad, of your husband going to prison. Wondering if you were enough. If he'd still have chosen you. Do you know what it's like to live with the knowledge that you abandoned your child? That you left her unsafe?'

'Then why didn't you come back for me? At any point you could have come back and got me! You could have sent social services, you could have reported him! Something, *something* to show you gave a shit about me!' I yelled. I watched as a porter arrived out of the corner of my eye, standing in the doorway, but Nina waved him away, like she was the queen here, allowing a subject's outburst. He nodded and stepped out into the hallway.

'It's easier to live in other memories. Ones where I'm not the bad guy. Ones where I left you with a kind, loving father who would look after you. Where you were better off. I was seventeen when I had you!'

'And I was sixteen when I watched my dad die on the living room floor, brain bleeding into the carpet. I was sixteen when Sharon took me in because they couldn't figure out where to put me and I had no other family. When I went every week to a prison to visit my boyfriend because they decided he killed someone. Don't talk to me about being too young.'

I paused, looking at her, the way she sat in her chair suddenly so much more like the old Nina, rather than this new regal, calm creature. She pulled a hand through her hair like she used to, like she was pulling it out. She tapped the pack of cigarettes she had down the side of the chair, but resisted lighting up.

'Do you even really have Alzheimer's?'

She almost laughed at that. 'Yes, penance. Misremember the past on purpose, and they'll take away all of it.'

There was something she wasn't saying.

'But…?'

'It's not as advanced as they think.'

'You lied.'

She half shrugged, looking out of the window again.

'Tests showed I have it, didn't say how bad it was. People assume. Just like you did.'

'What *on earth* could you possibly have to gain from that? Come on, there must be an angle, Nina, you always liked a good con, didn't you?'

'I'm going to get there anyway,' she sighed, flicking her pastel pink nails, 'this way at least I have a roof over my head, and a sister who feels obliged to look after me. I'll have some family before I'm completely lost.'

'I actually can't tell what's worse – leaving me with him, or making me believe he was a good man all these weeks. Filling my head with these memories that never existed, making me feel like I'd destroyed a man's life when all I'd done was tell the truth!'

'They *did* exist. There *were* good times. We went to the fair, and he cried when you were born and he asked me to marry him on the carousel. They were all true. I just didn't want to remember the bad times. I wanted to give you something good.'

What use was good? What use was remembering that he liked candy-floss when suddenly every other memory came flooding back? The smell of beer and cigarettes, the screaming fights they used to have, the split-lip smiles and tiny circular burns on her arm? I remembered the fear viscerally, hiding under the bed and trying to climb out of the window, wondering if I could break my arm because then *someone* would have to *do something*. God, how could I just have forgotten all of this? How could I have believed they were good? The floodgates were open and it was like everything I'd ignored or pushed away for decades was suddenly returning to me. Every memory that was too painful, that I thought had been safely snuffed out, had come back.

I rushed to the toilet and was sick, nothing but spit and bile, as my stomach convulsed and tears streamed from my eyes. I suddenly remembered those evenings at Sharon's, doing my homework at her kitchen table, her eyes clouding over when I mentioned my mother.

'Why are you so angry at her?' I remembered asking, but Sharon wouldn't give me an answer, just put a cup of tea and a sandwich in front of me, and ran her hand over my ponytail.

'Mothers have one job, they put the safety of their kids first. In the animal kingdom, in the human world. That's all they've got to do. Keep them safe and keep them loved.' I remembered Sharon's words, but couldn't recall when she'd said them. After Dad died, when she took me in, or those Saturday afternoons I used to sit with her because I didn't want to go home?

When I wiped my mouth and my eyes, I made sure to stand tall, walking to the door. 'You didn't want to give me good memories, you wanted to pretend you weren't guilty. You're selfish, the same way you always were. Using me for your amusement, the way you always did.'

'But I told the truth! I told the truth when I saw how guilty you felt, how heartbroken you were! I assumed you remembered what he was like. I wanted to let you know you could still miss him even if you hated him!' Nina stood, babbling in her desperation to be understood.

'That's funny, that's how I always felt about you. Goodbye, Nina.'

As I walked out of the door, I heard her yell, 'Wait, are you going to tell Kit?'

Of course, like all liars, all she cared about was being found out.

I kept walking.

Chapter Eleven

I knew I should be more upset, but it was like I was in a bubble. Like I couldn't figure out who I was, and what was true. All I knew was: I hadn't lied. I hadn't tricked him.

I would probably always feel guilty, feel responsible. But there had been a reason for Daniel to come to my flat that night. I *had* needed saving.

Strangely, I decided to stop off at the bakery in town and picked up some cake for Kit, because somehow it seemed that I had to provide sugar to counteract the sour truths I was going to deliver. Or maybe she'd laugh at the silliness of the gesture, and that would mean something too.

I nodded at Fraser, on the bridge again, and he lifted a hand in response, tapping the brim of his hat. I still needed to ask him why he was there. Or maybe I needed to mind my own business, because I had more than enough trouble of my own to deal with.

It's funny, but I felt calm. I knew I should have been disappointed, I should have keenly felt the loss of a woman who had suddenly filled that mum-shaped hole. But the truth felt like relief – the world was upright again.

Kit was busy when I arrived back, and didn't seem to want to stop her tasks. It was like she sensed I had news she didn't want. Perhaps she was trying to put off my departure.

'I need you to sit down.' I put my hands firmly on her shoulders, and pushed her into a chair.

I sat down opposite her, paused, and then got up to get the whisky out of the cupboard, and brought over two glasses.

'Taz, this is a way to scare someone. If you're here to tell me you're going home, I figured the time would come. I don't need all the amateur dramatics,' she snorted. 'You're welcome back anytime, hen, you know that.'

She seemed so natural to me then, like I'd known her all her life. Her hair pulled into that fluffy plait and her naturally severe features softened as she smiled.

'It's not that…' I swallowed, focusing on those three prominent frown lines on her forehead, that stayed no matter what, perfectly fixed like she was a cartoon character. 'It's about Nina. I went to see her this morning.'

It spilled out like rain onto pavement – aggressive and unstoppable. That she had lied, that she wanted to keep Kit close, keep her paying, make her look after her.

Somehow, I expected her not to believe me. Nina had been banking on that, of course. Who would dare accuse a woman with Alzheimer's of faking it? Who would be so disgusting as to suggest someone with a confirmed medical diagnosis was lying? It was pure Nina – audacious. Go big or go home, baby.

But there was no laughter, no suggestion of confusion or misunderstanding. She just sighed deeply, met my eyes and nodded.

I had expected anger, frustration, outrage. Perhaps embarrassment for being taken in, sadness at how much money and time she'd wasted? Instead, all I found on her face was relief. I knew that feeling. I felt it myself.

'You're not surprised,' I said, and Kit offered me a sad little smile.

'The best stories have an element of truth, like you said,' she shrugged, sighing deeply. 'You know I actually felt *relieved* when I saw she was ill? How disgusting is that? To be happy that your sibling has an awful disease? But she was… it was like she was the person she might have been. A blank slate.'

Kit poured two healthy helpings of whisky and held up her glass to mine as a toast. 'You know, my ma always used to say, if you give people the chance to show you who they are, they will.' Kit sipped and sighed. 'But all this other stuff about your memories and your teen years? Why didn't you talk to me?' she asked.

'Because I thought it would drive you to drink,' I snorted, and raised the glass before glugging, '*slainte*.'

Kit rolled her eyes, 'Come on now.'

'Because I was ashamed. And I didn't want you to see me as weak,' I sighed, irritable. 'Plus, there has been more than enough going on, and I feel like I've been spilling my guts left, right and centre. You already had a sick sister, you didn't need a dramatic niece turning up in the middle of her marriage breaking down.'

'Wee girl, we're family. If you don't share your problems, you're not giving people a chance to be there for you, understand?'

'I don't—'

'Nope,' Kit held up a hand, 'no arguments. Understand?'

I laughed, nodding. 'Okay.'

'Now, are you gonna call your husband?'

I shook my head, 'Ya know, I just need a few hours of not talking about this. I'll call him later. He didn't believe me anyway. He never wavered, never doubted.'

Kit nodded, topping up my glass, and sat down opposite me. 'So, you'll be alright then, you and him?'

I laughed, 'You know, Effie was wrong, you are incredibly nosey and want all the gossip.'

Kit rolled her eyes and jutted out her chin, 'Only when it's family.'

'Convenient. And what about you, about Nina? You're the one paying for her to stay there.'

'Aye,' she sighed. 'Nina never was one to make it easy to love her. You always had to jump through hoops.'

'And are you gonna keep jumping?'

Kit raised her glass to me and said, 'I don't know love, but what I do know is that we are not going to let her stop us from getting dolled up and going out to get absolutely shit-faced in the ample bosom of the friends that love us. What say you?'

'Aye!' I raised my glass, and Kit nodded like she was about to lead us into battle.

We walked out and round the back of the house, heading away from the car. 'Please don't tell me we're riding the horses down to the pub, because I don't think I could handle it.'

'Har har,' Kit rolled her eyes, and pulled out from the back of the stables an old bicycle that barely looked like it could roll straight down a hill. She pushed it into my hands and went back for another.

'You expect me to ride this?'

'Well, not without some complaint, I imagine,' Kit bared her teeth at me in a poor impersonation of a grin.

'Come on then, the sooner we go, the sooner we have booze and a good meal to soak it up, and some kind people to exclaim at our tale of woe.'

'Except for Effie,' I said as I mounted the bike.

'Except for dear Effie,' Kit nodded, 'who will tell me I'm a soft touch, my sister was always a bitch and I need to wake the hell and accept it.'

'She'll be gentler than that, I'm sure,' I said, not sure at all.

'That's very nice of you to say, and yet completely unfounded,' Kit grinned again, before pushing off and mounting the bike seamlessly, 'and we're away!'

There was a manic energy to her, one that I recognised from my childhood, and while I was all about *doing* things when terrible stuff happened, there was this niggling doubt in the pit of my stomach.

It was still light, the grey skies softening in the face of the trees and greenery along the path. We seemed to be going through private land, and yet Kit didn't care. She nodded and smiled at everyone she met, but when they passed I saw the tightness in her face. It was like she was holding it together until she was with everyone, so she didn't have to relay the story twice. She was waiting to receive her 'I told you so's and get on with her life.

She must have texted Effie something before we'd left, because the whole lot of them were waiting in the near-empty pub when we arrived. All except Sarah, who hadn't replied to the invitation. Jakob looked concerned at that, but everyone else said she was probably taking the chance for a sleep whilst the baby was settled.

Fraser nodded at me as we arrived, lifting his hand to his mouth, offering a drink. I nodded, giving a thumbs up. 'Two beers. Big ones.' I made a face, and he widened his eyes and nodded, getting to work. He spared a small smile for me, but I knew he was worried about Kit.

When everyone was seated, Effie impatient for an answer, Kit stood before them all.

'Don't tell me, you've decided to move to England to be nearer your niece and you're giving up the country life?' She rolled her eyes.

Kit nudged her with her elbow, 'Oh yeah, me in an office, sure. What can I do except chatter to horses and feed chickens?'

'And dress up alpacas,' I added helpfully, smiling at her, willing her to find the words.

When Kit told her friends about my mother's secret, there was an audible gasp, followed by the usual questions.

'Well, I'm not surprised,' Effie said obstinately, hands on hips as she stood by the table, apparently too enraged to be seated any longer. 'That woman would spear the arsehole out of a donkey.'

I guffawed, and Kit rolled her eyes, 'Effie…'

'Well, you don't look after yourself! Putting yourself out for people, putting yourself at risk!' Her forehead crinkled and collapsed into sadness, 'So it's my job to protect you.'

Kit smiled at her, tired, but satisfied that she'd taken a softer approach, 'Well, I'm glad to have my loyal bull terrier.'

Effie squawked, 'Excuse me, you'll find I'm an Irish Greyhound, svelte and fast.' She presented herself like a model, as if to identify the lie in her round, soft frame.

'Either way, you have teeth and your bite is definitely worse than your bark,' Kit put an arm around her, and then turned to the rest of the group. 'So, friends, will you drink with us in this time? Will you share a meal and remind us of all the goodness and kindness in the world? Will you tell us stories and share our laughter until the day falls into darkness, and tomorrow we can start again?'

'Bloody hell,' I laughed, 'all that? I thought you just wanted to get shit-faced, not start an uprising?'

'A regular poet, our Kitty,' Fraser said quietly, raising his glass to her. We raised ours in response. To Kit, who deserved a better sister, but did not regret her kindness.

The afternoon whiled away into evening, as we drank and laughed and reminded Kit that she was not at fault. She shared memories of my mother, not just terrible ones but funny ones, as if she was mourning her. I understood what it was to say goodbye to the memory of someone, to the hope that they might prove you wrong.

That evening could not have been more of an

exorcism if we'd dowsed ourselves in holy water. The spirit of my mother, the memory, the possibility, was truly gone. In her place, she left a sad story we would tell of a spiteful creature who would use anyone and anything to get what she wanted.

But we didn't want to focus on her, we wanted to focus on Kit. Kit who held Effie close to her, affectionate and softened by the haze of whisky and good friends. Jakob told us all funny stories about the different places he'd worked, and the first few times in the café when the Scots couldn't understand his accent. He spoke about Sarah, and how good and kind she was, how strong she was for her son, and we did nothing but giggle a little as we noticed how he blushed.

Fraser simply clapped him on the shoulder and shook his head, a smile on his face.

'Oh dear, lad…' Effie shook her head.

'What?' Jakob looked embarrassed and confused.

'The heart wants what it wants,' Kit said, only slurring slightly, 'and I applaud that. I hope that wilful, wonderful girl figures it all out. God, I do.'

She wasn't to be brought down though, and it was Kit who led the charge into joyfulness. By the time evening came, when we had sobered over hearty meals heavy on potatoes and meat, satiated and relaxed, the singing started.

Whether they were local songs or completely ancient, I had no idea. I just knew that sitting in that pub surrounded by these people, some I knew and some I'd never met, all singing songs of freedom and history and love… my heart felt fit to burst. Something brought people together, and it was more than geography, or history or shared pain. It was love, and loss and heartbreak and being painfully, beautifully human.

I stepped outside for some fresh air, finding the drinks had gone to my head. I felt untethered, and it scared me a little. I hadn't even messaged Dan to tell him what had happened, what I'd discovered. But I'd left my phone back at the house, so pointless as a point of connection out here. I'd wanted real people, not picture perfect photos of family holidays and pregnancies announced to the world, their baby's growth shown in images of fruit and vegetables.

Yet, it also felt a bit much, these people who had taken me in, part of Kit's crazy family.

I heard the door to the garden open, and felt someone sidle up. I desperately hoped it wasn't a drunk patron wanting a chat, or someone who heard an English accent and wanted an argument.

But it was Fraser, who just leaned on the wall next to me, looking out at the darkening garden. I twitched my lips as an attempted smile, and didn't try to talk. I didn't expect he had anything to say. Already this evening, his occasional interludes had offered more than I'd heard from him so far.

'You've seen me on the bridge.' His voice croaked

slightly, but it was warm and gentle. The kind of voice you'd kill to hear tell bedtime stories. 'You always look a wee bit concerned, as if you don't know whether to check on me.'

I nodded, scared to say anything in case I disrupted this moment.

He took a deep breath. 'When I was a young man, I was an idiot. I had something to prove. And I was out driving, drunk as a skunk, and I crashed.'

I turned to face him, expecting the worst and wondering why the hell he was mentioning this now.

'I crashed right by that bridge. Just me, no one else. I was in hospital for a few weeks, busted up my leg, cracked ribs, the whole lot. I couldn't stop thinking, "What if I'd hit someone? What if I'd killed someone? Killed a child?" And it turned into this dark, dark thing inside me. That guilt, even though no one else was hurt, it twisted me up.'

Fraser paused, his features softening, 'And that was how I met my Rosie. She was the nurse on the ward that day, and she kept an eye on me. Whenever she saw me going inwards, she wagged her finger and said, "We didn't save your life just to have you disappear, Fraser Forsythe, so you do better now." She kept that up, for weeks.'

He laughed dryly, nothing more than a chuckle, but his eyes glistened slightly as he stared into the distance. 'She was a nightmare, sweet one moment, stubborn the next, but she made sure I survived. She made me laugh. And the day I was discharged from the hospital, I took myself down to a jewellers and came right back that afternoon to ask her to marry me.'

Fraser paused and said nothing for a moment, as if he was trying to recall what his point was. 'We had forty years together. Wonderful years. And it never would have happened if I hadn't been a nineteen-year-old idiot.'

'Sometimes good things come from bad things,' I summarised, and looked at him to check I'd got his meaning.

He smiled and nodded, 'That would have been the quicker way to say it, but I thought I'd better make it big and meaningful. A proper story.' He smiled at me and I laughed.

'But why go to the bridge? Why not go to the place you got married, or places where you had memories together?' I wondered if it was rude to ask.

He pointed at me like I'd asked the right question. 'Because I'm not just grateful for the woman and the life I had. I'm grateful for the moment that brought me to it... And sometimes I like to stand and wonder "What if...?"'

Fraser reached out and gently squeezed my arm, 'Your mother did not deserve you or your aunt. But her lies brought you to each other, and that's worth thanking her for. Whether she meant to do it or not.'

I smiled, touched, and he nodded at me.

'Well, that's quite enough of that. I'll be back inside, lass. Don't catch cold.'

In the last twenty-four hours so many unbelievable things had happened, but I struggled to decide whether Fraser telling me the whole story about his past was more crazy than my mother exaggerating her illness. Probably not, but it felt that way.

I slipped back into the group and breathed a little easier. I thought about Dan, and everything that had brought me to him. I still felt guilty, and I wondered if Fraser's story would be different if he had hit someone in his car that day. But today wasn't about that.

Today was about Kit, glorious Kit and the wonderful people who wanted to make sure she was okay.

After much hugging and singing and yelling, we decided we'd cycle back to the farm. We were offered multiple lifts and yet Kit was insistent. We had a few cups of coffee and she said the breeze would knock the cobwebs out.

'As long as it's not a car knocking those cobwebs,' Effie had scowled, but hugged us both fiercely.

Biking home in the dark, half drunk and Kit hooting to keep animals away, was one of the funniest journeys I've ever had. It was dangerous, and yet we weren't smart enough to care.

Kit put as many lights as she could on the bikes (she'd briefly considered wrapping them in fairly lights from the pub garden) but it barely made a dent in the darkness of the Highlands. There was darkness, and the stars, and us.

We wobbled and laughed, merrily stupid as we made our way home. Kit sang old songs and I tried to join in, getting the words wrong, but there was no one to disturb us beyond the birds in the trees, and perhaps the odd sheep. I almost fell as I jumped off, striding into the cottage with relief.

There would be tea and biscuits and bed. That was all I wanted.

The sight of Sarah, sitting at the kitchen table, clutching Lachlan to her chest, shocked me into soberness. But not as much as the bruise forming over her eye.

Chapter Twelve

'That bastard.'

Kit's voice could kill, but there were tears in her eyes as she approached Sarah.

She moved in the way she did with the animals, trying not to spook them as she got close enough to help. Sarah just watched her, eyes moving even as she stayed frozen.

I waited for Sarah to defend him, to make the same tired excuses, but she said nothing. She was shaken and bruised but there was something in the set of her jaw that made me proud of her. She was a lioness with her cub, there was nothing she wouldn't do to protect him – she was primal and powerful.

'I won't go back,' she said finally, her voice croaky. I wondered how long she'd been sat there in the dark, whilst we'd been drunk in the pub.

She met Kit's eyes like an act of defiance, daring her to say she'd told her so. But Kit had feared those words herself earlier in the evening and I knew she wouldn't dare.

She just nodded.

'Take the room, I'll sleep on the sofa,' I said. 'Do you want tea?'

'I'd not say no to something stronger if you have it.'

I poured her a drink and watched her hand shake briefly as she reached to take it.

'Do you want me to take the wee lad?' Kit asked gently, but Sarah frowned.

I watched the first signs of recognition in her eyes, bracing myself for what was coming. 'I… I can't seem to let him go. I can't put him down. I don't know what's wrong with me. He almost, he almost… Me, it's fine but not him. He's only a wee'un, he's done nothing to…'

'To deserve it?' Kit winced. 'And what have you done, except be a good mother, a kind person, someone who loved him?'

'I knew it was coming, I knew, and I didn't want to believe. I wanted to be wrong. I was leaving, Taz knew. I was leaving, wasn't I?'

That's when the shaking started, and for some reason it all felt very familiar. I fetched her a blanket, wrapping it around the two of them, trying to infuse as much love into that gesture as I could.

'You did it,' I said to her, trying to smile, 'you did it.'

She didn't look like she believed it yet. I kept forgetting how young she was, as if stubbornness and motherhood could hide it.

When Sarah was settled, Kit made a call.

'The police?' I asked quietly, hovering at her side as she held the phone to her ear. I watched Sarah from across the room, smiling at her son to show that everything was alright. As if she could convince herself by convincing him. How strange that a smile was all in the eyes, that without truth it was just red eyes and bared teeth.

Kit shook her head, 'They'll know soon enough. But we have ways of looking after our own around here.'

I knew what that meant. I'd seen it enough times on the estate. The pride, the pack, the code of honour.

'Who did you call, Kit?'

'Fraser. He loves that girl like she was his own. He'll take care of it.'

I wanted to tell her to be reasonable, to call the police and let it be handled properly. But I didn't. Because Sarah was sweet and kind and I could see why everyone would do anything they could to keep her safe. To stop her from feeling powerless in a court, looking at a man like Murray as he smirked like she was nothing.

It was a community, and if you broke the rules, you paid the price.

'Don't look at me like that, they're not going to kill him! They'll just make it clear he's not welcome here anymore. She deserves to feel safe in her own town, don't you think?'

I watched Sarah settling herself on the little sofa, stroking Lachlan's hair even though he'd since drifted off to sleep.

'She's lucky to have you.'

Kit looked at me, briefly taking my wrist in her bony, rough grasp. 'If I'd known about you, I would have been there too, you know? When everything happened.'

'Well, we've had enough dramas to share since, I'd say.' I nudged her with my hip. 'Been quite a day.'

'Normally, I'm a fan of understating things, but I think that's a bit much,' Kit sighed, shaking her head. 'At least the day's almost over.'

Kit spoke too soon.

I knew it, the moment she said it. Bad things happened in threes, that's what Mum always used to say. *Never tempt Fate unless you're willing to pay the price.* She was strangely mystical like that, and I always wondered why she never thought about karma. That said, no one thinks they're the villain, do they? If anything, maybe we were the villains in her story. I certainly was now.

Eventually Sarah handed Lachlan to me, nodding and giving me a small smile as she went to the bathroom. I took it as an honour, a symbol of trust, and Kit nodded like she was proud of me, that small smile on her face, if only for a second.

When she came back, Sarah didn't immediately reach

for him, instead busying herself cleaning up in the kitchen, tidying anything she could find until eventually she lay down on the sofa and fell asleep.

About twenty minutes later, just as Lachlan was settling into sleep in my arms, and his mother dozed almost peacefully on the sofa, the phone rang.

I stopped breathing, so sure it would be Fraser, or whoever else he was in charge of, to say that it had all gone horribly wrong, that Murray had got away, was on his way to us, was making demands. Or perhaps someone had been hurt. I went through every possible scenario in the ten seconds that the phone rang before Kit picked it up.

I watched Lachlan, his little bottom lip quivering with the threat of tears, even before he'd opened his eyes. I shushed him, rocked him, desperately prayed that he wouldn't start crying, because I was sure I would start crying too at any point, the way this day had been going. Even just looking at Sarah's face, so white against the rapidly changing bruise, her brow furrowed in sleep as if she knew she wouldn't sleep uninterrupted… it made something in my chest ache.

'Hello?' Kit's voice was soft, and I saw her take the phone out of the back door, her voice muffled as she stood facing into the distance. 'This is she.'

'I see,' I heard her say, 'right… well, yes, I see.'

The other person spoke for a little longer, and all I could hear in Kit's tone was bemusement. 'Right, well, thank you for letting me know.'

The voice on the other end said something, and Kit huffed, almost snorting in that irritated kind of amusement.

'I can imagine it's been quite the ordeal. You can let my sister know I plan for her to be at St Michael's as long as she is willing to stay. Please tell her I'll be there tomorrow. Yes, goodnight.'

'What did she do?' I tried to whisper but ended up hissing, when Kit stepped back inside the room. 'What's she done now?'

Kit shook her head, almost laughing as she exhaled. 'Your mother, in what her nurses are calling *a fit of confusion*, decided to try and make a great escape.'

'Right…'

'After relieving a few of the other residents of their cash, jewellery and other valuables,' Kit snorted. 'Always loved herself a good bit of drama, did Nina. Good to see things haven't changed. She didn't make it past the main gate. They've got her back in her room now.'

I closed my eyes in embarrassment, 'Are they going to prosecute?'

'Of course not, she said she was confused, and apologised. Apparently she asked after me.' Kit shook her head, 'I told her to get comfortable. I'll go tomorrow and straighten things out.'

I tilted my head in surprise. 'You're not going to

punish her? Stop paying for the facility? Send her packing? It must be costing you a fortune, and—'

Kit held up a hand, and shook her head, but her smile took the sting out.

'Sometimes when people test you to see if you'll stay, it's worth letting them know you will. My sister did not deserve to have you, my love, and you do not have to have anything to do with her ever again. But for the sake of our mother, I'm going to look after her as long as I can.'

Kit seemed to have this ability to be able to hold the awful things about someone alongside the good things, and just do what needed to be done. Pure acceptance, even if you didn't agree.

'Family first,' I nodded.

'Family first,' Kit agreed, 'whether blood or chosen. Besides, I've decided to have a little hope in humanity. We'll see what the world does with that.'

Sarah and I spent the next day together, and whilst she was clearly shaken, the strength of that young girl was still in there. She just didn't feel the need to put on a pretence. She wasn't happy, and she needed time, so that's how she was going to be.

She smiled for her son, singing to him and playing with him. She brushed the horses, and as long as she could see Lachlan at all times, she was fine. But I knew she and Kit had their own relationship, and I wanted to let them have their time together.

And I'd missed my morning gossip with Effie.

So I made my way into town. Partly I wanted the distraction, but mostly I wanted to know about Murray. Whether anything had been done. I was hoping Effie, at least, had forced someone to report the incident to the police.

'He turned up earlier, black and blue and angry as a bear with a sore head,' she said to me without further greeting. 'I refused to serve him.'

'I bet that went down well.' I'd only seen Murray from a distance, but he wasn't small.

'Jakob stepped in,' Effie looked to the back of the café where her cook was frowning at the fryer, his eyebrows down low. 'I'm not sure Jakob knows what to do with himself, bless him. I think he would have liked to have been the one to hurt him, but he doesn't want to overstep. He still thinks he's an outsider.'

I shook my head, keeping my eyes on him.

'He wanted to run over to Kit's to see her, but I convinced him to give her some space. Lass doesn't need anyone else's amateur dramatics right now, aye? She just needs help and space and time.'

'I agree… but didn't anyone want to tell the police?' I asked, desperate for just one person to be official, to trust the system. So Sarah would be safe, so he would be put away. In my head, that was what happened. If Dan could be sent away for punching a man who fell and hit his head, surely what Murray had done was actionable too?

'Oh lass, take three guesses where Murray's da works.' Effie's dark eyes darted back and forth as she waited for me to understand.

I sighed, holding up both hands in defeat. 'Okay, fine. Clan business, as Kit says.'

'Don't be like that. You work to the system that gets results. That bastard on his way out of town with his tail between his legs is a result. He won't mention whatever happened to his da, and Sarah will feel safe again. It may not be official, but it's justice, of a sort.'

'And what if he comes back? What if it didn't scare him?'

Effie shook her head, 'I know the lads in this town and how they deal with… that sort of thing. All they'd been waiting for was permission. Young sweet thing like Sarah with her wee lad and her brave smile? She could have started a war round here growing up if she'd wanted to. One cheeky grin sent to the wrong boy and she could have had them all chasing. But she kept to herself, had dreams of going to university to study. Maybe now he's gone, she'll do that. When she starts to believe in herself again.'

It was easy enough to see it in Sarah's mannerisms now, the hesitance when someone complimented her, as if it might be a trap. The dismissal of any words of encouragement. The idea of someone like Sarah having been systematically worn down over the years, until she truly believed she didn't deserve her dreams, was horrific.

I could see why everyone had banded together to protect her.

'And how are you, hen? What with… everything?' Effie's head tilted like a concerned owl.

'I am… figuring it all out, I guess,' I sighed.

'And what about that lovely husband of yours, what are you doing about him?'

'That is an excellent question.'

I hadn't spoken to Dan yet. I hadn't told him about my mother's revelation, or how I was wrong. Because none of it mattered to him. He had believed me from the start. *I was there, Taz.*

And he was right. He had been there too. Making choices. He hadn't been the marionette, and I was not in control of our story.

I might always feel guilty about what happened, but he'd always told me he never regretted it. I'd believed him, right up until his parents returned, until our new life started. And he was right about that too – I knew exactly who he was and what life he was expected to lead. Maybe it had even seemed perfect when I was a teenager. But I knew I couldn't do it anymore. Not even for him. Biting your tongue just left bruises.

Effie's face was kind as she patted my shoulder, 'Real

love is a rare and wonderful thing. But it's not the *only* thing.'

I nodded, and she gave me a quick hug. 'We're all going to come over tonight, a big group dinner. Be there for Sarah.'

'And for Kit.'

'And for you,' she nudged me, 'no getting rid of us now.'

'Well thank goodness for that,' I grinned. Effie managed to pack me up with multiple sandwiches and cakes for Kit, Sarah 'and the wee lad', even though we were seeing her later. It still made me smile.

When I was driving back to the farm, Dan called.

'Hi…' I was wary, unsure even where to start.

'Hello my beautiful wife,' he said, his usual lilt, usual tone. As if nothing had happened.

'Hello my wonderful husband,' I gave the expected reply, even as it made me want to cry a little.

'I just wanted to check in.' *After your absolute meltdown.*

'That makes sense.' *After my absolute meltdown.*

There was silence for a moment, and Dan suddenly said, 'Guess what my favourite meal is, Taz.'

'What?'

'What's my favourite meal? My absolute, makes-me-happy, last-meal type meal? Guess.'

I laughed, going along with it, enjoying this moment of normality. 'Easy, buster. Chateaubriand with potato dauphinoise and minted spinach at Serafino's. With a fancy pants red wine.'

He made a buzzer noise, 'Eh, wrong! Try again!'

I frowned, trying to think.

'Ah, okay. Terrifyingly rare burger at The Shack, with a beetroot bun, extra-crispy bacon and a side of truffle mac and cheese?'

I could hear his smile widening, 'Nope, I'll put you out of your misery…' He slapped out a drum roll on what must have been his desk, '… tuna pasta bake.'

'Horse shit.'

We'd lived off it in the studio flat in Tufnell Park. I'd make a big batch of it on Sunday and we'd eat it for days. It was the only thing I knew how to cook, something cobbled together from cheap ingredients that could satiate a growing teenage boy who was accustomed to big meals at home.

Eventually, I learnt to add chillies and soups and stews to my repertoire, anything we could make in a batch to fill our bellies. I was proud of how I'd find cheap ingredients and make it last, loved to tell Dan how much I'd spent and how many meals we'd got from it. I was proud to be thrifty. To care for him.

'We haven't eaten that in years.' I couldn't remember the last time I'd eaten something so basic. 'I don't know what point you're trying to make here.'

'Those days were the happiest in my life. Maybe it didn't feel like it at the time. Maybe I was worried about money and my parents and my future. But sitting with you, eating tuna pasta bake and watching VHS tapes we'd bought from the charity shop… that was happiness to me. Still is.'

It was easy to get lost in it, our love story. Our history. Our rags-to-riches, first love, young marriage, ultimate sacrifice kind of story. It's why the journos loved it, why they reached out every few years. I was the girl from the wrong side of the tracks and he was the boy who was destined for greatness. It was a good story.

But that didn't mean it made sense anymore.

'Look, I think when I get back we need to have a proper discussion about everything, about what we want to do.' I breathed. 'Just like you said.'

He completely ignored that, 'I'm assuming you haven't received your parcel then?'

'What parcel?' I shook my head, 'No, listen, we have some decisions to make, and I know I haven't made things easy—'

He interrupted me, 'Taz, honestly, don't make any decisions until you've seen what I've sent, okay?'

'Dan, presents aren't going to solve anything, all the money—'

'Taz! I've known you most of my life. I know things have been very weird, but can you maybe trust that…' he trailed off. 'You know what, never mind. Just wait until you receive the package, okay? Give me that much.'

'Okay.'

'Good, thank you.' He sounded different, sure of himself. Perhaps it wasn't my decision to make anyway, perhaps he'd already made it for me. Which was what I'd wanted all along, wasn't it? For him to come to his senses and prove me right? I was just like Nina, waiting for people to leave and testing them until they gave in. 'I've got to go now, but I love you. Call me when you get the package. I want to know what you think.'

'That's suitably cryptic.'

'Just keeping the magic alive, babe.'

I laughed in surprise as he hung up, and clocked the tour bus approaching as I pulled in to park in front of the cottage. I ran in to join Kit, preparing all the bits and bobs to welcome the tourists.

It was second nature by now, taking photos, sharing stories, listening to people. It was easy to watch them and see what was going on with people. The new couples, unable to be separated, always reaching for each other, the older couples nudging and pointing things out. The ones in fights, the friends who had been travelling together too long. The hen party forced on an educational journey by a well-meaning organiser, desperate to offer something not centred around alcohol. The solo travellers, separating into two camps: those quietly taking it all in, and those eager to chat, knowing that they got the best stories from people rather than places.

I reeled off interesting facts, and encouraged funny poses, and made kissy noises until the cows edged closer.

I told them what to taste for in the whisky and where it was made. That I was heading home myself and taking a few bottles back with me (true) and that it was hard to get anywhere else (less true). I cherry-picked moments of history and knitted them into stories, the ones I knew they wanted to hear. But I made sure they were real. People want flare, sure, drama and romance and excitement. But they want it to be true. And history has that, if you know where to look and how to tell it.

When they left, Kit turned to me in awe.

'You sure you don't want to move up here and help me? Make it a family business?'

'You have no idea how tempting that is,' I smiled, putting an arm around her, 'but I've got a few chapters to close back home. Things that need to be put right.'

'And have you decided what to do?'

I made a face, 'I've decided to be honest. I'm going to stop pretending everything was perfect and I was happy, because I wasn't, and this wasn't the life we designed or planned for. And if it's what he wants, and we have different lives we want to lead, well… we had a good run. We were happy. We grew up together.'

I smiled at her, even though talking about us in the past tense made my heart hurt.

Kit chucked my chin, 'You're pretending again.'

I shook my head. 'I'm not. It fucking hurts. But a smile isn't a lie. And I've still got hope.'

That night we had a barbecue out the back of the

cottage, with all of our friends coming. Fraser left the pub in capable hands, and Effie arrived with Jakob, who greeted Sarah so carefully, like he thought she might break. Lachlan reached for him, and he obliged, happy to be hanging out with 'my little buddy Lucky', as he called him. Effie fussed over the food, Fraser wrestled control of the barbecue and all that was left for Kit to do was help me bring the table outside onto the lawn and sit drinking beers as we soaked in the view.

The sunset was a mass of pinks and oranges, promising a beautiful day tomorrow, and a chill this evening. The lingering warmth of the day faded, and the smell of smoke took me back to summers sat on the flat roof outside our window, watching everything with a cup of tea, and burning sausages. There had been picnics in the park, and work friends' summer birthdays, and festivals. All these memories evoked from charcoal and lighter fluid.

When we were full, moaning at how good the food had been, how much we'd eaten, and, actually, could anyone even think about dessert, I started clearing the table. Effie and I washed and dried together as she tried to teach me a Scottish song. I failed miserably to join in, but we laughed a lot. When the last of the plates were put away, we looked at Kit, sat out at the table, smiling in the candlelight, relaxed as she bounced the baby on her knee.

'She's going to be okay, right?' I asked, feeling foolish.

Effie smiled, 'Och, she'll be fine. Her sister is a troublemaker, always has been. But Kit's got a lot of love to give, and she'll give it whether it's wasted or not. There's no stopping her.'

'I guess at least she knows the truth now,' I said.

'I think she probably had an inkling all along. Your mother was always playing games, and people are complicated. They're not absolved of their sins just because they get sick. It's why we can still be so mad at people and still miss them when they're gone.' Effie nudged me with her hip. 'And what about you?'

'What about me?'

'Are you going to be okay?'

I smiled, 'Kit thinks I should go to therapy.'

Effie laughed so loudly and for so long that I thought she was going to stop breathing.

'I know!' I said. 'The strong and silent type all for the healing power of talking.'

'Well, she does have long chats with those animals, I just thought she liked winning an argument for once.' Effie grinned at me, her bright eyes wild with mischief. 'You know, she loves you very much. She's a soft touch who takes in strays all the time, but it means a lot to her to have family.'

I gestured to the table outside, 'She has family.'

'You know what I mean. I've been with your aunt twelve years, and I've never seen her cry the way she did when she learned what you'd been through. When she found Nina and looked you up. It's been a regret for most of her life that she didn't somehow find you sooner and swoop in to save you.'

'Well she saved me this time round, so I figure…' I paused. 'Wait. With her twelve years?'

Effie smiled and raised an eyebrow.

I closed my eyes, 'Oh god, I'm such an idiot! Why didn't you say anything? Why didn't Kit?'

Effie shrugged, 'We're private people and some in this town are still a bit old fashioned. We're women of a certain age, companionable old maids, as most of the farmers think.'

I pressed my hand to my forehead, 'I thought it was weird you always cooked breakfast and arrived so early… Please don't tell me that I chucked you out of your home during this time?'

'Dunna fash, pet. I keep my flat above the café in case I get sick of your aunt's moods and it's best to leave her to her cows and chickens. It was no bother.'

'I feel so stupid, I'm sorry.'

'That's because you assumed she was a crotchety old bag who lived alone. Who knew she could still be so grouchy as part of a couple?' Effie put an arm round me. 'I'll look after her, she'll look after Nina and you look after yourself. Whether that's talking to a human or a couple of alpacas, I'll leave it to you.'

'Easier to find a therapist than an alpaca in London.'

She nodded, 'Very practical.'

We went to walk outside and rejoin the others, but Effie suddenly took my hand. 'I just want you to know that everything's going to be alright. I don't know if anyone's told you before. But you are kind, and loving, and have a lot to give. And you are going to be alright.' She clasped my hands between hers, and briefly kissed my knuckle before patting them.

I felt a lump rise in my throat, and saw her eyes watering, before I pulled her in for a hug. 'Thank you,' I whispered, and she gave me a squeeze.

'Okay,' Effie said, wiping her eyes as she pulled back, 'now I definitely think it's time for a drink. Let's get Fraser to make cocktails!'

Time passed unheeded, different to our drunken rampage at the pub days before. This was relaxed, friends talking, laughing and doing nothing much except being together. Kit brought out blankets and I pulled on Daniel's hoodie, snuggling down and surreptitiously sniffing at it, comforted by his scent. I knew it was almost time to go. I would wait for Daniel's mysterious package, and then I would go home to have The Conversation.

The thought of living without him was painful, it felt like being ripped in half, but I didn't feel so much like I owed him silence and smiles anymore. It hadn't been working anyway. Nostalgia, obligation and guilt don't make a marriage. We had the love, probably the greatest love I'll ever know, but sometimes love isn't enough. We focus so much on that big star of the show, that we forget the small things that make it possible – practical things like time, and dreams, and values. Shared goals. There's no point walking side-by-side if you need to go in different directions.

We had a choice to make, but I wouldn't just be dragged along in the tides anymore. I'd steer the ship. And if I had to do it alone, I absolutely could.

People always feel like love stories don't count if they don't have a happy ending. But that's not true. Ten happy years aren't cancelled out by an ending. Those memories happened. They exist. They might be a little dog-eared, but they can't be deleted.

Even if I didn't get to have Daniel as we aged, watch him be a father, see the grey at his temples pepper the rest of his hair, or see him chase his grandkids, I had him at all the other ages. I had Daniel at seventeen, at twenty-three, at thirty. I had a lifetime of memories that would live forever.

If that had to be enough, then it would be alright. I'd survive.

I knew that now.

Chapter Thirteen

The next morning started the same way every other had. I got up at 4:30 a.m. and pulled on my clothes, met Kit in the kitchen where we offered silent, bleary-eyed good mornings to each other, sipped our coffee, and headed out on the rounds. That morning everything seemed significantly more loud, that bastarding cockerel shouting his head off like an auctioneer not getting enough interest.

Fraser's bloody cocktails. My tongue was still blue.

I patted the cows and said hello to Winston, who seemed to have forgiven me for going rogue when I gave him an apple. I had a chat with the chickens, who didn't have much to say. I felt like I was saying goodbye, and though I was waiting for Dan's parcel, I knew if it didn't arrive today I would start my journey home anyway. When you're finally ready to do something after months of stasis, staying still feels like torture. Kit asked me that morning whether I wanted to say goodbye to my mother, and I shook my head. She left it at that, and not for the first time, I was grateful for how she never needed a justification, never tried to talk you into anything. She respected my choices and left me to them.

Nina got to keep her sister, she got a chance at rebuilding that relationship. It was probably more than my mother deserved, but I was pleased for her. Because she would get nothing from me. No hatred, no thoughts, no regret. Nothing.

When we got back, Effie was preparing food as usual, but this time she stayed in her pyjamas and dressing gown, and I smiled as Kit put an arm around her. Sarah had padded down the stairs with Lachlan in her arms, and smiled as she said, 'Mmn, bacon!' She was still wearing the jumper that Jakob had lent her the night before and she blushed when Effie said how nice it was of him to lend it. I almost didn't want to leave, I wanted to watch as this new potential bud developed, but the way Effie raised an eyebrow at me, I knew she'd be keeping me in the loop with all of the gossip. Possibly whether I wanted it or not.

When the postman knocked, poked his head around the door and left the parcel on the side, I almost jumped out of my seat. 'Just leave these here for you, see yous later!'

I stood up.

'Hey, finish eating,' Kit said sternly, nodding towards my plate. It was so incredibly parental that despite my desperation, I smiled and sat back down. But I kept my eyes on that parcel for a full minute, chewing slowly until eventually Kit rolled her eyes, and said, 'Oh, go on then!'

I scrambled over to the front door and ripped open the packaging, struggling with the tape. What could he possibly have sent me that would fix anything?

When the heavy book fell out into my hand, I recognised it instantly. The black leather cover was more worn than when I saw it last. He had filled it already, in a few weeks? All that talk of work, and being too busy to make art anymore. Was that what he was saying, that he would make the time?

'Is that a photo album?' Sarah asked, and I shook my head, opening it.

'It's a sketch book. I gave it to Dan when I left.'

I could feel them exchanging quizzical looks, but I ignored them, opening the book and flipping through it. He must have been sketching non-stop. There were line drawings and paintings, charcoal sketches. He drew our history, from the moment we met in the library, to the drawing of me cradling our son in the hospital, heartbroken and numb. He had painted our wedding day photo, the real one that sat on our mantelpiece, with him in that silly top hat and me in my Oxfam dress. Further on there were sketches of the other wedding day, he'd captured how my mouth was a thin line, my eyes anxious as I looked out at the crowd of guests, but he had only been looking at me.

There were moments I didn't even think he remembered, curled around each other in that mustard armchair in the studio flat, and the Cava we sat and drank by the river when he got his first commission. Some of these were painted from photos, but others were from memory, complete with detail that blew my mind.

He had been watching, had been paying attention. There was a cartoon of me pulling a tuna pasta bake out of the oven, him looking eagerly over my shoulder. There was a comic strip of him walking to work, and every day he got lower and lower, smaller and smaller until eventually He was just a stick figure in a blue suit, standing before a huge building. There was a sketch of him in the baby's room, head bowed over the cot, face in his hands. His way of grieving.

The last one was a sketch of me, curled up in an armchair, smiling at him.

On the last page, he'd written a note in bright blue ink:

You told me to draw the things that matter. So that's what I did.

I skipped back through the drawings again, tracing them with my fingertips. There were moments there I'd forgotten about, the ones where we laughed or cried, stupid arguments and delicious meals.

There was us, celebrating our positive pregnancy test, me in the bath with my bump popping up through the bubbles. There were burnt birthday cakes and cycling through the countryside and getting lost in Rome. Our first Christmas tree in a little pot with a sad single star on it, and me on a ladder, painting Callum's room, singing to the music.

A lifetime of memories, of just being us.

Not a single fancy dinner, not the expensive holidays, or those people we pushed into friend-shaped spaces.

The things that mattered.

I pulled out my phone to call him. He answered before the first ring had ended.

'Hello?' I could hear the smile in his voice.

'Hello,' I said tearfully, 'I got the sketchbook.'

'I gathered. Did you like it?'

I nodded, pressing my lips together to stop myself from weeping, then cleared my throat. 'Yes.'

Daniel laughed, 'You know, that's what I love about you. Stoic woman, few words wasted.'

'It's a lot, Dan. I'm just… we still need to talk about things. About where we go from here.'

He sighed, 'I know, but I think we should do that in person.'

'I agree.'

'Good,' he said again.

There was a knock on the door.

'I'm sorry, I've got to go—' I started to say, and Daniel laughed.

'Yes, get the door, I bet it's very important.'

When I opened it, of course, he was standing there. My handsome husband looking every bit the saviour he had when he was seventeen. He grinned at me.

'Oh, look how proud of yourself you are!' I laughed, and he nodded.

'Too right, I've been sat in the car for forty-five minutes waiting for the bloody postman to arrive. Got some very funny looks too!'

I wanted to hold him, to throw my arms around him and not let go, but it wasn't so simple. A romantic gesture after months of distance, of confusion and grief and loss… Happy endings didn't last forever. Real life got in the way.

'Uh oh, you've got that overthinking look in your eyes,' he said, and took my hand, before peering behind me and waving, 'Hello!'

Kit, Effie and Sarah mumbled and made noises as they pretended not to be watching us like we were the latest TV drama.

'So here's the thing. We lost our way, and I'm here to make sure we find it again.'

I shook my head, 'I think we want different things.'

'You told me to fill that book with the things that mattered. I filled it with you, with us. Our memories, our life. The things that made us,' Dan grasped both my hands, those blue eyes so desperate as he argued. 'And there was one more drawing I had to add, but I had to wait. So here, add this to the last page.'

He reached into his back pocket and unfolded a piece of drawing paper, handing it to me.

It was in colour, the entrance to our flat, with a big red 'sold' sign outside.

'Confirmation came through this morning,' he said, waiting for me to respond. I could feel his eyes on me, 'Are you happy?'

'What are your parents going to say?'

'Well, I imagine they're going to be more concerned about the fact that I quit my job.' He grinned at me, desperate for me to be pleased.

'You quit your job? And sold our flat?'

Dan nodded, 'I'm not making up for things anymore – we didn't do anything wrong. We loved each other, we went through some shit, we lived the way we wanted to. You've spent all these months biting your tongue because you wanted me to be happy. I wanted them to be proud and they're never going to do that unless my life looks like theirs. I don't want their life, I want ours.'

'So what, we go back to living in damp studios, living off tuna pasta bake and counting our pennies?' I snorted, 'You're not going to miss skiing in Aspen or drinking with your work buddies, or going to the races with your dad?'

Dan shook his head. 'Babe, you were in the worst

place possible when you came up here, and still you got me a notebook to remind me to create something. You've always put me first, you've always fought for us, made sure we survived. I knew nothing about how to do anything before you. So it's my turn to fight. You're going to get your dream job, and I'm going to go back to my commissions and we will live simpler lives, if that's what makes you happy.'

'And your parents?'

'I told them they can come and visit us in whatever hovel we're living in.' He squeezed my hand, hope in his eyes. 'You still don't believe me? Okay, one more magic trick.'

Out of another pocket he produced my engagement ring. My original one. The opal set in silver that he bought from Camden market and gave me that morning on Primrose Hill. I had missed that opal ring, the one I'd been so proud to wear until Miranda convinced him it wasn't appropriate, and got him to replace it. The diamond had never felt right.

'You never tricked me into loving you, Taz. It was never a bargain I made. It was something that happened beyond my control, just because you're you. I don't regret anything. I never did.'

There would be conversations to have, ruffled parental feathers to smooth, arguments and silliness. But I put out my hand and let him take off that ridiculous ring, replacing it with the one I'd always loved.

'So what now?' I asked him, an echo of that same question he'd asked me all those years before. 'Where do we go?'

He smiled at me, interlocking his fingers with mine. 'Anywhere we want.'

Epilogue

People called us 'brave' for changing our lives, but it was with that air of derision and concern, like when people ask if you've got a pension and why you're not preparing for the future. Like you're behind at being an adult.

We didn't care. The real people stuck around. Angela was excited for us, and it was true how few real friends we had in that group beyond her. She helped us with her connections, and Dan started doing his murals again. Within a couple of months we were travelling around the world, going from place to place so he could paint feature walls and unique designs.

I acted as his booking agent, protecting his art just like I'd always done. But I'd also been training as a counsellor. After a few months of therapy, I felt lighter. Jenny, my therapist, wasn't like those pinch-faced school counsellors, and I didn't have that fear that I was going to be seen as I really was. There was no one to take me away from, no one to run from. No need to trick me. Jenny reminded me of Kit in many ways, shrewd and forthright, which was exactly what I needed. When she suggested I consider training to counsel people myself, it felt like the right fit. An extension of working on the grief helpline. No need to tell stories, just listen and say the right words that made them feel safe, unlock those inner worlds. Use my persuasive powers for good. Funnel the grief into something else, slowing the rush down to a trickle, until the river was manageable.

We lived an amazing life, travelling through European cities, road tripping through America. We collected stories, made friends with strangers, curled up in basic hotel rooms at the end of each night (or fancy ones provided by Dan's work if I had been very good at negotiating). We often wondered what our teenage selves would have thought of this life, and agreed they'd be so impressed.

We knew it couldn't last forever, but we were enjoying it while we could. We still came home for stilted, formal dinners with Dan's parents every couple of months, where Miranda criticised my clothing and Timothy talked about equity and risk, but it was a fair price to pay. She hated me even more, but she had to accept he'd made his choice this time. No trickery, nothing to do with class or anything else. Just a man choosing the life he wanted. We gave back the flat deposit, which seemed to annoy them more than anything, but it didn't seem right to keep it when we'd rejected everything else that came with it. But we got to see Dan's siblings, see their kids and watch them grow up. He was still part of the family, a black sheep rather than an outcast, and I think he liked it even better than briefly being the golden boy.

We were frequent visitors to the farm. We'd spent a month or so in the Highlands with Kit before leaving for our travels and Dan had created a beautiful sign for her, advertising to any passing travellers on the road that 'Scottie McTavish's Excellent Farm' was open for business. 'Fudge, Drinks and Wee Knick Knacks' it proclaimed on the sign, and Kit laughed for a full thirty seconds when she saw it, and then gave Dan a pat on the back.

She liked him, they all did. It's hard not to like someone who makes a grand romantic gesture on your doorstep, but it was mainly because they saw how happy he made me. 'Bloody hell, it's like someone's plugged in your batteries,' Kit had said, and served Daniel up a plate of food.

Christmases are spent at Fraser's pub, all of us at a long table.

Life changes little by little, but when we're all sat round the table, none of that seems to matter. Effie still makes the world's best breakfasts. Sarah still has that way with horses, and Lachlan loves his mama's new boyfriend. Kit and Effie still squabble in a way that only speaks of years of love. Fraser still says very little (except when he can't miss an opportunity for a good punchline).

Kit spends one day a week sitting with Nina, chatting. She doesn't tell me much about it, because I don't want to know. But she's doing okay, they're talking. Nina sends me a birthday card every year. She knows my favourite cake now.

I won't forgive her for what she put me through, but it doesn't torment me like it did. Seeing those birthday cards doesn't feel like obligation. It just feels like a form of love, however misshapen.

As we sit around the table, everyone wearing party hats and chatting loudly, wine flowing, Dan takes my hand and grins at me. We're going to tell them we want to settle down up here, close to them. To be part of all this. We're going to need a settled home and friends and family around us when the baby comes. It doesn't have to be us against the world anymore.

I squeeze his hand, surrounded by these beautiful people, watching snow settle on the peaks in the distance, and I feel at peace, like I was always meant to be here. Like I'm living the life I designed, the happiest one I could imagine.

And more than that, I feel like I deserve it.

Acknowledgments

Some books take longer to become who they're meant to be. They're a little like people that way. *The Things That Matter* was a book I started working on as a writer-in-residence at Red Door Studios in around 2012. I was in love with the story, but a few months in I realised I wasn't old enough or experienced enough to write it. I wasn't ready yet, and neither was this book. So it had to wait. Over the years it popped up in a variety of guises, trying to become a time lapse story, a YA book, even a thriller (which led me to my wonderful agent). This book has been trying to become for almost as long as I've been a writer, and there's something very special in allowing it to finally go out into the world.

Big thanks to Hayley Steed, my agent, who saw the potential in these words even when they were in the wrong genre! This book wouldn't be what it is now without the skilled vision of Hannah Todd, who helped me craft it into something that had hope and love at its core, the way it was always meant to be. To Bethan, Charlotte and the OMC crew who have looked after it since, thank you!

To the usual band of wonders, mainly the TSAG and Savvy Writers Snug groups who always are there with a kind word and lots of advice, to Lynsey James, my writerly cheerleader, and to my mum, who always listens to me outline a story with unbelievable enthusiasm: thank you.

Finally, a thank you to Shaun: for the endless cups of tea, the kind words, the plot lines questioned and the walks around the block when I needed to think it out. Falling in love with you inspired this book, and growing in love with you helped me to finish it.

YOUR NUMBER ONE STOP
ONE MORE CHAPTER
FOR PAGETURNING BOOKS